HIM

By: Amanda Sohan

HIM

By Amanda Sohan

Him

Text Copyright © 2016 Amanda Sohan
Printed and Published by Amanda Sohan
ISBN 978-0-692-61914-8
eBook ISBN 978-0-692-61915-5
www.athomewithateacup.com

Other Works

By Amanda Sohan

The Slipper

Love In Black And White

JOURNEY

*The utterance of my name from your lips sets my feet
to path*

From whispers on wind, I come

Wait for me

The love I bear knows no barrier

Not even death can keep us apart

Dedication

For Suzy and Roger

Sister and brother

from another

mister and mother

To My Teacups

A special brew of women

Rowena

Shamin

Sheri

Delilah

Tracey

Table of Contents

The Beginning

The moment I saw him I knew he was trouble. In a space of a moment, you know that moment, when a man looks at you and you look at him and you both know in some animalistic way that you belong to each other. In that moment, a span of a few seconds, flashes of naked flesh, lips locking, entwining bodies and moans of ecstasy flash through your mind's eye. You want to hear that particular man say your name in a dark room while pressed up against you. Yes, you knew he was trouble, trouble you would gladly give up one of your lungs to get into.

But what stops you? Certainly not the fact that you're married. Oh no, don't be so quaint. Truth be told, you and the French have the notion of marriage quite right. It's a game for three or four, any less is simply not enough players on the board. Oh, don't judge, just read. Let's hold the morals until the end of the story, shall we? No, no, no. That is not what stops you. What stops you is the fact that he did not come alone. In point of fact, he walked in with what is commonly referred to as a frenemy. Yes, in point of fact, that trollop used to be a friend of yours. A fascinating woman by all accounts, well spoken, quite pretty in looks, spoke several languages (a quality you secretly envied but never let on), blah blah blah.

It was a few years ago that you and she met. She was just another pretty bartender friend of a friend back then. We all used to frequent said friend's bar those few years ago. It was our jump-off, and let's face it, said bartender hooked us up lovely! Drink $100 pay $40—those numbers would have others performing sexual favors in the back. But there's something to be said for a pack of beauties frequenting your no-name bar. We bring the boys, and once word gets around, they bring their wallets. Next thing you know shots all around and your no-name bar is, pray tell what? Pop-U-Lar and jumping. Everybody's happy! Anyhoosie, I digress … Frenemy was a lovely gal at that point. She was not one of us, West Indian, brown, long black hair and pleasantly thick, but oh how she wanted to be. Looking back now, I can't believe I missed all the signs. I mean, desperation to belong to our group. It was as if she studied us, mimicked us, became part of us and then left with the hard gained knowledge of us. You know the type. The ladder climber. The girl that meets a friend of yours and jots down the number hoping if she puts in the work they'd become a friend of hers. An infiltrator. A collector. Two months later she's hanging with them and hardly remembers your name. Yeah, that bitch. Too bad she didn't see that anyone outside of the circle didn't matter all that much to us anyway.

It took her a long time to figure us out—apparently she's a slow learner. She was an integral part of our group for about two years. So of course when she started to pull the disappearing act, we didn't see it right off for what it was. Oh certainly not! Why, she must be preoccupied, busy, participating in life-altering decisions, of course. She can't be bothered to come out with our alcoholic asses every weekend, n'est pas? We laughed it off. We drank our weekends in perfectly slanted wine glasses and danced our video vixen fannies into the wee hours of the morn. Not a care in the world.

We toasted to her and kept it pushin'. That is until we saw her canoodling with my girl's new love interest. Say what now? Need I say that was the beginning of many an eye opener when it came to that bitch. After that it was a polite hiya and bye-ya, and that's if I was in the mood. Later I came to grips with the fact that she is who she is and you got to live and let live. So I was polite to her whenever I saw her. Gave her a peck on the cheek that I would also grace a rotting corpse tucked in a coffin and followed through with the "so how's everything," hardly stopping long enough to obtain an answer. She was no fool—anymore. She was just as cordial, and for a while I thought almost wistful, as if she missed being around us. But as the kids these days would say, whatev. I ain't tryin' to Dr. Phil your ass, so—see ya.

In any case, now that you have the backstory, let's get back to the real nitty gritty. Him. Ray. I never actually knew a Ray before. And I can safely say he's not the kind of man that every girl would immediately break her neck to get a glimpse of. In point of fact, I may be one of two. Yeah, I said it. But there was something, something about this guy that made me ... quiver.

Now I don't know about other women and their experiences with men, but for me there's never been a question. I see you, it hits me like a ton of bricks ... bam ... I'm caught, I'm done. And by the by, this doesn't happen to me on a regular. Nope, not at all. I like all guys. I'm a natural flirt. People actually pronounce the word flirt when talking to me as if it's a dirty disease. I just laugh and reply, yeah, I'm a flirt. I flirt with men, women, boys, girls, dogs, cats, occasionally fish and trees if they're passing my way. What's wrong with that?

Flirting is a lost art form. Flirting is practice for being an engaging and interesting human being to other human beings, well mostly. And for those that don't know (and I've had to school many), flirting ain't fucking. I am always amazed at how many men are willing to admire a girl that is willing to get down, but meanwhile shaking their head with such disdain at a girl who simply flirts. But I'm onto those douchebags (and I should say boys not men)—

13

because they interpret flirting as being cheated out of a fuck, that's all. Mystery solved.

Anyhoo, I digress. The frenemy entered the club with this delicious devil on her arm. She introduced him to our group, who couldn't look less interested. Luckily, my group of teacups (oh, you'll learn about the teacups as we progress, that's what I've dubbed my lovely group of women), we're hardly ever into the same type of dude. Never a conflict of interest, and if there was, we'd be more likely to have a "you take him, no you take him" conversation than any other. My teacups are one in a billion.

Even I had to admit the beeatch looked good. She put on some weight and had curves in most of the right places. She could use a little more upstairs and she hadn't acquired the bootylicious, but she had it goin' on. She accentuated her fair skin with a curve hugging red strap dress that had a deep slit practically hinting at her nether regions. She added tone on tone brown highlights to her hair and had it styled classy like Jen Ann.

I raised an eyebrow in reluctant approval. She smiled knowingly and introduced. "Ladies, this is Ray." The girls took less than 2.3 seconds to size him up while managing a chirpy "hello." He did the usual quick sweep, but his peepers lingered for a few seconds longer when he reached moi, and a slow, seductive smile crept across my face, quite without forethought or permission. Bam. The bricks have been laid. Any chance I could be Ray???? Oh yeah, every wicked thought bounced betwixt us in the span of a finger snap. And then he turned back to her and they were off. But I never forgot him. I wouldn't say that he was constantly on my mind, but he was definitely in there somewhere.

When I spied him about a year later in one of my favorite clubs and a mutual friend of ours, Mike, reintroduced us, we both smiled in secret recognition. And what did I do instead of giving him the customary kiss on the cheek? Well, I was feeling deliciously wicked and dangerously sexy; after all, I was celebrating my birthday. I was rocking a dress that was made for me, a form-fitting black and red halter slinking just past my knees. To complete the sexy siren roaring 20s look, I rocked some very high black heels. All of that along with my silky smooth, long, jet black straight hair—well, let's just say that night, boys stood at attention all over (wink wink). Ray was no exception to this rule, but he was so cool about it.

You wouldn't know that his flag was at high mast to look at him. Oh no, he couldn't be more cool, but that twinkle in his eye that I swore I knew so well from a time before, I caught that. I reflected that. And as I leaned in toward him brushing past his cheek, I playfully bit his ear ever so gently before pulling away with a wicked little giggle. He broke into a sexy smile. He had a little scar on the left side of his cheek that I wanted to kiss. Damn, he smelled so good. He shook his right pointer finger at me and leaned back against the bar. He shook both finger and head and said, "You. I like you." I can still remember every single detail. And just like that a small fire ignited and I was hardly the same for the rest of the evening. I smiled seductively in response before my crew and I moved on, though not far.

That night the joint was on and poppin', as my girl Charmy likes to say. The bartender's nimble fingers were busily grabbing bottles, shakin' ass and mixin' cocktails. The waitresses were gliding here and there with large hookah setups. Soon Skittles and Mint flavors would envelope us in a soft, fragrant fog.

Gorgeous girls were waiting for their drinks, batting their perfectly feathered lashes, happily chatting with their girls while handsome men on the other side of the bar were making arrangements to pick up their tab, posturing for a chat and a whine. The DJ was tight with it, mixing all of our favorite oldies with the new popular dance jams. This was the golden era. West Indian men were throwing money around left, right and center to impress the ladies. And the ladies were equally impressed and impressive. The men looked good and smelled better. These were the days when men were suave as opposed to a nuisance. They bought you a drink, they conversed, they danced, and if you weren't feeling them beyond that, they smiled and moved on. There wasn't a hangdog face in sight. A perfect atmosphere to celebrate my birthday.

That night we were out in full force and rollin' deep. All of my teacups and some of the extended crew came through. And one of my crushes, V, already set up shop in one of the poshest VIP sections. White sheer curtains enveloped our section while still making the sights and sounds of the rest of the club accessible. The L-shaped ebony leather sectional was littered with members of both our crews. A favorable scene indeed. V had already taken the helm and arranged two small tables layered with an assortment of bottles and hookah pipes. He left no stone unturned.

Since we normally celebrate our birthdays together, I guess he wanted to turn it all the way up. I naturally assumed V was going to make my night, but that all ended once Ray walked through the door. It quite shocked me at just how abruptly. Damn the Patron (oh, do act like you know). Yes, I will blame it on the liquor which totally had me on DIVA behavior. After I oohed and aaahhed, greeted and thanked, I abruptly left poor Veran waiting in the wings while I sauntered over to the bar to tempt Ray some more.

I left a shit-ton of liquor to come here and let this handsome, mysterious man buy me a drink? Says a lot. I could tell that it amused Ray to witness me leave my entire crew and dismiss a dude to come spend time with him. The arrogance was written all over his face. This diminished my power some, and I knew instinctively this was not a man that I could toy with. He hadn't seemed obviously pleased, only slightly amused. I wanted him to reveal much more than that. I sensed I was well beyond my depth.

I wasn't playing this right. I should have said hi, pass him and head to the bathroom, after all, he wasn't encouraging me to stay. One could gauge his actions as merely being polite. I began to panic a little and backpedaled. Since I couldn't think of an elegant exit, I mimicked his movement instead, casually propping myself against the bar rail. Mike faded into the I know not where. He, Ray … I liked turning over his name in my mind. Ray glanced over his shoulder back toward the VIP section.
I followed his gaze and could see V shrugging his shoulders as his friends asked him to no doubt explain my absence. There was a whole lot of vigorous head nods and finger pointing over to the bar. It would take me a few minutes to smooth that over. I wasn't overly concerned. When Ray swung his head back in my direction, his expression was unreadable. I arched an eyebrow wondering what he thought about the whole shebang.

"So is he your boyfriend?" He nodded in V's direction.

"No. He isn't." I could hardly explain what V was. That would just open the door to too much other shit. I decided less was more. More or less.

He's so damn cool, he held back any response. Instead, he rewarded me with a sexy grin and asked me to name my poison.

Feeling a bit chastened by his resplendent show of class by not calling me out on my bullshit, I decided against being shot girl at this juncture. (Applause for the tiny fraction of saving grace.)

"I'll have a Malibu and pineapple, please." I smiled back and fiddled with my hair in proper Cher manner. Only God stopped me from licking my lips. (Discontinue applause abruptly as I am back to displaying idiocy.)

Perhaps he couldn't quite make out what I wanted or wasn't the type of guy to order a drink; whatever the reason, he bade me to order and just as I was about to, Mike reappeared. Apparently he was behind me the entire time. Oh joy! Like the genie of spirits, he ordered both Ray and me a drink and one for himself, paying for our pleasure. Yeah, Mike is a baller! This I always knew. There's not a whole lot of people I don't know, truth be told. You can't be in the West Indian community, in this game, run in the circle and be this friendly without knowing a thing or two about everyone. Don't get it twisted as they definitely know a thing or two about you, but that's the game, truth and fiction. I can dig it.

Drinks came, we three clinked glasses and took a swallow. I glanced past Ray and saw my VIPs were getting a bit nervous, wondering whether I'd developed a permanent residence at the bar and whatnot. I smiled and waved at them with my one-minute finger. I could do this and gauge Ray's reaction all at once. If he was disappointed, he didn't show it. I'm sure I did. All my cool points have suddenly left the building.

I turned to Mike and thanked him for the drink, offering my customary "you fellas be sure and join us at the VIP whenever you're ready" speech. One could hope. Of course, when I turned to Ray, I could see that I would need more than hope. Perhaps a wing and a prayer, because this here man was nobody's fool. He was however, sweet to me in any case. He smiled as if to say, "thanks, but no thanks." I kissed him on the cheek and went my way. Several times during the course of the evening I could feel Ray staring at me as I danced with my girls, as I danced with V, as I sipped my drink. He stared. I stared. But we never came together that evening again. It was sweet torture.

When I pulled the covers to my chin that night, snuggling next to my sister, closing my eyes, it was Ray's face that I saw. It was Ray's voice that I heard. I replayed the entire scene several times until I finally went to sleep with his face underneath my eyes, and his name on my lips. Ray. Ray. Ray.

Homebound

I woke to the smell of apples and fried potato. My sister was already up and at 'em, making us breakfast. What a charmed life I led. What a luxurious birthday party last night. I threw my arms over my head and stretched on the bed like a languid kitty. Thoughts swirled and twisted around me like the crisp, fragrant sheets. What a delectable fancy feast I could make out of that man.

Ray. Mmmm, if I had nine lives I'd be destined to spend at least one or three with him. I closed my eyes and stayed in bed a few minutes longer to replay the evening from start to finish, stretching out each scene that contained Ray and fast forwarding the ones that did not. I fabricated one audacious detail, a kiss to rival Bogie and Bacall. My fingertips brushed my lips and my imagination morphed into a sensual wish. I could almost smell him. Damn! I flung the covers off with violent will. It was time to get up.

I made the bed in meticulous fashion, sharp crease tucked here, a comforter wrinkle smoothed there. Nikki was a perfectionist. Any less and chances are she would sneak in here and redo the entire thing. Luckily there wasn't much of a need to stress; we were both cut from the same cloth, even if hers did require a bit more starch. I could hear her quietly humming a tune I couldn't place as I silently padded across the hardwood toward the bathroom.

By the time I brushed my teeth and concluded my necessaries, Nikki laid out the food with all of the elegant fanfare of a state dinner. I raised an amused eyebrow. The gal believes in presentation! The stark white serving plates held delectable apple filled empanada-like pastries as well as toast, fried potato and scrambled eggs. Two fine China mugs were filled three-quarters with fresh, steaming hot coffee and tea. All this white against the dark mahogany of the table and I began to second guess my pajama ensemble.

I padded over into the kitchen to see if I could be of any help, but she quickly shooed me away.

"No, no, no. Everything's done. I don't need any help, baby. You just have a seat and I'll join you in a minute," she chirped, reaching past me to rinse the frying pan.

"Are you sure, lil bunny?" I inquired, already halfway out of the kitchen. It was rare that she ever needed my help, and truth be told, I definitely took advantage when I was by my baby sis. She required me to do as little as possible, and I was nothing if not obedient to a fault. I'm such a little stinker!

I settled into one of the four comfy pub chairs and fiddled with my placemat. ADD is not a condition as much as a trusted and valued friend. Next I set to straightening the already straight utensils. And people take medication for these fabulous little rituals? Say it ain't so.

True to her word, she pulled out her chair a few minutes later. We both said a quick prayer and dug in.

"Oh my gosh, girl, what are these? They are delicious!" I exclaimed, biting into my third apple empanada thingamajig.

She smiled her sweet, shy smile when being praised. "Oh, you likee? I just made those from scratch, and you wouldn't believe how easy they are," she mentioned while maneuvering her knife and fork.

"Did you have fun last night, Nikki?" I asked in between coffee and potatoes.

"Girl, I had the best time as usual during your birthday. You know when it's your birthday, for some reason we all feel like it's our birthday and we have the bestest time ever." She sighed.

"I know that's right!" I giggled in agreement.

"Did you see that guy Princess was talking to?" Her eyebrows went up, her chin folded into her chest as she nodded in my direction.

"No, girl, after a while I hardly noticed anything except Patron and the dance floor. Why, what happened?"

I wiped the crumbs from my mouth with a napkin and took a deep sip of coffee.

"Nothing, girl, except he was fine as hell and all over Princess, as per usual."

We burst into giggles knowing there was nothing unusual about that scene. Princess, our cousin, was younger by a few years, a teacup through and through, and a stunner. She attracts more men than subways do rodents. And not just any man. Oh no, men of quality, fine like wine men, men with means, money and swag. We tease her about this fact all of the time and constantly joke about how we're going to kidnap her before an event just so the rest of us stand a chance. Don't laugh. We just can't figure out a way to do it without getting caught … yet!

"Not surprising at all, girl. Sorry I missed that," I said in a way that implied I wasn't sorry at all. "But did you manage to see who I bumped into?" I asked, shooting her a wicked grin.

She stopped her fork midair and smiled conspicuously.

"No. Who?"

"Mike was there."

"Who Mike? Tricia's Mike?"

"Yeah, girl."

"Well, that ain't no shock, he was following Trish most probably." She chuckled and daintily placed her fork in her mouth.

"Yeah, I know that girl. Who really cares about Mike? It was who Mike was with that I found very entertaining." I snickered, grabbing my coffee mug for another swig.

"And just who was that?" she asked.

"Ray, girl."

"Ray?" She crinkled her brow in confusion. "Who dat?"

"Girl, Ray. Ray that used to go with that trick Shiela."

"Oh, that boy that you liked from way back when?"

"Yeah, girl, that one."

"So what happened?" She pushed her empty plate back and reached for her teacup.

"Girl, you won't believe what I did to him."

"What'd you do?" She jerked her head back, preparing for what I was gonna' hit her with.

"Well, Mike didn't realize that we had already met, so after he introduced us, you know how we usually do the kiss on the cheek?"

"Yeah," she said and sipped her tea, her eyes following me above the rim.

"Well, instead of kissing him, I kind of bit his ear, just a little," I divulged and fell into giggles.

"You what, bitch?" my sister stated, incredulously.

"Yes, girl, I surely did. I could hardly help myself. I had every intention of kissing him on the cheek, but the next thing I knew I decided his ear looked way too tempting and I went in girl." I chuckled and slid my chair back. "I'm gonna' need another cup of coffee to continue this. You want some more tea?"

"No, not yet. I'll get it later. So don't leave me hanging. What did he do after you bit him?"

And that's how our morning went. During our two cups of tea and coffee, I recalled every tiny inconsequential detail of the Ray chronicles, and my sister, in truest sisterhood fashion, gave me her undivided attention. I'm sure I bored her to sobs, but she coped like a soldier, God Bless Her. When I was finished, she sipped her tea and said, "Well. I can't believe I missed that whole scenario. Where the heck was I?"

"Girl, you and the rest of the teacups were on the dance floor. Which was great, in retrospect. I'm glad I had that moment to myself."

She nodded in understanding. "Yeah, I'm glad you did too. Who knew after so long and on that particular night you would end up seeing Ray? Thank God, 'cause you really looked stunning!"

I nodded in agreement. "I know, right!" I'm not being conceited, but there are nights when you're on, and then there are the other kinds. The nights when it's a week before you're riding the crimson wave, you've gained a ten-pound tire round your middle and there ain't a dress, tights, sweater, top in the world that can make you look human, much less attractive. Truth be told, that also usually happens around my birthday, but luck was on my side last night!

"Thanks, bunny. We all looked amazing as per usual. But last night everybody turned it up."

"Well, you know that's how we do when it's your birthday!" She smiled and squeezed my hand.

"Girl, I bit him because he was so irresistible, but I also bit him to get back at Shiela a little bit too."

"Really?"

"Yeah. I know it's childish and foolish, but after the whole Marcas thing, I was kinda feelin' myself when I saw Ray, you know what I mean?"

She nodded while sipping her flavored tea.

The Marcas thing. What a fiasco that was. A few years ago, after the whole Shiela and Teacups breakup, well, needless to say we did not hang in the same circles after that. Marcas is one my boys. Not just any boy, mind you. Marcas and I are as close as two people can get without the benefit of sex. I've known him forever.

We met many years ago. He was always in the club, I was always in the club, and one night he developed balls and starting chatting with me. If he wanted more from me he never said. We had a silent understanding from the jump. We didn't screw with what we had, and we didn't worry about what we didn't. We enjoyed the flirtation. In short, I dug him.

As the years went on, we grew closer. If I was out, nine out of ten he was out. The girls found Marcas easy to be around. He was practically one of us, but where we had two large up top, he had two small down low. It was a perfect union. We could all bump up and enjoy the simple pleasures of the evening … dancing, drinking, and talking shit. Like I said, it was the golden era.

To have Marcas as a kindred spirit, well, that was a gift. He was married with two kids. I was married with one. His eldest son and my daughter were about one year apart. We were like two sides of the same coin. Like I said, Marcas and the Teacups and I were inseparable. When Shiela was hanging with us, naturally she got to know Marcas. One night when I was home on a Friday night, a rare occasion indeed, Marcas was out, though we found ourselves texting back and forth.

A few minutes later when he popped into another spot, he informed me that my home-girl Shiela was present and with several male companions. Interesting. She wasn't my home-girl at this point, but why correct my boy? It was of no consequence. That is, until she went up to my Marcas and bought him a drink. Sniff Sniff. I smell Skkkkank. Her opening line—payback because he was always generously plying us with drinks. Simultaneously, Marcas was breaking down the entire scenario for me via text. Gotta love that technol-O-G-.

Both Marcas and I were cracking up because it was common knowledge he was a cheap bastard. Sure he was inclined to spring for my drink, but definitely did not have baller ability to spring rounds for our entire crew. My teacups and I totaled six. Once we get a round of shots and drinks, it's roughly about $100 a pop. Did I mention we drink like the Irish??? Do the math. When we do encounter ballers, which in those days, were many, they would be all too glad to buy our whole crew a round and we'd always sneak a drink in for Marcas. He was our boy, it's how we roll.

Shiela's weak lame ass line was seriously trifling, and while it amused Marcas, it worked my damn last nerve. She already made this play with a love interest of one of my girl's a while back. Now my girl loved Shiela, where the rest of us liked her well enough. My girl Ashley is the sweetest person on the planet. She will wait and see how things pan out, analyze and assess her play long before she makes it. Me? Well, not so much. You screw around with me and it's a wrap. I'd rather apologize for being hasty than curse inwardly for acting too late. Anyhoosie, back to the heifer. Not only did she buy my boy a drink, but she invited him to follow her to the next joint she was going to. Is this bitch freakin' for real? I was beyond pissed. I wanted to ring this chicken's neck.

27

Luckily, when it comes to Marcas, no explanation betwixt us is necessary. He intuitively knows the score and understands me in a way that very few people do, even fewer men. He knew this whole scene was pissing me off, even though my text responses were more sarcastic than acidic.

He accepted her initial drink and then proceeded home. I'm sure she amused him but Marcas had a type, and I was it. She wasn't worth the risk. (Take note, boys, 'cause this is what we tend to call grown man behavior right here.) If you picture T.I. saying that line, it will do down as smoothly as single-malt scotch.)

You'd think the horror would end here, but it continued. A few weeks later, Shiela contacted Ashley. She said she missed her and wanted to chat for a bit over lunch. I made it my business to accompany Ash, not because of Marcas, necessarily. I had no plans to bring up that trivial bullshit. I knew that my girl still had a soft spot for this viper. I wanted to be certain she wasn't gonna' act like a timid rabbit and end up boiling in a pot, 'cause this attraction was fatal.

When we got to the diner, there weren't many occupied tables. We took up residence on the six seater, bench on one side, three chairs on the opposite. Once we got comfortable in the back of the 50s-style diner, the owner John sent over our favorite waitress. Ash and I both decided we'd stick with water without the lemon until the messy business was over. We promised we'd order something filling once our guest departed. Satisfied, our waitress set off to cater to a new set of customers up front.

Minutes later, I saw Shiela coming via the wall-length mirror in front of me. She didn't bother to look impressive in her old jeans and misshapen sweater. Girl looked a little rough around the edges truth be told. I wasn't surprised given an account of the company she'd been keeping.

Unfortunately, I could see Ashley's eyes visibly soften. I was rolling mine. Oh lawd, here we go. She chose to sit across from my girl and to my right. They greeted each other with a hesitant hug and kiss on the cheek. I didn't get up and barely mumbled a hey. She hadn't even bothered glancing in my direction. Touché.

She seemed nervous, jittery. Perhaps she was hoping to get Ash alone. Who knows, who cares? I was ready to show her the door. I sat in stoic silence as she and Ash had polite, blasé, catch-up convo. Then she got around to it. Shiela explained how she missed her, not the girls, just my girl, in rather hushed, pained tones. Ash, as per her usual fashion, didn't say much. She held her tongue until the end of Shiela's spiel and then made me proud. She explained to Shiela in matter-of-fact tones that although she missed hanging out with her as well, she thinks they're not as close as they once were for a myriad of reasons, none of which she deemed necessary to get into.

My girl further mentioned that if she saw Shiela in passing, she would always be glad and warm to her. I said not a peep. I shared no such sentiment. Shiela was polite though visibly surprised. She swallowed hard before saying she understood and would always be glad to see Ash anytime, anywhere. And just when I thought the bitch was going to leave and we could order and finally eat in peace, she set to ruining my appetite.

Still without glancing my way, she said, "Oh, I saw your boy a few weeks ago. What's his name?"

Ashley cut a worried glance in my direction and visibly tensed. She knew me too well and was worried that I was close enough to the heifer to inflict irreversible damage.

"You mean Marcas, don't you?" I said flatly, checking her reaction through the mirror.

"Yeah, that's him. Marcas." She smiled, absently fiddling with the place setting.

"Yeah, I know. Who do you think he was texting the whole time you were chatting him up?" Now, any other person would have instinctively realized the lethal tone and texture of my comment and backed the fuck out of the diner—never taking their eyes from me, similar to that of a gazelle trapped among a pride of lionesses. But oh, common though she was, sense was in severe deprivation, and the heifer actually continued down the treacherous path.

"Yeah, he gave me his number and I was going to call him, but I lost my phone and his number, so I couldn't."

Mind you, the whole time she's regaling her tall tale, she hadn't looked at me once. Truly, I amazed myself at this point, because I remained in my seat. My hands were neatly folded in front of me. There was no blood or hair under my fingernails. Quel dommage! "Why in hell would you take my boy's number or call him, Shiela?" I spat while turning my body toward her.

I suppose at this point the heifer regained her senses, because she mumbled something that I couldn't make out, threw a hurried good-bye at my girl and bolted out of the diner like her ass was on fire.

30

And that is 50 percent of the reason why I bit Ray on the ear. The other 50 percent was purely lust. Who cares, anyway? I hope the heifer hears about it. She had it long time in the coming! Yes, it's more than a bit trifling and childish. Nobody's perfect. Now you have the backstory.

About an hour later, I packed my overnight bag, kissed my sister good-bye and climbed into my '98 black CRV. I popped in my favorite reggae CD and headed back home to South Jersey. I was glad to have a three-hour trip in front of me. I should be home by 1:00 p.m., plenty of time to recount the past evening's frivolities.

By 1:30 p.m., I'll be back to being wife, mother and medical records clerk in boring but stable good old Runnymook, as Keithy would say. Truth be told, I was kind of digging my double life, so to speak. I treasured my workweek in South Jersey, I loved our apartment, my husband, my kid, our two dwarf bunnies and the cat.

But once a month, my trip to NY, where I could party with my girls, let my hair down, hang with my boys and just be Catherine, those were equally treasured for the exact opposite reasons. I've heard it said that women are a contradiction born and our hearts are but a deep ocean of secrets. I couldn't agree more. Bite me.

Monday, Monday

Monday morning. I dropped Gaia off to school. It was too far to walk, and she's been having some difficulties with some girl in school. This wasn't a girl in her class, so thus far, dropping her to school and picking her up seemed to temporarily solve matters. Kids are not exactly forthcoming with information. I wasn't sure if things really were okay or if she was protecting me and really stressing on the inside. Since this just happened at the end of last week, I was going to question her subtly, keep my eyes open, eavesdrop on her telephone conversations with her friends and keep a close watch on her behavior. For now.

If I happen to hear something I don't like but her safety or well-being is not adversely affected, I'm going to have to hear and do like I nah hear, as we West Indians would say. After all, I'm not trying to repeat my parents' mistakes. Every time they caught me in some bullshit, I simply honed my skills and became a better criminal. They had the best intentions, which only served to make my rebellion that much more hellish. I don't need to create that in Gaia. She's a good kid, we trust each other and have a very tight relationship. I accept that I don't know everything that goes on in her life.

Maybe I'm strange, because I'm all right with that. I'm her mother not her friend. As long as her safety is secure, she's doing good in class and her friends aren't hell raisers, I'm good. My childhood was much like a survival course, and if I didn't have my JC lookin' out for me, I wouldn't have made it out alive. Sounds dramatic, but I'm not exaggerating. Needless to say, my Jesus and I have many a conversation. Making moves without seeking his guidance produces ill results. Sometimes I forget this fact, try to manage everything by myself, and that's when things start going left. So right now, I'm praying, dropping the kid to and fro and keeping my eyes and ears open. Now it's a wait and see game.

She gave me her customary kiss on the cheek before leaving. She didn't appear nervous or scared. I watched as she caught up with one of her girlfriends, Faith, and walked through the open middle doors. She laughed at something Faith said and did a cute little skip hop to better adjust the weight of her book bag. When oh when will we catch up with the rest of the world and figure out a way for our kids not have to carry twenty pounds on their backs every day? And they wonder why some women suffer miscarriages and can't carry a pregnancy to full-term. Hmph. I've got my theories.

Said a quick prayer and shot off to work. I love, love, love my drive to work. I pass this huge, lush, green pasture, or maybe it's a real old-fashioned ranch (as if I would know the difference). Sometimes it's empty and in the distance you can make out some deer grazing. But when I'm lucky, I catch a glimpse of the horses. Who would have thunk it? Me, Cat, born and raised in NYC, worked in the city since I was seventeen, would ever wind up in Runnemede, South Jersey?

Who would have thought that as I head to work, instead of seeing millions of suits and skyscrapers and hot dog stands and street vendors, would instead bear witness to deer, horses, chickens and geese? Hell, there's a beautiful little man-made lake with a fountain in the middle right by my job with a lone swan gracing the waters. It's downright magical, and even though we've been here for three years now, these sights still feel like a gift from God every single day.

I have ten minutes to spare, so I pull into the CVS parking lot next door to get some hostess muffins before heading to work. Can't wait to get my coffee on.

I swipe my time card at 9:03 a.m.—no biggie. We have ten-minute grace. I came in through the back which leads through the kitchen, passing the doc's office before branching out into the medical records area. Mondays, Wednesdays and Thursdays are most assuredly my favorite days of the week. Two of the hottest docs work that schedule, absolutely completing my bliss. Eye candy is nothing to sneeze at. Oddly enough, one of my docs is fair skinned, practically blonde, features I don't typically find attractive in the least, but there's something magnetic about him. And as I've mentioned before, I kind of just like what I like. Rhyme or reason does not seem to enter the equation.

The doc's office door is slightly ajar. I spot Dr. S reading a report off of the computer and inwardly sigh. Mmm mmm mmm. This morning is just full of gifts! He hears my footsteps and turns his head toward me. We exchange a perfunctory smile, but there's a little subtle, almost wink betwixt us. He knows I dig him. I tend to stare at him intensely every now and again. He does the same, occasionally dashing convention to the wayside, but for the most part, he's warm yet professional. Damn the 90s and all of their sexual harassment suits. Chase me around the X-ray machine, why don't ya? It's all good, though. I need very little to make my work day joyous. Oh for Pete's sake yes, I'm flirting. I thought we established that!

The day goes by pretty quickly. We are, after all, Cooper Orthopedics, and you wouldn't believe how many people break their bones. Patients file in and out faster than the buffet line at Golden Corral. Charts make their way from our hands to the nurses to the docs, around to coding and accounting and finally back to us to record and rectify the changes.

This particular job is new to my resume. I've been doing it for about two years now and discovered it quite suits me. Although it's a new title and some new skills, it still falls under the admin umbrella. I've always been good at dealing with people and pushing paper. This was a good fit and a hell of a great deal better than the first job I had when we moved here, which I affectionately refer to as "the dungeon." Don't ask. I'd need at least two glasses of wine to get into that one.

The office politics around these parts, however, are far beyond me. We all make chicken feed, so one wonders how anyone can afford office politics, but never underestimate management. Thank God my husband acquired a real job with real money, or we wouldn't be able to afford an apartment, groceries, date nights or anything else. In point of fact, I can't quite fathom how anyone makes it out here at all.

My coworkers, for the most part, have homes, mortgages, kids in school and 'tis a mystery to me how they manage it on our salary. But I ain't that curious and won't lose sleep over it. It is one of those questions I've stored up to ask God when I get to heaven. Yeah, I'm an optimist!

Let me break down office hierarchy. Bear with me. Jenelle, whom I love and adore, is my boss. She's fair, forthcoming and straightforward. Following that are my coworkers, starting with Jason, and he's the best. We all adore him. He, like me, sings to every song there ever was and he is totally the office fav. We've all picked him to be the next American Idol; unfortunately, he's just over the age limit. Damnation! We think he'd be a cinch. First off he looks like Vanilla Ice, which is to say he's a hotE, plus he's the sweetest guy ever. He'll help you out with anything and everything. I know what you're thinking, and nope, no attraction there whatsoever. Go figure.

There's Brianna, sweet girl, quiet for the most part, but can be chatty at times. There's T—young gal, smart, beautiful, lively and a bit competitive. That is how the young are. I can dig it. There's Jane, smart as heck, a little older than myself, big family, and a woman that can deal with a lot of stress. She's an amazing coder and funny as hell. Then there's Laura. Laura is a sweetheart, chatty, witty and a darling. I like my coworkers. They're a great bunch of hardworking, genuinely nice people. The docs are great, talented, skilled and usually very personable. However, under pressure they've been known to be a bit asshole-ish. I forgive Dr. S for anything and everything. People like to tell stories about his rather diva behavior on occasion. And the stories are accurate, but me, I laugh it off. Perfection has its price. If I break a bone, I want Doc S. Period.

Now the trouble is my boss's boss. Cassandra. (Now you have to say her name like Mary would in the show 227, 'cause if you don't know what I'm talking about, you may not get the complete effect.) Cassandra is one of those bosses that are simply unable to allow my boss to do her job, even though my boss is more than capable. Personally I think Cassandra is just afraid of Jenelle shining a little brighter than her. It's a shame, really.

The moment Cassandra comes into the office, the very air around my boss changes. At first she used to just nitpick subtly. After a while she started openly undermining Jenelle; and lately it's just been nonstop. I can see that it's taking quite a toll on Jenelle, who is actually a new recruit. She's only been with us for about a year. Prior to that Laura was running the office instead of being "second chair."

On more than one occasion while working late, I've overheard Jenelle on the phone to one of her old coworkers complaining about her situation. I feel bad for her and can't help but wonder why she doesn't just tell Cassandra to back off or go above her. But of course, I don't have all of the pieces to the puzzle. I am not in the know, and therefore I sympathize silently and give Jenelle the best support I can give her professionally. You hate to see good people get shyted on, but it is what it is, not much I can do about it.

I bum a ciggie off of Jason and take a smoke break. I text Veran and we go back and forth with a little bit of harmless banter. I shudder, the air is crisp, and it's colder outside than I thought it would be. I pull my hoodie over my head and grin as I read V's text. It's fun, but I've still got Ray on my mind. I hear a sound and look through the slanted blinds inside of the break room. Dr. S is getting a cup of coffee. He gives me a very doctor-patient smile and I return it automatically. I finish my fag and head back inside. A few more hours and it'll be time to pick up the kid. As I walk toward my desk I can see Jane rolling her eyes and motioning for me to look in the back. Cassandra is "explaining" yet another policy to Jenelle. I roll my eyes and shake my head in Jane's direction. Crap, it's gonna' be one of those days.

Monday Evening

I hear my husband's key in the door just as I put the finishing touches on my famous chili over rice. A few seconds later he's in the kitchen kissing me on the cheek and giving me a hearty hug.

"Hey, babe, smells good." He smiles while unzipping his jacket.

"Thanks, honey, I'm almost done. Should be ready in about five. How was your day?" I ask, stirring the pot to keep the bottom from sticking.

C heads to the front hall and opens the closet. "It was okay. They're giving me a lot of work, and some of these clients are really starting to piss me off."

I roll my eyes skyward. Immediately I think to myself, come on, man, you've only been at this job for about a year. We were seriously struggling before that. Is it really that bad? Of course, I don't say anything. I swallow my thoughts and instead try to put a positive spin on my feelings. "Well, babe, hang in there. Hopefully it's just temporary."

"Yeah," he mutters unconvincingly and heads to the bathroom.

My mind wanders happily to my NY distractions for a minute or two before turning off the burner and gathering the plates to dish out dinner. I poke my head through Gaia's door with her plate in hand.

"You okay, lil mama?" I kiss her on her forehead as I pass the plate.

38

"Yeah, I'm good." She goes right back to her computer and digs in hungrily.

I study her for a good minute trying to assess if anything seems off with her behavior. I remain unconvinced either way. Further investigation is required.

I fold out the little tray tables and put the plates down. C plops down on the futon and reaches for the remote, turning to our favorite show. I close my eyes for a moment and travel to Iraq on the words of the opening song, and I can't help but smile sadly, experiencing both the excitement and sorrow the character storylines always bring.

One day we decided to give the series pilot a shot and we've been hooked on it ever since. The series depicts a US Army Third Infantry Division on their first tour of Iraq, and you cannot imagine how unique and unapologetically real the characters are and how invested in their stories you become. C senses the change in my emotion, squeezes my hand and smiles at me in the cutest way.

This, of course, finishes me. I fall in beside him marveling at my blessings. We've come to the end of our evening, coincidentally our favorite time of day. We can finally sit down together, chat about our ups and downs, regale each other with As the World Turns episodes of our work mates, watch TV and snuggle. Simple pleasures.

Afterward, we load the dishwasher and head to the shower together. It's a routine that preserves our sanity and renews us both for the following day. Yes, I love my NY distraction, but this quiet life we've built here together, I cannot deny its charms. Odd how one life can make you so fond of the other and incomplete without both, though they are such polar opposites. And later that night, when I'm lying in C's arms, I'm not thinking about NY or Veran or Ray. I'm thinking about C and Gaia and whether I'll catch a glimpse of that grazing horse in the morning.

Hump Day Horror

"What do you mean they're at the apartment? Are you freakin' kidding me right now?"

I got the phone call from C while at work. I try to remain calm as I brush past Jane, walk through the kitchen and out the back door, digging into my pockets for a cig. I light it and inhale quickly. My smoke stream cuts through the air in a cloud of dirty white. Damn, it's cold. I throw up my hoodie and begin pacing while listening to C explain in detail the scenario before him.

Even though we've been diligently taking turns dropping off and picking up Gaia from school while eavesdropping and checking for any sign of depression or worry and subtly probing for information, it all came to a head today. Like a pack of wolves, the girl gathered her friends and descended upon our apartment complex. Her fella, if you will, determined, brazen little bastard, is presently threatening my husband in the courtyard.

They heard through the grapevine that Gaia was at the library with some friends and decided it was a good time to accost her. The library—blessed temple of books and all that is gracious and wise—is directly across the street from our apartment. It was like a dream come true for me and played a huge part in our decision to rent our apartment.

We know the librarian and staff so exceedingly well that they called my husband the minute they saw the mob outside surrounding Gaia and her lone friend, Faith. Gaia's other companions had already left for home before the mob collected. As fate would have it, C was home early and came downstairs to protect Gaia and find out what the hell was really going on. He called me to keep him from pounding little man into the dirt and no doubt ending his evening in handcuffs.

I talked my man down and told him to call the cops and relax. I was on my way home. I checked my watch, a little after five. Should be no problem to leave work about twenty minutes early, and if it is, I'm really unconcerned 'cause I'm leaving come what may. Cassandra's in the office today. Oh joy. Write me up, if you must, bitch, but I'm out. I spritzed myself and make a beeline for the bathroom to wash my hands. C doesn't appreciate cigarette smoke, so deception is necessary.

I want to quit, but I have to do things in my own time. Ultimatums serve only to ensure my deception. I learned that growing up. I want my cake and eat it too, sue me. By now it is already 5:10 p.m.; twenty minutes early shouldn't be a big deal. I explain briefly the situation to Jenelle, who is more than reasonable. She wishes me well and tells me to clock out. She'll see me tomorrow.

I think I peeled my tires heading out of the lot. A little dramatic, but I'm pretty worked up at this point. I know not what I'll find when I get home, and I'm worried, angry and upset all at once. I don't notice the farm animals tonight. I turn off the radio and say a small prayer. I'm gonna' need it. No. They're gonna' need it. I don't feel too much better, probably because I'm too pumped and my prayer wasn't as sincere as it should have been. I turn the radio back on and hit the gas.

By the time I pull into the complex there's no one in front of the library or the courtyard. I snag a parking spot in the back of the building, sprint across the lot and shoulder past the teens hanging out on the stairwell. It's just the neighbors' kids. I like them all but I can't stand the hallway hangouts. I mumble a quick what's up as I pass by.

C opens the door before I'm able to get my keys out. He must have seen me pull in through the window, which means he and Gaia were in her room mulling things over.

He grabs me in a bear hug and immediately whispers, "It's okay. She's okay."

I exhale in relief and we go inside, shutting the door behind us. I pull away from him gently and head into Gaia's room. Faith, God bless her, stayed. The sunlight from the window hits Gaia's face revealing a trail of dry tears. My heart breaks and I run over to her and give her a huge hug. I look over at Faith and ask her if she's okay. She looks fearful but nods. Poor girl, brave friend. I'm glad she was there. It sucks to be alone in all of this. There's my elusive silver lining.

I release Gaia and maneuver her over to the bed. We sit down and I raise her chin to look at me. "Gaia, what happened?" I can feel C enter the room. He hangs back by the door. These are the things I love about C that makes every other man pale in comparison. He knows his presence is reassuring, but he hangs back far enough so that he's not intrusive. Oh Lord, when this is all over, can he teach "How to be a Good Man/Amazing Stepdad, 101?"

Gaia swipes at her eyes in true frustrated lil mama manner and just like me becomes instant Italiano. Chow Francesco Rinaldi. Her hands start going in all directions, telling the story.

"I don't know why this girl hates me so much. I never did anything to her. She said that I gave her an attitude and some look in the hallway and that I was talking to my friends about her. But I don't even know her. I don't know what she's talking about. I tried to tell her that she's wrong, but she won't listen. She wants to kick my ass, Mom. She and her friends are determined to kick my ass over nothing." After sputtering all of this out, she deflates and her hands go limp.

I look over at C and he folds his arms across his chest and leans into the wall, confirming Gaia's version of events. Clearly he'll fill me in on the details she missed later, but for now, this seems to be the gist of things. I exhale deeply and kiss Gaia on her forehead.

"Did they hurt you or Faith?"

"No," Faith mumbles.

"No. When I came out of the library, all of a sudden I was surrounded. The girl was screaming stuff at me and the rest of them were just snickering and laughing. They didn't touch me or Faith, but they were scary. Two minutes later, Christian came downstairs and they started in on him!" Gaia said incredulously.

"Okay. Faith, are your parents coming to get you, or do you need a ride home, sweetie?"

"They won't be home for another two hours. I told them I was hanging out with Gaia at the library and we were gonna' do our homework together." Faith shrugs.

"No worries, sweetie, you'll do exactly that and stay for dinner and then we'll drop you home around nine, okay? You can call your parents and let them know that we'll take you home."

"Thank you."

"Of course, hon." I turn my attention to Gaia and kiss her on her forehead and hug her close.

"Gaia, when someone's after you like this, when you have a problem with someone or they have a problem with you, I need you to be honest with us. I need you to tell me what's going on so we can help."

"Mom, how are you going to help me with this? You can't make this girl stop coming after me."

"Gaia, I know you think that there's no solution to this problem, but that's because you're only fourteen. With your limited life knowledge, you can't see a solution. That's my job, honey. I have to fix this, not you. When something's too big for you to handle, you're supposed to give it to your parents. It's up to us to figure this thing out together. You can't fix this by yourself. Things will only get worse and spiral even more out of control. You could get seriously hurt."

"Mom, what are you going to do about it? Talk to my teacher? Talk to the principal? You really think that's going to make her stop?"

"Gaia, that's a good place to start. And truthfully, I don't know if that will make her stop. But I do know one thing. It's my job to protect you, and that's exactly what I'm going to do. If I had to quit my job and be your bodyguard day and night, then that's what I'd do. If I have to call Auntie D to come out here and the two of us have to put on ski masks, kidnap this girl, threaten her to leave you alone, then that's what we gotta do. But you have to give me a chance to help before you decide that I can't, okay? That's fair, isn't it?"

She considers this for a moment. That's my Gaia, always thinking. Appealing to her sense of fair play is a win-win.

"Okay." I can see the relief wash over her as she transfers all of the weight she's been carrying over to me. I've been slacking. I didn't notice it until this point. I'm going to have to be on my A game with this kid if I'm going to be a useful parent.

I kiss her forehead one more time. "I'm going to make dinner, your favorite, chicken and mushroom casserole, and I'm even going to bake cupcakes, vanilla and chocolate. You guys work on your homework, okay?"

"Okay," Faith coos a little more enthusiastically. It's the cupcakes. Faith loves my cupcakes.

"Hey, Mom?"

"Yeah, honey." I turn on my heel and look back at Gaia.

"When things are too big for you, who do you give it to?"

"God," I say without hesitation.

Gaia nods and smiles as if she knew what my answer would be but just wanted to confirm. I return the smile and C follows me out.

And as I close the door gently behind me, I think to myself, God, here's another one for you.

Thursday Game Face

I called my job and let them know I needed to go to Gaia's school and see the principal and would be late to work. Jenelle wasn't in so I left the message with Jane, our early bird. I don't know how she manages to be on time every day without fail. It's a skill that's escaped me my entire life. Time and I can be friends, but when it comes to employment, he abandons me entirely and somehow making my bed just right becomes priority.

Jane confides that Cassandra's back in the office again. I frown through the phone. She's been here practically all week. What is it with this woman? Jenelle is going to be at her wits' end. When I get in, I better mind my p's and q's. No smoke break until two-ish.

I was afraid that Gaia might be right, that going to the principal and having the school talk to this girl and her parents might not be enough. But after praying, I always get clarity. This is the proper first step. If this doesn't work, we will proceed to plan B, though I'm not entirely certain of what plan B entails at this point. More prayer is required. I lost another hour dealing with my guilt. I kept thinking that Gaia was carrying this weight for far too long and I wasn't perceptive enough to take it from her sooner. More prayer, I forgave myself and finally slept.

It turns out that before I got home last night, the librarian did call the cops. They broke up the children of the corn and were good enough to write a report and warn the kids about coming back. I figured this would be helpful in keeping little miss mob rat in check, God willing. I did a lot of praying last night. I wasn't exactly sure how to proceed in this situation.

47

After speaking with the principal that morning, I was extremely satisfied. They were very concerned about Gaia (she was the only West Indian in the entire school) and her safety. They brought the "young lady" into the office to explain her version of events. She confirmed that she was present at our apartment complex last night. She said that Gaia was giving her all kinds of looks during the school day and she was certain that Gaia and all of her friends were making fun of her and talking about her during lunch (the only time the two kids were actually in the same place at the same time as they shared no classes together.) Odd, I thought.

The principal concurred and concluded that little miss thang simply wanted to bully someone and Gaia seemed like as good a target as any. The principal then proceeded to have a candid chat with mob wife in training, threatening to have legal action brought against her and her parents on not just our behalf but the school's as well. The principal also made an appointment to have the aforementioned parents called in. Mob wife junior looked properly stricken at the prospect. Awesome. I looked over at Gaia and she seemed very happy and relieved with this plan of action.

Before leaving, Gaia and I had a moment alone together.

"So do you feel any better about this situation, lil mama?" I asked her seriously.

"Yeah, I think she might stop now, Mom." Gaia knitted her brows together while answering.

"I think she will too, Gaia, but just to be safe, I want you to keep your eyes and ears open. We'll still be picking you up and dropping you off for a while longer until we're sure, okay?"

I could tell that while optimistic, Gaia still needed and appreciated the safety net.

"Okay, Mom." She gave me a big hug and kiss and then carted herself off to class. I watched her silently until she disappeared into the stairwell and sighed. If this didn't work out, I was more than prepared to call D and kidnap that little wench. Guess I was clear about plan B after all.

Saturday Date

We make it through the rest of the week without incident. Halleleuer! The only thing any of us want to do now is kick back, breathe easy and have some fun. C is taking Gaia and her friends to Deptford Mall while I catch up on some housework before we go on our date. I see them off and then sit down on the futon with my second cup of coffee, allowing myself a ten-minute reprieve.

I flick through some channels and come to a halt on 112. Perfection! HGTV's Divine Design is on! I am a complete closet pillow fluffer if ever there was one. I totally dig that show. After watching Candice come up with a plan for the couple's dreary basement fix, I check the time and realize as I down the last bit of coffee that it is time to get to work.

I blast some Indian music and start loading up the dishwasher. Oddly enough, I've never had a dishwasher before, but one certainly gets used to luxury in a hurry! I don't know what the routine is supposed to be, but in my house if you use a plate, when you're done, you put it in the dishwasher. Before I go to bed, I run it. In the morning I unload and put all of the dishes into the cabinet then we start the whole process back up again. I think it's bloody genius! I make the beds, vacuum, and do a bit of dusting before I hear the keys in the door.

During the week, Gaia takes care of her room, makes her own bed, but on the weekend I like to change the sheets, straighten and dust more thoroughly than she would. I'm so wrapped up during the week with work and other tasks that doing the small tasks for her makes me feel like I'm earning my mom points. I think that these are the things that she will remember when she grows up.

The weekend solidifies my mom status. During the week I'm more focused on work, and when Gaia is with her friends it frees up my time to hang with C, solidifying my role as a wife. But I don't feel like I'm doing anything much for her with the exception of taking her to school and serving her meals. I guess that's why my double life is so important to me and I feel like I can be selfish about it because the rest of the time, even though I wouldn't have it any other way, my time, my life belongs to everyone else. When I'm in NY, that's when I can just be me, Catherine. And I'm not gonna' lie, I need that to feel whole. I need that.

My chores took about an hour and a half, so I know that after dropping the kids off C went to the car wash. He's so cute. I shine the house and he shines the car. I am comforted by our sweet routines and rituals.

C spies me puffing up a pillow and placing it on the futon. "You about ready to shower baby?" he asks, coming up behind me and wrapping his arms tightly around my waist.

"I'm just wrapping it up, perfect timing." I smile, turning into his arms, kissing him.

As we soap down, C cracks me up regurgitating the conversations Gaia and her friends were having on the way to the mall. It's so funny how I end up tuning the mass of screaming teens out and listen to the radio, but C not only listens to their chatter but participates in it as well! Now, I listen to the kid even when I'm too tired to listen, but every now and again I'm more than happy to pass the baton over to Christian.

Forty-five minutes later he heads downstairs to start the car while I look for suitable shoes that go with my outfit. I decide on a pair of ankle boots and take them out to the hallway so I can sit on the bench and put them on comfortably. Two minutes later I'm squishing through the staggered pyramid of teens on the stairway. A few of the teen boys arch their brows and smile shyly as I pass, some of the girls look awkward and intimidated. I smile at the girls reassuringly. In a year or two they'll bloom and won't regard women my age as anything other than an old lady. Don't worry girls, the boomerang will be coming back your way.

As I sit in the car, I smile and give C a big kiss. He tucks my hand in his while pulling out of the lot and smiles back.

"Thank you baby for putting on my butt warmer." I giggle.

"It was a little nippy out so I knew you would appreciate it."

Got to love das auto, heated seats and a man who is so thoughtful! I happily settle into the bucket seat and we're off to the mall!

We park in the lot and leave our jackets in the trunk. We can brave the cool temperature for a few minutes as we make a mad dash inside. We love makin' our rounds or walking through the entire mall and neither one of us felt like being weighed down with our heavy jackets.

We enter holding hands like a couple of teens in love. One thing about C and me is that we're almost always touching. We're very affectionate with each other. Soooo opposite from my ex-husband and me.

I've dated a few younger guys before marrying Christian, and in my opinion there are some striking differences between younger and older men. The younger men seem fascinated by everything that involves being together no matter how mundane the task. Whether I was doing laundry, grocery shopping, trips to the doctor for checkups, hell, whatever, the young guys just seem to want to be with you, near you. I found this more than refreshing, I also found it appealing especially since my ex-husband seemed to want to be anywhere but.

This surprised me. Until then I'd always considered myself more of an independent gal, the kind that loves to do it on her own. I didn't realize I had to do it on my own which is why I became that gal. When I met Christian I experienced an epiphany, turns out I wasn't that girl, not even close. When I married C, all he wanted to do was be my partner in all things. And I finally understood the definition of the word helpmate. I reflect on this while sneaking a glance at C and pressing myself to him affectionately. That's how I am, a complete mush at the oddest of times.

We walk the entire mall, peaking in this store and that, chatting amiably, window shopping and people watching. After a few hours we start talking food and decide no fancy restaurant today, we're keen on the budget and settle on Cajun, picking a prime spot by the carousel to plunk down.

We notice a bunch of Asian teens in Final Fantasy haircuts laughing and talking and we remark on how nice it is that the mixed group of guys and girls can have such a good, carefree time together. They seem the picture of old-fashion teen fun, hanging out and sharing some laughs. Practically vintage!

After a quick trip to the bathroom, we're ready to visit our favorite cookie stand. They guy who manages it has a little crush on me and always gives us much more cookies than we order without ever charging us extra. How sweet, all pun intended. We've recently discovered the mini chocolate almond cookies and are completely hooked. It's been a long week so we skip the movie and head home. Faith's parents have pickup duty this week so we have time for a little lovemaking. They haven't invented a more perfect way to end a date night as far as I can tell.

Later that evening, when C makes love to me, tenderly, softly, I can't imagine my life with any alterations. I revel in this man above me, inside of me. He makes me feel loved and yet not quite desired. Maybe that's unfair. Maybe that's how I feel because I know my heart has small pieces that don't contain C at all, just my own selfishness. I push these thoughts to the back of my mind and enjoy the feeling of being a woman in love and a woman being loved by a man who loves her.

All else seems trivial at our moment of climax. After a few minutes of lying quietly in each other's arms, we take a shower and get dressed for bed. I finish first and put the kettle on the stove. C places two nesting tables in front of the futon and turns on the TV. He reaches into the cabinet to get two plates and divides our favorite cookies. I make the tea as he turns the channel to HGTV.

I smile as I put down the teacups. Does it get better than this? This comfort that we two share, isn't that what love is all about? I kiss him on the cheek just as I hear a familiar jingle. In a matter of seconds Gaia bursts through the door, plants herself in front of us practically acting out her mall tales and displaying her random items of purchase. I look over at C who never is bothered by any of her interruptions and smile inwardly. Suddenly Gaia stops when she notices the cookies.

"Hey did you guys …" and before she finishes the question C points to the microwave.

"They're in the microwave Gaia."

She giggles like the tween that she is and promptly drops us for the confection of perfection.

I laugh to myself as C and I accept the resuming of our peace as easily as we did the interruption. Whatever I feel might be missing, I am aware of what I have and that it tips the scale one way. And just like the blanky Christian covers my legs with, I am warm and comforted by that last thought.

Abundant Life

Oh crap, is that the alarm? I was in the middle of a great dream. Nooooo. I grunt and reach over, disoriented, hitting the snooze. It's only 7:00 a.m. We could sleep another half hour and still make it on time. I could get ready in a hurry if I absolutely had to. I snuggle closer to C who didn't even seem to hear any of the ruckus. He's always so warm and my feet are always so cold, even if it's 90 degrees. I shove my toes under his calf and he stirs a bit while mumbling some incoherent protest. I pay no attention and before I can analyze anything further, I fall asleep.

Seven thirty and the alarm goes off again. This time, I know exactly what it's about. And just as I do every week, I turn it off as quickly as I can and then look over to see if there's any sign of life in C. He's onto me this week, though, and practically has a song in his voice as he flings the blanket off us both, hollering, "Rise and shine, it's time for church!"

I groan. I have very mixed feelings about church. I have no mixed feelings about the Lord. I love the Lord. I have no doubts about my savior. But the house of worship seems to invoke the lazy in me. Sometimes C is too tired to go himself and we stay home and sleep in, but today, today isn't one of those days. My husband, son of a pastor, has definitely got his game face on. This man is revving to hear the word, smile at fellow worshipers and sing some Godly hymns. I, however, not so much.

I am not so foolish, however, that I don't realize when C is in this mood, there is nothing to do but get into a fight (of which I will not be able to sleep afterwards in any case) or get up and get dressed! I decide on the latter. What's worse is getting Gaia up. She's been raised as a Hindu for the better part of eight years, or the entire time I was with her father. Since her dad and I split, I've gone back to my Christian roots. Ever since C came into my life, my Christian roots have become stronger. Marrying the son of a pastor has its influences, not all of which I fully appreciate. As my child, Gaia has been thus affected. While I haven't forced her to change her belief system, I have instilled a "my house my rules" type of situation and also told her that I'd like to expose her to my religion and that way whatever choice she may make in the future, it would be an informed one.

Needless to say, Gaia was unhappy with my enforcement, lapse as it was. We wouldn't attend church every Sunday, sometimes I was in New York, or sometimes it was just plain laziness. But when I had to wake her on a Sunday for it, she was most displeased. She obeyed, but not without the "tude." Between her tude, my ambiguity and general lack of proper Christian enthusiasm and C's quiet forbearance, we made for very strange worshippers. But the Almighty did say come as you are. Indeed, and in deed.

When we finally enter the temple of the most high (no sarcasm), I smile at our entrance greeters in what I hope appears pleasant, though I detect a hint of uncertainty in the return. I distrust what I think I feel or see because my guilty imagination tends to have its way with me. There are moments I feel like a fraud in a religious setting. I tend to wonder if those around me have really caught the Holy Spirit or simply drank too much spirit from the passed chalice. But in this particular church, Abundant Life Church, I don't feel anything but genuine joy. The hardest part is getting me here.

These people seem to be genuinely ecstatic about coming to this place on Sunday and singing not about but to our savior. I know I've got one foot in the world and one toe in the Lord but being here makes me desire more Jesus less world.

My mom always tells me that it's not the perfect people he came for but those just like me, the sinners. I am that lost sheep the shepherd left the perfectly obedient herd to go find. All of these thoughts swirl through my head as we're shown to our seats and given the pamphlet for today's goings on. Gaia sits down while C and I continue standing and join in the hymn already in progress. C use to tell me that I should make Gaia get up and join but I told him that's pretty useless. I can't force her to sing to a God she doesn't believe in with words she doesn't mean. It's enough that she's here and she's not sulking while she reads along in her Bible. He doesn't like it but doesn't push the issue.

Being married a second time, yoked with a man who is not the father of my child, definitely has its challenges. Luckily, I am a tiger when it comes to Gaia and because C also comes from divorced parents, he is more sensitive to Gaia on that level than perhaps another man would be. This line between these two loves of my life has not been an easy one to walk, but we have a pretty good system. If C has an issue he brings it to me. We discuss it, and if I feel I need to bring it to Gaia's attention, I do just that. Not we, me.

For all intents and purposes, I maintain control when it comes to Gaia. C and I don't always agree on what's best for Gaia. Thankfully I had some foresight and had frank discussions with C before walking down the aisle. He's quite aware that if we disagree on any course of action concerning Gaia, my decision will trump his, bottom line.

He didn't like it. I don't think I can ever really make him understand my reasoning. What I had to make him understand is that he doesn't have to understand in order to comply. In the end I think he realized that most of our decisions were in sync. C's a good man and he loves Gaia separate from the love he has for me and thus far we're doing all right.

Two hours later, my favorite preacher was wrapping up the sermon and we stood to sing the last hymn. It always amazes me that Christian never has to look at the screen for the words. He knows all by heart. Me, I hardly recognize any of them. My mom took my sister and me to church when we were little but I can't remember one word to any of the songs we sang. As usual, the choir loathes to quit singing at any point and by the time they're on their third round of a chorus that should have ended two stanzas ago, we're making our way out. C is merciful. My back is aching and we're all starving. Can't wait to get home and heat up last night's leftovers. Chicken, rice, veggies and cheese casserole, yummy! My soul is filled to the brim with good, wholesome thoughts; now it's time to let my belly catch up.

Planting a Seed

It's been a wretchedly hard week and thank God there's only two more days left to it. Cassandra has been around every single day harassing Jenelle right along with the rest of us. I've about had it with her. I'll never understand why the powers that be place the most unsuitable people in management positions when they have absolutely no clue how to effectively manage or communicate with others.

Everyone should know that in order to lead you must first have learned how to follow. Duh! Unfortunately this seems to be a cancer-sized issue. I don't think I can remember but one or two companies that I've worked for who seemed to have gotten the infrastructure and managers correctly appointed. One day, when I rule the world Pinky. My earpiece buzzes as I reach into the freezer pulling out the beef stew to defrost. I press the button to take the call.

"Hello?"

"Hi babycakes, how are you doing?" My sister's sweet, chirpy voice sings into my ear and all prior thoughts of work are banished.

"Hi my lil bunny, I'm great honey, how are you?"

"I'm doing great also. You have time for this conversation?"

"Yeah, no one's home. Gaia is over at her friend Skye's house and C is doing some overtime. What's up?"

"Oh nothing much but I wanted to go over a few things with you and then run something by you."

"Sure. Shoot." I knitted my brows while peeling away the plastic and plopping the beef in a basin of warm water.

"Well girl, you know last weekend the girls and I went out."

"Yeah I know. Wish I could have joined ya'll but you know."

"Of course, girl please, I just wanted to give you the low down."

I open the cabinet and reach for the rice pot, simultaneously hitting the electric kettle. I'm definitely gonna' need to sit down with a cup of joe once I get dinner started.

"Well, don't keep me in suspense girl, what happened? First of all, where did you guys end up?"

"Well, first we went to Rum Jungle. But they were kinda dead so we hopped around to a few other spots, in the end settling on this little hole in the wall called Roy's."

"Roy's?" I wrinkled my forehead trying to search my memory banks. "Have I ever been there?"

"No girl, never. We just discovered this joint that night." She laughed. I could hear water flowing on her end as she turned on her faucet.

"Forgive the noise, I'm refilling my kettle. I need a cigarette."

"No worries, I just put mine on a minute ago. I could use a ciggie myself but no can do right now."

"Aw, I feel you." She sympathized, knowing Christian would give me an earful if he detected the faintest hint of smoke.

"Anyway, what happened at Roy's?"

"Girl I saw Ahmed," Nikki said, practically breathless with excitement.

"Say what? You saw Ahmed?"

"Yes girl, and he looked soooooo good."

"Doesn't he always? Oh my gosh, what were you wearing?" I inquired, while washing the rice.

"Well that night was no exception. Oh thank God I looked good. I was wearing my orange cut up Marciano top with black pants and black heels."

"Umhm. Yeah, girl, I know that top. You look amazing in that outfit."

"Thanks Cat. I did look good if I do say so myself. Matter of fact, we all did."

"Did everyone make it out that night?"

"Yeah girl, even Charmy."

"Wow, ya'll was rollin' deep."

"Yeah, girl the whole crew was out, but we all missed you like crazy."

"Girl I know. Don't sweat it. Next time. So anyway, what happened? Did you do something crazy girl?"

Hearing the sound of her laughter I could picture her clapping a knee, doubled over in glee.

"You'll be happy to know that I did not embarrass myself this time. I didn't even know he was there. Princess had to point him out. But anyway, he came up to me while we were at the bar, bought us all a round and then pulled me aside to talk for a bit."

"Well that was nice of him. What did he say?" I turned on the stove under the rice pot and set to making my coffee.

"He asked how I was and told me how nice I looked, blah blah blah. I hardly noticed. I was too busy staring into his eyes. Damn girl, he really did look good."

"Well, how did it end?" I asked while scooping the Folgers into my coffee cup.

"He gave me his business card," she said, clearly annoyed.

"Well what's wrong with that girl? At least you can call or text him now," I said, not understanding what the problem was.

"Yeah, that's true but he shouldn't be waiting for me to call him. He should call me."

Lord have mercy, more proof that my parents found me under a rock somewhere because there are times (case in point) where my sister and I are so far apart in thought that I have to check myself before responding.

"Well what's wrong with calling him? I really don't see the issue honey," I said, probably a little too abruptly.

"Girl, don't you know if a man really likes you he doesn't leave the ball in your court but takes the bull by the horns and gets your number?"

I pursed my lips and squinted my eyes in a "seriously" fashion. If men are from Mars and women are from Venus, I'm certain I'm from Pluto, 'cause I don't get none of this right here.

"Well girl, I don't know. I don't see much difference in who gives or gets the number. As long as it's been got then there's a chance one of you will give and the other can receive." I chuckle at my own perceived cleverness.

"Well whatever. I'm glad I got to see him. I just wish he'd take more of the initiative," my sister said, disappointment evident in her voice, probably from my reaction as well as Ahmed.

I feel a big sister pang and make restitution quickly.

"Girl he's probably more nervous than you will ever be. You know he thinks you're the shit. He probably doesn't want to give you a chance to shoot him down. I mean, what if he asked for your number and you said no? He probably doesn't even want to take that chance so instead he played it safe. Don't you think?"

"Hmm. You know, I never thought of it that way girl, but you could be on to something." Success. I could hear the perk back in her voice.

"Of course girl, that man has been chasing you forever. I'm sure that's it. So you gonna' call him or what?"

"I don't know. I want to, and then I don't. I'll see. You know he's always got these chicks surrounding him, and I get the feeling that he's married."

"Well girl, could turn into something fun. You will never know unless you give it a whirl." I blow my coffee and take a sip while seating myself on the sofa.

"That's true. I'll think about it. Anyway, I wanted to run something more important by you."

"Oh yeah Nikki, what's that?"

"Well." She paused and I could hear her exhaling the Newport. Jealousy surged through me along with an innate need for nicotine.

"I wanted to readdress maybe you moving in with me and coming back to New York." She takes another long drag.

"Oh that." I laugh, not really taking it seriously.

"Yeah girl, that," she states all too seriously.

"Girl I don't know. I want to move back to New York, of course, and these days I do think about it more than not but I don't know if it's something Christian will even consider. I think Gaia might be onboard, but honestly I haven't even had a proper discussion with either of them."

"Well maybe it's time you do," she pushed.

I sighed.

"Listen. I know it might not be an easy thing to talk about with C but you might be surprised. He might be down with it. Haven't you told me that lately he's been griping about his job? And didn't you say that Gaia isn't really thrilled about her school?" She pushed a little further.

"Yes, all of that is true but that doesn't mean that they'd be willing to pack and move back to NY. Plus Nikki, the whole money situation. We really just don't have the funds for all of that."

"Well, I worked that out."

I could hear her lighting another cigarette. I took another sip of my coffee and crossed my legs Indian-style on the couch. This was gonna' take a minute.

"Pray tell, how did you accomplish that?" I asked, clearly skeptical but willing to hear her diabolically ingenious plan.

"You and C could move in with me, and Gaia could stay temporarily with her dad, until you get some paychecks under your belt and get on your feet. Then you guys can get a place of your own. Everyone's together under one roof in NY again! And, everyone's happy! Ta-dah!"

I could just picture her doing the Ta-dah hop, skip and spirit fingers.

"Girl I don't know. It sounds simple enough and I really can't thank you enough for even entertaining the idea of putting us up but Nikki, you got a one-bedroom apartment. We'd be all up in your grill. Wouldn't you feel put out?"

"Now, I'm not gonna' lie and say it would be an ideal situation for any of us three but girl, you being all the way over there and the rest of us being all the way over here is just not working. Mom, Dad, me, the rest of the crew, we want and need you home. Come on, it's been three years already."

"Girl, I hear you, and frankly it is what I seem to want more and more. But let me talk it over with C. I don't think we could seriously entertain the idea right at this point. Gaia's in the middle of her last year of junior high and C's job is taking care of most of the bills. My job pays diddly squat, but at least I've got one. I haven't got anything in NY."

"You act like finding a job in NY is hard for you." She inhales impatiently.

She's right of course. Finding a job has never been hard for me. If I was going to come up with an excuse, it was going to have to be better than that.

"True. You're right. Well listen, I really appreciate you putting this offer on the table. It's extremely kind and generous of you, lil sis. Let me talk to C and Gaia and see what they think about all of this. We'll chat later on in the week, okay?"

"All right Cat, sounds like a plan. But I really want you to talk to them. I want you to take this seriously, okay?"

"Okay, okay. I promise I'll talk to them and get back to you."

"All right, sounds good. I love you."

"Love you too little bunny."

I hang up the phone feeling both dread and excitement. Oh damn, the rice! I run into the kitchen just as the water is about to spill over. I lower the heat just in time and stir the rice, most of which is stuck to the bottom. I decide that I'll talk to C and Gaia Saturday. This week has been too much of a doozy to figure anything else into it. Thank God tomorrow's Friday!

Subtlety Required

I thought that maybe I could have a chat with Gaia and C about moving back to the Empire State on the weekend, but last night C's mom called and invited us to a family get-together at his grandma's house on Saturday. I think I might have to postpone our chat until Sunday. I know one thing for sure, after a two-and-a-half-hour drive to NY and a two-and-a-half-hour drive back, C is definitely not going to be able to muster the strength for church the next day.

This might just be the opportunity that I need. Frankly, I don't even feel like going to the get-together. His family is great, don't get me wrong, it's the timing. I'm mulling this over as Brianna walks out of the doc's office wearing a long face. I scowl, dreading my turn as I step inside.

This morning Cassandra decided to pull us all into the doc's office one by one to discuss Thursday's early dismissal. I really can't figure this crazy bitch out, except to say she's on a power trip from hell and we're all along for the ride, all but Jenelle. She wised up and quit Tuesday. She finally decided the force was indeed against her and made arrangements to reacquire her old job. Cassandra had the balls to act as if the situation was a surprise instead of a natural result from her own incessant interference and lack of ability to allow someone competent to do their job.

The New York option was starting to grow on me. Staying started to seem more like an unappealing nuisance. Christian was doing more griping about his job since last week. Every day there seemed to be more pressure to serve an impossible client, and new business seemed unlikely. His company (a small family-run business) was talking about closing up shop for good.

Fate was arranging all of my ducks in a row even before I had a chance to open my mouth. But I knew how stubborn C could be. On one hand he'd be happy that I already had an option in play, on the other he hated moving, and I wasn't sure how he felt about New York anymore. He loved being here, the quiet, the fact that no one interfered with our lives. It was just us. His brother and his family split a while back and have moved in different directions.

It really was just us out here in no man's land. But that sword cut both ways, and I could sense that he might sometimes be just as lonely as I was. I hate to resort to trickery but it was all in the presentation. If I spun this just right, he might actually think he came up with the idea and, well, there wouldn't be much I would need to say after that.

I tuned back in to Cassandra just as she crossed her legs, showcasing her cheap, brown, ugly orthopedic-looking shoes which actually went perfectly with her hideous brown pants suit. I nearly chuckled out loud thinking how badly this chick needed a good stiff one, a drink, and would benefit immensely from a head-to-toe makeover.

"I'm sorry, what was that?" I snapped my eyes from her shoes back up to her tightly pursed lips.

"I asked what made you think it was appropriate to leave the office at twelve noon yesterday after I specifically left instructions that no one was to leave until their work was completed for the day?" she asked in exasperated tones.

"Cassandra, I'm afraid I don't understand the problem with me or anyone else. After Jane announced that you left her in charge and said we could leave once our work for the day was done, that's precisely what we all did. There wasn't anything leftover for today. We hardly have any patients on the roster."

I'm sure I sounded like I was speaking to a damn fool and probably should have softened my tone, but I could barely suppress the urge to reach over and choke the life out of this woman. With visions of New York and a proper paycheck swirling in my head, I could hardly be expected to contain my abhorrence. I was fairly convinced no jury in the world would convict me.

"That may be Catherine, but I cannot believe that anyone, including you, would interpret 'you may leave early' as permission to leave at noon when the work day normally ends at 5:30. Wouldn't it be more reasonable to assume I meant 'by early' perhaps three o'clock or 2:30, but noon?"

Oh sweet heavens, did she actually use air quotes? I had to inhale deeply, ask Jesus to check me, and then answered.

"Cassandra, you left Jane in charge with a note that stated in black and white that we all had permission from you to leave once our work for the day was complete. You did not specify a time in which you were personally comfortable with. We in turn did exactly as we were told from your limited instruction. Perhaps if you wanted us to do something specific you should have been more specific in your note." I crossed my arms over my chest in absolute "I can't be bothered with this bullshit" stance.

Needless to say, my attitude did not foster any further conversation. What I received instead was a lecture from a jester who clearly didn't know if she was coming or going, most of which I unmistakably tuned out. She dismissed me with something of a vigorous nod and a loud hmph at the end of it all. Prior to this "meeting," I was certain I was on her hit list, but now, I've managed to move myself up a few rungs to her shit list. Under normal circumstances I might have felt uncertain, scared, nervous about my ten-dollar-an-hour job, but today I felt freedom. In that moment, I knew we were moving back to New York, even if I had to paddle all the way with one oar and a canoe.

Getting the Hell Out of Dodge

Surprisingly, C did not offer up much resistance to the idea. At this point, he and I were running neck and neck in the "who despises their job more" race. Some days he would get the cookie, other days ... well, I'm sure you get the idea. A week ago my aunt called with news that my uncle was sick. Apparently he wasn't feeling well and went to the doctor who, after a preliminary checkup, made an early diagnosis of lupus. Of course, he couldn't be certain until he ran some more tests.

Frankly, I found his lack of common sense appalling. How could you possibly give someone that kind of diagnosis before you're absolutely certain is beyond me. On the other hand, of course, my uncle was a stubborn man and could have pressed the doc for more information than he was willing to give, perhaps forcing the doc to state among many other theories this one. Whatever the case, from that point forward, my uncle started behaving as if he had received a death sentence.

I took a few days off to drive to NY and stay with my parents while the family tried to find out the whole story. You can imagine how well that request went at work. Frankly, I didn't care. I was hoping they would can me. My mom looked as if she was getting tired of my hearing about my uncle's pity party attitude. She was a strong woman of faith, reassuring her sister that my uncle, her brother, was going to be fine, and that he was only making himself sick.

Frankly, I wanted to side with my mother, but after you get a diagnosis from a medical professional, it is rather hard to ignore. Still, I wished my uncle had a more balanced attitude until we knew for certain. My sister and I did what we always do, research. We talked to the docs, comforted my aunt, uncle and parents while trying to figure out who my uncle should consult for a second opinion.

Whilst all of this was going on, Nikki and I started making more definitive plans about my moving back to New York. I hadn't shared any of this with my parents yet but I could tell they would be completely onboard, especially after this situation. By the time I left New York and headed back home, we still hadn't heard anything from the second doctor.

When I went back to work the next day, I requested a meeting with Cassandra. I played the grieving niece to a tee. With my uncle's health in question, I really didn't know what the future held. Of course, if things got worse I would have to consider heading back to New York permanently. Cassandra nodded with perfect understanding that she clearly didn't feel.

There was no surprise there. West Indians were very close to their families, which baffled many other cultures. My uncle was as important as my own father. I was actually worried about him, but of course it wasn't the entire reason I was taking the next two weeks off. I had plans to go back to New York and acquire a new job within that time frame. I had a Dustin Hoffman Kramer vs. Kramer deadline that I had every intention of meeting.

Cassandra was all sympathies and smiles when she granted my emergency request. She probably had plans to replace me during the same two weeks. It mattered very little. We both had our strategy. It'll be down to last man standing. I looked down at my feet while Cassandra gave my shoulder a sympathetic pat. Game on.

Best Laid Plans

"What can I get you?" my sister asked, reaching into her wallet and whipping out her credit card.

"My usual hon." I smiled, swallowing a bit of my pride. We always were generous to each other when it came to dinners, drinks, just about anything. But this time she was taking on a little extra. That's just the kind of girl she was. She'd hardly ask me for a dime until I was gainfully employed in the Big Apple.

There were sisters, and then there was my sister. I squeezed her hand in subtle thanks. She squeezed back and engaged the bartender. "One Malibu and grenadine and one dirty martini, actually, make it filthy, and if you could throw in some extra olives that would be awesome!" She handed over the card and smiled at the bartender in a way that would win wars. People loved to do things for Nikki. She had a way about her that made you want her approval. Don't look at me. I hadn't acquired the gene.

"So what'd Cassandra say when you told her you needed two weeks off?" Nikki arched her brow in question, fishing out the fancy toothpick and peeling off an olive with her pearly whites.

"What could she say, the beeatch?" I shrugged, taking a sip of my sweet concoction.

"She didn't have much of a choice. Frankly, she probably didn't wait for me to leave the parking lot before making calls to find my replacement."

"Really?"

"Yeah girl, but it's all good. I don't intend to drag this on. I'm getting a job within the next eight days, if it kills me."

"Speaking of, how did the interview this morning go?"

"Great. You mind if we go outside and have a ciggie?" I asked, digging into my purse. Old habits die hard, and I picked up right where I left off the minute I crossed state lines.

"Of course. Let me ask the bartender Tricia to hold our drinks. You got ciggies?"

"Yeah, girl, I picked up a pack yesterday before I got to your house," I answered, opening my purse wider, scanning for my lighter.

A moment later we were out in front of Ticks, the night air a little chillier than an hour ago. She shivered slightly as I lit up.

"You want to go back in and get your jacket?"

"No, no, I'm good. So how'd it go? Continue." She smiled as she exhaled a thin stream of cloud.

"Girl, I think I'm practically in already."

"Whaaaaat?" She smiled.

"I actually met with two recruiters, well, it's their company, they run it. Anyway, after an hour of chatting, they set me up on my first interview and told me to call them the minute it wrapped. And when I called them, they told me that I had another a few blocks over if I was game! I was like, hell to the yeah! Can you believe that?"

"Wow, those guys are good."

"I know right? I can hardly believe it myself." I smiled, staring across the street at the Maxima parking.

"The first interview went well but even if they offered me the position I don't think I'll take it. It's a lot of work, the guy I'd be working directly for seems very demanding and a perfectionist. I'm not really feeling the vibe."

"Well girl, nix that. I know you've got a deadline but you don't want to land something only to be looking for the exit two weeks later."

"True that." I inhaled deeply right before my eyes went wide and I choked. Classy!

My sister went into near panic mode, patting my back vigorously which no doubt served to make my coughing progress to a dry heave. What an awesome sight, just as Ray glided past us with two of his friends. Please Lord be merciful and don't let him notice us. I was doubled over. He might not have recognized me at that angle. I wasn't brave enough to sneak a side glance through my curtain of hair. Once they were safely inside, I managed to compose myself and whirled at my sister excitedly.

"Omgosh did you see that?"

"See what?" my sister screeched. "Girl, I'm one second away from calling an ambulance. Are you all right?"

I laughed, coughed, sputtered then laughed some more.

"Yeah, I'm all right. Girl, I choked because I saw Ray!"

"Ray?" my sister questioned, completely clueless.

"Ray, girl! He just passed us and walked inside with two of his peeps. You didn't know that was him?"

"Girl, how the hell would I notice anything other than you when you're coughing up a lung like that?"

I rolled my eyes and threw my hands in the air. Truthfully though, I couldn't blame her. I did have allergies and a slight case of asthma that did act up on a fairly regular basis. If you're gonna' give me the lecture, save it. I use to smoke like a chimney. I only do it now when I'm drinking. For now, that's as good as it's gonna' get, so work with the kid.

"True. Well, whatev. He's in there now. I just pray he didn't see me hacking away like a cat with a fur ball." I flicked the offending cig while Nikki took her last drag. We took a moment to collect ourselves and went back inside.

The lights seemed dimmer. It was a Wednesday night, around 9:00 p.m.-ish. There weren't many patrons, but enough to make me have to scan the area conspicuously. Damn, nada. He's probably playing pool in the back somewhere.

Nikki and I resumed our seats. Our gorgeous blonde bartender Tricia already had our drinks in front of us. That girl was always on point and though I bat for the team with two balls, it must be said, Trish was marvelous eye candy equipped with a West Indian hot pepper attitude that made you enjoy the tongue lashing she was always dishing out. My sister took a sip, spun her stool and leisurely scanned the back.

78

"He must be in the back playing pool," she said, clumsily fishing for another olive that managed to evade the toothpick, safely resting on the bottom. Between my hacking up a lung and her fishing for olives, we didn't exactly make the top ten list of whom to spend your evenings with. I made a noise in between sips that concurred with the idea. Ahhh, sexy.

"Listen, why don't you tell me what happened on the second interview, we'll finish our drinks and then go to the bathroom real casual like and see if he's back there?"

I nodded. Unless he came up here, what other option was there? I finished telling her my story about how well the interview went. Not only did I interview with two people, but they insisted that if I had the time could I wait thirty minutes for John who approved all hiring. Apparently, he was in a meeting.

Of course I waited, and I felt just as comfortable with John as I did the other two. We all seemed to have a nice flow going and by the end of it they wanted to know my salary requirements and start date. They needed someone to fill the position immediately, which fell right in with my plans.

Seemed like a perfect fit for all involved. Time will tell. I spoke to my guys at the agency. By the end of the day they received positive feedback from both clients. They instructed me to come in tomorrow around 10:00 a.m. dressed for interviews. They expected to have at least two more lined up for me.

So far, everything came up roses. Nikki, of course, was extremely pleased for me. We decided to go have another cigarette after we finished our drink, then we'd head to the bathroom, and if the mood struck us, have one more for the road. Just as we were lighting up outside, Ray and his two boys appeared like mist. This time, we locked eyes and smiled at each other.

"Hey, I thought that was you earlier." He smiled, pointing at me.

Crap, I should have known he recognized me. I'm not Mystique, for Pete's sake.

I nodded sheepishly and exhaled to the side. "Yeah, you know, I wasn't 100 percent sure it was you, but hey, how's it going?"

He smiled in that sexy, unaware way. "Good, good. These are two of my friends from Canada. I just got off of work and picked them up for a quick drink." He pointed them out and politely introduced them to my sister and me. I hardly glanced at them. I wasn't trying to be rude, but I couldn't tear my eyes from his beautiful face. It's been a long time that a man had this type of effect on my person. It took me back all the way to junior high. You can't bottle this stuff.

His pals noticed and were much cooler than I gave them credit. They stood closer to my sister, lit up and chatted with her amiably, leaving Ray all to me.

Ray pointed to my cig and I thought, here comes the lecture. Instead he surprised me and asked me for one. He allowed me light it for him. Unusual. Most men preferred to light it themselves. I couldn't predict the smallest detail about him. It only served to intrigue me further. We made small talk, and I tried my best not to sound like an idiot. I can't tell you how I did because I hardly remember. I was unbelievably happy to simply be near him. Ray was not the kind of guy that was out and about all of the time. Whatever stars aligned to make this meeting happen, I couldn't say, but I wasn't questioning it. He finished his smoke faster than I, and looked over at his friends. By now they appeared ready to go. He turned back toward me and smiled.

"It was nice smoking with you, Catherine. Good night."

I smiled, properly puzzled but managed a "Good night Ray."

And just like that he was gone. No kiss on the cheek, no see you another time. I watched him walk to the car with his friends. He looked back at me only once, after he opened the driver's door, right before he got in. I smiled, slightly. He didn't smile at all but I swear his eyes glittered. If he was checking to see if I was checking to see, then I suppose we both get a cookie.

My sister turned to me and smiled. "Should I light up another?"

I hadn't bothered to answer. I saw the fire flicker.

"Well, looks like this entire day went well for you." She smiled and took a drag. "New York has welcomed you back with a little present your first day!"

I smiled back and took a drag. "Girl, the last time I saw Ray was about two months ago."

"Yeah? So?" She shrugged.

I sighed. "He remembered my name."

You Can't Go Home Again

I was a bitch. I couldn't help it. It's rare that I show my ass, however ... I actually waved my new hire contract like the flag of freedom it was.

"Well, that's great. We are very glad everything worked out." Cassandra smiled tightly.

If she had her way she'd probably toss one of her ugly shoes at me. But sorry, Sandy, the day belongs to me. This one's for you, Jenelle. I wish she could have been here to celebrate this little victory but alas, it would seem we're both moving backward to fly forward.

"Yeah, who knew things would happen so quickly?" I feigned innocence so ridiculously that my gloating was nothing short of obvious. "I'm just glad the timing all worked out as it did." I smiled, pushing the kitchen chair back. "I suppose I'd better say good-bye to my peeps and clear out my desk. It's been a pleasure, Cassandra. Thank you for all you've done for me. I really appreciate it." I extended my hand.

Got to give her credit, she looked at it a full three seconds before deciding to shake. "Well, thank you for all you've done here at Cooper. We wish you the best."

I nodded curtly and quit the room, bumping into Doc S on his way in. He gave me a wistful smile but didn't stop me. I returned the smile in kind and continued on my way. I always saved the best for last. A few minutes later I was hugging some of my coworkers and making promises to keep in touch.

Some were genuinely happy for me, some not so much. I didn't blame anyone. Since Cassandra came onboard with her policy changes and her stifling aura, I've been a pill. I talked about moving back to NY nonstop and bitched and moaned about everything. I was almost sick of myself. Word spread about my new salary and of course that wasn't really inspiring the warm and fuzzies either. I made it short and sweet, grabbed my gear and headed out to the parking lot.

A few minutes later, when the crowd thinned and I knew doc would be writing reports in his office, I came in through the back. I missed my guess. He was in the kitchen making his seventh cup of joe. He hadn't troubled himself to look up, and in that instant I knew he had been waiting for me. Funny number two, the kitchen door was closed. I smiled at him as if he had been mine his whole life.

"I suppose I can't count on your to find those patient files anymore, Catherine. Received a better offer, I've been told." He tucked his arms into his beautiful chest, crinkling the pinstriped Brooks Brothers shirt. The man with the beautiful shirts, I thought absently. He smiled but his lips hadn't told his eyes.

That's the second time this month a man I lusted after said my name. I savored the moment, closing my eyes a second longer than necessary to blink. I felt the heat from his nearness, and when I opened my eyes, he held out his arms.

Without hesitation, I folded into him. When we finally pulled apart, he caressed my cheek. I kissed my Doc S for the first and last time lightly on his lips and squeezed his hands. "Give 'em hell, John." I smiled sadly and fled the scene like a murderer. I did not look back. Whatever hadn't happened between us never would, and it was enough that he would miss me.

That night, when I recounted the scene, it did not surprise me that a doctor I had been working with for two years, whom I passed at least three times a week, eight hours a day, felt something for me. Truth is always stranger than fiction. In a moment of mad bravery, we shared a precious thing, acknowledgment.

Out of my whole Cooper experience, he's the one thing I still carry with me. And just like that, an old chapter in my life closed and a new one began.

Wildin' Out

The Big Apple. Cars honking, millions of people hurriedly commuting, yellow cabs shouting at rickshaw drivers, coffee and donut carts on every corner, all before 8:00 a.m. Rewind to South America, British Guyana, some forty years prior, a tiny village from where my parents hailed. If someone had a radio in the entire village, that was something to talk about. And yet, my father had the foresight to settle down in quite arguably the center of the universe, New York City. Some years later, I was born, in the heart of the city no less a genuine New Yorker with the attitude and mindset of the city, a hustler, a winner.

It ain't easy makin' it in New York. For one, New York is wicked fast. You're always on the go. You wake up, choke down your coffee while getting ready for work, fight the millions who are on the bus and subway hustling just like you to rush to a cubicle and push paper.

I am acutely aware of being part of the energy of the city that spins the world. And I'm finally back where I belong. As much as I appreciated the horses and chickens and pastures as the backdrop just a week ago, I hadn't realized until now that the concrete, noise and suits are exactly what I was missing. I was ecstatic to be back in the center. I was home.

Today was the start of my new job. I left C to tidy up things back home. He still had two weeks to wrap things up, and Gaia had two weeks left of school to finish. We had already packed up every room in the house, with the exception of the few items they would need to comfortably function. I took off an extra day to tack onto the weekend we were moving so there wouldn't be such a horrific time crunch and we could breathe a little easier during the move.

Once we put everything in storage, we just had to trek over to Nikki with our essentials. Gaia was actually looking forward to spending some time with her dad. It wasn't an entirely new transition as she already spent summers with him and had her room redecorated the previous summer. Everything was in place. Of course, that was next weekend! This weekend, the girls and I were gonna' celebrate my homecoming big time!

The coffee at work was amazing. They had a Keurig machine. With one touch of a button I had fresh brewed java! I bought a chocolate croissant from the deli next door and was ready to get to work. I totally dug my setup. I occupied the reception desk in front of the office. I worked independently, greeted and seated all guests, took care of all office and kitchen supplies and made travel and lunch arrangements for the big boss, John. It was easy! I had done this for several years, training was unnecessary and everyone verbally appreciated the fact that I did whatever needed to be done without the need for instruction. I silently said a prayer.

This was absolutely the right fit for me and working here, getting to know my coworkers, reinforced my decision every day. One of the interviewees was a young lady named Kris, my junior by almost ten years. We hit it off right away. I could tell we would eventually socialize over drinks during the coming weeks and become buds.

Things couldn't be better! Every day was filled with little challenges but for the most part each day was very much like the last. I found stability in routine and the paycheck was a Godsend. Forty-five K a year would definitely get us on our feet in no time. I still find it hard to believe how we managed on the paltry sum I was making at Cooper. I shook it off. I had to leave the past where it belonged. Nowhere to go but up!

Friday came much quicker than I imagined. I had a pep in my step walking from the train station on Fifty-Third and Lex. The sun was shining and I felt beautiful! I was wearing one of those outfits that flattered in every way possible, my hair was perfect, my makeup flawless and yet today the attention of everyone seemed extra. I was no stranger to admiration but this seemed a tad much. It was as if the entire block confused me with some celebrity. Not until I paused waiting for the light to change did I stumble upon the real McCoy. As I turned to my right to check the streetlight, I was blindsided by this Amazonian beauty who looked as if she just stepped off the runway in Milan!

Do you know the type of which I speak ladies? Well, she's the type of woman that has you conversing with yourself as if you were a player on the losing team and needed a pep talk. Yes honey, that woman. She was absolutely flawless and, believe you me, I was looking.

Oh all right, I was gawking! She was a foot taller than me, she looked like she bathed in Chanel and was made of money. From her head to her toes, this girl was a walking Vogue ad. What's even worse is that nothing she wore was overtly anything. She rocked a beige silk jumpsuit, a leather vest, simple strands of gold chains, leather sandals and a sun hat. Yes, you heard that right, a sun hat.

Who can pull that off in uptown Manhattan on a Friday morning? This Chiquita banana, that's who. My morning that started off so promising was quickly spiraling south. Don't get me wrong. I dug Ms. Thang. I truly did. I'm not a woman hater by any means but after walking another block in her presence, the pressure was simply unbearable.

I couldn't help but question why I was putting myself through it.

What exactly was I trying to prove? That I could stand in the presence of this rose and not feel like a wilting carnation? I am a confident woman. I know I'm beautiful in my own right, but hot damn the way people (including myself) were reacting to this chick, well, it was as if a unicorn was walking down Lexington Avenue. I crossed the street and breathed a sigh of relief. Thank God these beauties were dispersed in small doses across the city, because it was just be too much to bear on the regular.

When I finally got to the deli on the corner, I thought twice about that chocolate croissant! I had a nutri-grain breakfast bar instead and a delightful cup of java. A few hours later, when I was in the midst of ordering supplies, I got a text from my best friend Draia inquiring of my plans for this evening. I texted her back that I had none as of yet, but was down for anything. She was going to pick me up at midnight and we were going to bar hop!

I sent out a blast to the rest of the girls, however, everyone else had plans. Looked as if it was just gonna' be me and my bestie tonight. Things were definitely looking up! What was even better is that tonight was preliminary. Tomorrow we were rollin' deep. All of the girls were coming out in full force to celebrate my homecoming at our favorite West Indian Club, Maracas. I couldn't wait! This was definitely going to be a weekend to remember!

****

Was that the doorbell? I ceased towel drying my hair and poked my head out of the bathroom, straining my ears. Yup, that was definitely the doorbell. I gave one more furious tug on my hair and slung the towel over the rod, making sure to open it up all the way so it would dry. Nikki's house, must bear in mind Nikki's rules.

"Browsers, don't you look hot, beeatch!" I exclaimed, brushing an affectionate kiss on Draia's lightly rouged cheek.

"Why tank you, tank you, my darling," Draia returned, locking the door behind her. She was the only one of us that was mixed between Spanish and Black and probably a little bit of everything else and yet the only one of us who could actually pull off an authentic East Indian accent. Oh the shame of it.

"Can I get you anything hon, I need about ten more minutes." I gestured toward the kitchen.

"No, no, I ate already. Just finish getting ready and I'll just park myself over here and wait. Take your time, it's not even midnight." She pulled out the dining pub chair and made herself comfortable.

"Draia, you look amazing hon. I love the outfit, the shoes and the makeup," I appraised before heading to the bedroom. She always looked spectacular, but tonight she was rocking understated elegance. She had her hair in a very chic 20s bob. Only Draia could rock wigs and look natural.

"Thank you. I actually tried today. Raj took the kids out to get a haircut, so I had the place to myself. And you know how rare that is."
I paused with the eyebrow brush in midair to answer.
"Girl, for you, yes I do." Draia had three kids, one son, grown and out of the house, and two girls, age five and age

thirteen. Being mom to three was not easy. She was always busy running here and there, doing this and that, not to mention working and taking care of house and hubby. It never ended. Thank God we girls had each other and could squeeze in some chill time in betwixt the paycheck and the dusting.

"Yeah, so you know I said I have my bestie all to myself tonight, so I'm gonna' have to turn it up."

I could hear her laughing and joined her.

"Girl I know that's right. We'll see the rest of those beeatches tomorrow but tonight it's just you and me. I can't wait to get our drink on. Where are we gonna' hit up first?"

"For real, but we should take it easy on the drinking because we're gonna' do this again tomorrow. Cat, your phone is beeping. You got a text."

"Yeah, you're right. I don't plan on drinking more than like three drinks tonight. We'll go light. I just wanna have some fun. Draia, I'm putting on my lipstick, and then I'm gonna' run some gel through my hair. Can you see who's texting me?"

"It's Veran," she shouts.

"Oh really?" I'm surprised. I didn't expect to hear from him. I chucked my lipstick in my wristlet, checked to make sure I had my ID, some cash, my ATM card and my Triple A card before joining Draia. I smiled at my girl while reaching for my phone.

"Wow, you look great, Cat." Draia smiled.

"Aw, thank you, baby. I gotta match my girl," I said, smiling and punching my code into the phone, reading the text.

"What did he say?" Draia asked.

"Apparently he and his boy are leaving a party and heading over to Mingles. He wants to know if we're going out and can chill with them for a bit. What you think?"

Draia shrugged noncommittally. "It's up to you girl. You know I'm down for anything."

I thought about it for a second and a half and texted V back. I turned to Draia and smiled wickedly.

"Said we'll see him in about twenty minutes!"

Draia shook her head and chuckled.

"Cat, you're too much."

Hidden Agendas

We arrived in Mingles a little after 12:30 a.m. and things were just starting to jump by the looks of it. Couples and singles lined the bar like horses at the starting gate while a fair amount of attractive ladies and gents occupied the VIP areas. The single dudes posed GQ style, drink in hand, surrounding the pockets of interestingly clad females gyrating on the dance floor. Thus far I dug the vibe.

Draia and I checked our coats and made the rounds. We spied a few of the usual suspects, cheeks were graced with our friendly kisses and offers spiked from one group to the next on dibs for our first drinks. Didn't look like we'd need to spend a dime tonight. Draia's budget and mine were about the same, wouldn't take but two rounds to empty our pockets. A good friend of ours, Ty, took the lead and bought us our first round. I reminded myself to go light and opted for a Malibu and pineapple. Draia settled on a Corona. And though our generous benefactor offered, we declined on the Patron.

"Hey Ty, where's Carmen?" I smiled, raising the glass to my lips.

"I'm not sure actually." He smiled sadly and took a slow sip.

I opened my mouth to say something but then thought better of it. I heard through the grapevine they were having some marital troubles. This wasn't the time or place. Instead I smiled and squeezed his forearm in silent support.

Draia nudged my arm. It was time to leave this scene.

I kissed Ty on the cheek and smiled. "You're a prince."

He raised the Heineken to his lips hesitantly. "You think so?"

I nodded. "Don't you forget it," I threw over my shoulder as we swept passed him and headed toward the DJ booth where Veran and his crew staked their claim.

"What took you guys so long?" V inquired, quickly circling an arm around my waist and pulling me against him in a warm embrace.

"Sorry, I was actually in the middle of getting ready when I got your text." I smiled apologetically and clinked glasses with him.

I glanced behind me and noticed one of his boys wasted no time and was already chatting up Draia. He wasn't half bad. She looked pleased. All was right with the world. We finished our drinks, gently pushed past the crowed and headed toward the dance floor. Veran was a very tall, attractive young man with the kind of body that I admired, a man's body, no skin and bones on this fella. I put one arm on his hip and slung the other over his shoulder, playfully twirling his hair. He hooked both hands around my waist and pulled me close.

In no time we surrendered to the music. In this arena, we left everything else behind and enjoyed the dance. Twenty minutes later he led me off to the side and made certain I was comfortably seated before making his way back to the bar to order round two.

As he walked, I observed a number of ladies admiring his gait. As he leaned against the bar waiting for our drinks he noticed a number of males appreciating his absence. He smiled at me knowingly and I had to smile back. It was all part of the game, the ambiance, the company and the drinks made it all the more intoxicating. I closed my eyes and savored the moment. It was good to be back in the thick of it.

Some minutes later, while V and I were deep in chat, I looked up and noticed Draia standing in front of us.

"Hey sweetheart, you ready for another drink?" I asked, all smiles. The liquor was definitely coursing through my veins, making me feel warm and giddy.

"No, I just wanted to get away from that dude. He's nice, but he's talking my ear off. He really won't shut up." She gestured to Veran's friend, who looked a little embarrassed and kept his distance.

"Come on, don't be like that. He's probably just nervous because he's really shy. He's one of my best friends, and I can tell you, he's never talked to a girl as beautiful as you."

Doth my ear deceive me? Do I understand the words that are coming out of this dude's mouth? Was I completely soused, or was V actually flirting with my girlfriend?

"Aw that's so sweet of you to say, but frankly you're more my type than he is," Draia cooed, flashing her million-watt smile, dropping a hip and punctuating the statement with a schoolgirl giggle.

Now I definitely was on planet what the fuck because I could swear that my best friend was flirting back. Oh hell no, this is not happening. I felt queasy and it wasn't from the liquor. A flash of jealousy seared through me. I knew that if I didn't get a hold of myself I was going to make this bad situation worse and look a hot mess. I excused myself and headed to the ladies room. I needed a minute. I could hear Draia toss V something witty just before she spun around and followed me.

As soon as we burst into the bathroom, Draia fired questions at me like a semiautomatic. I ignored her, brushed rudely past a girl coming out of the stall and locked myself inside while doing my best to drown her out. Was it possible that Draia didn't realize the "thing" betwixt Veran and I? I had been away for a very long time, I reasoned.

Perhaps she hadn't realized that he, much like Marcas, was one of mine. It was the cardinal rule. Don't mess with someone else's flirt. None of us had ever broken it or even come close, probably because our tastes were so varied that we rarely found the same thing attractive. Needless to say, I was completely taken aback by the sudden interest, at least on Draia's part.

My head was spinning. How could I extract myself from this, keep V's interest in me while making Draia lose hers in him? There's no way to keep what was yours except by letting it go.

After pondering that strategy for a few minutes, I decided the best way to handle this would be to serve up Veran on a silver platter. HarA Va! Let her have him. Once V recognized that I wouldn't fight for him, he would undoubtedly realize that to lose me was unthinkable, reel himself in and fall in line. Nothing like a little liquored up logic!

I burst from the stall all smiles, the very picture of feline friendship. I practically purred the answers to Draia's legion of questions. Why yes, he did seem quite taken with you. Very handsome. I always thought so. He's gone for months at a time, in the Army you know. A special forces medic, of all things. Quite impressive.

Before I knew what was happening, I began encouraging the budding romance. At this point I honestly felt that I still had him, and whatever temporary insanity fell upon these two, it would soon be over. I must endure. Little did I know, fool that I had become.

The rest of the evening I wish I could say progressed in a blur but unfortunately I remember every single detail. Draia was no longer interested in vacating Mingles to bar hop. Veran was even less interested in leaving her side. Despite my best efforts, I played the petulant child to perfection. I sulked not so silently. What hurt worse is that my reactions (not to be confused with actions) were entirely ignored by both parties. I found it less and less likely that Draia was oblivious to my feelings for Veran. For whatever reason, this evening, she decided upon him. I watched them from across the table. Oh, did I mention we all ended up going to the diner for breakfast? Whose idea, you ask? I watched as Veran shyly suggested it, and Draia coyly accepted.

I was beginning to doubt my visibility. We were seated in the back, a four seater—cozy. Their first date tennis match banter made me dizzy. Funny, Draia mentioned Veran's friend was quite a blabbermouth. Perhaps he noticed what rotten company I was, because he was as quiet as a grave and very serious about his breakfast, I might add. Before the check came, I threw my last $20 on the table and mumbled something about the bodega across the street and cigarettes.

"Catherine, I've got the bill, and you're not going alone.

Give me a second and I'll come with you."
My eyebrows accompanied my "don't trouble yourself"
side grin. But I did catch Draia's eyes widen just so. A
small meaningless victory. I reveled in it for a moment
before departing abruptly. Visibility at long last.

Before I hit the door, V's hand reached out from behind
and pushed it open.

I didn't acknowledge his presence and half jogged across
the street. He silently kept pace. Damn army special
forces whatever.

"Why are you upset?" he asked when I was giving the man
behind the (what I assumed was bulletproof) glass my
stogie order.

"Upset, m-wahhh?" I touched my hand to my chest
dramatically.
He chuckled. "Catherine, what's the problem?" he asked,
reaching into his pocket to pay for my bad habit.

"Nothing. Nada. Zip. Zilch. Zer-O." I grabbed the fresh
pack and started unwrapping the plastic. I needed a hit. I
was acting like the fool that I felt. The situation had gotten
away from me so fast my head was still spinning. There
was no way to salvage the evening so I did the next best
thing. I made it worse.

He sighed and tucked his hands into his pockets.

I took a hit, inhaled deeply and watched the long cloud of
smoke spiral toward him like an accusing finger.

"You gave her your shirt."

He shrugged his shoulders and his hands strained forward, trapped in his pockets. "She was cold. The diner has the a/c on full blast."

I pushed the air out through my nostrils hard and shook my head.

"Always the gentleman, aren't we?" I blew more smoke in his face.

He winced. Better than what he was doing, blowing smoke up my arse.

"Whatever, this evening's a bust, take me home please. I don't wanna talk anymore."

He didn't say a word and followed me back to the front of the diner, just slightly a step behind.

"What happened to you guys? We thought you got lost." Draia exclaimed, all wide-eyed doe-like. It didn't escape me that she was still wrapped up like a Panini in his shirt. I didn't bother to answer, just walked to the car still smoking. We dropped off V's friend first and then Draia. I was surprised but not half so much as Draia; after all, it had been the driver's decision. I tried not to be happy about it. I was. Damned if I'd show it. Just before she closed the door, Veran asked for his shirt back. She acted surprised, as if she hadn't remembered she still had it on. At this point I was hard pressed not to scream "really bitch," but I bit my tongue instead and did that arched brow, roll my eyes, silently kill me thing.

"Catherine, come sit in the front."

"Nope, I'm good right here," I said tightly. The only thing that made me happy was that Draia was still in earshot, walking to her apartment. We were best friends, but neither of us was acting like it tonight. I chuckled inwardly. Maybe we're on a break. Veran refused to put the car in gear.

"Catherine, I am not a taxi service. Please. Come sit in the front." He said the words slowly, cautiously, with exaggerated patience, like he was dealing with a caged animal, promising freedom.

I sighed, removed myself to the front and sat down in a huff, as if to say, if my broke ass didn't need a ride home …

He smiled. "You've got goose bumps. Would you like my shirt?" He held it out like some sort of whacked peace offering.

I smiled as fake as I could, gently took the shirt, balled it up like garbage and tossed it in the back. I considered throwing it out of the window, but truth be told, I'd never played crazy. You wouldn't know it by my behavior tonight. I had been giving such a good imitation.

He arched a brow and smiled. Obviously he found my behavior amusing. Oh joy!
I barely gave him a chance to stop the car before jumping out.

"Well, okay, good night," Veran said, bending his head awkwardly in an effort to catch a glimpse of me through the passenger window.

I was already halfway up the path to Nikki's apartment. I turned around, threw my two fingers up in true gang sign formation and said, "Deuces."

My light fun evening turned out to be anything but. And in a few hours, we would be doing it all over again.

The Mother of All Insecurities

"Yes, Mom, my job is great." I rolled my eyes skyward in annoyance.

"Well make sure you dress good, and you get there on time. And exercise. You lost some weight but you have a good way to go."

My sister spied the look on my face and instantly put the kettle on. She also blessedly laid a fresh pack of cigarettes on the counter before heading to the bathroom. I mouthed a silent "thank you" before reaching for one of her green Crate & Barrel coffee mugs.

"Ma, you know I've got no issues with my weight. You have issues with my weight but honestly you're going to have to keep those to yourself. You know I don't discuss weight or money with anyone; I'm not about that life ma mere."

At this point I was on automatic. The woman never fails to get under my skin and pick at the scab until it bleeds. I try and try for as long as I can remember not to allow her words to bother me, to cause a reaction that will later have me talking to Jesus for hours, alas I remain unsuccessful. Today will be no different.

I have learned through my conversations with Jesus not to answer the insults by lashing out at her in my own defense. Not only is it completely useless, but we both end up in tears and I become the perpetrator and she the victim. It's an orchestrated circular mess of noise that has no rhyme or reason. After my night with Draia and V, my angel of patience was losing out and the little devil was doing cartwheels on my left shoulder. It was time to end this conversation.

"Okay, Mom, well, I've got a lot to do right now so let me let you go and we'll chat another time."
"So soon you have to go? I just called you," she said indignantly.

What's a matter? You just ran through five out of your eight insults, and because of your OCD you need to get through the list? I gritted my teeth and put on my strained little girl voice.

"Mom, I don't have anything new to report, we just spoke a few days ago. Everything's still great with my job. I'm still going back to Jersey to help Christian with the last minute details, and we're going to move here officially next weekend. Gaia will be at her dad's. That's everything on my end. So unless you've heard anything new about Uncle's condition or if you yourself want to tell me anything new, then yes, I've got things that I need to attend to. We're going out in a few hours."

"Oh gosh, you're going out again? I don't know how you and Nikki are always running to bar and club. Me, I never liked things like that. Christian doesn't mind you going out?"

It was over. The little devil on the left hacked the angel on the right to pieces and it was, as Ashley would say, on and poppin'.

"Mother, Nikki and I are young. We like to go out and have fun with our friends once in a while. Where's the harm in that, for pity's sake? Of course you don't like things like that. You're from a completely different generation. And if I needed permission from Christian to go out with my girls, I would never have married him."

"A-hi-rai. Catherine, you're really something else." I could see her chin pulling towards her neck and her eyes widening to an impossible degree. This was her stance when she witnessed a horror beyond all horrors.

"Mom, this is not what I would call conversation. This is foolishness. Do you have anything that you want to tell me that is sensible?" I huffed. I knew I would feel guilty later for my part in the conversation, but I planned like hell to drown it out with Patron. If I was going to have the guilts, it was going to happen tomorrow.

"Well go then, say good-bye. Get to what you have to do since you don't think I have anything sensible to say."

Was that a tremor in her voice? Oh for Pete's sake (sake, the Japanese rice wine)!

"Listen, Mom, you're taking things too far. I don't want to argue with you about silliness. I just have a lot to do and nothing to say that you don't already know." I was backpedaling as fast as I could.

"Well, okay, why didn't you say that instead of—I don't have anything sensible to talk?"

Must chew tongue completely off. I sucked in a breath and massaged my temple.

"Sorry. Next time I'll try that, Mom."

"Yes, you should. Okay, well go do what you have to do. I'll talk to you another time. All the best. Ba bye."

"Bye Mom. Love you," I said kindly.

"Love you too," she returned a little tighter than I would have liked. She hadn't forgiven me completely, but she was on her way.

I made myself a strong cup of coffee, grabbed the cigs and jogged downstairs. I sat on the stoop, took a healthy gulp. The coffee was delicious. I took my time and made it perfectly. I packed the cigs and lit up, replaying the entire conversation in my head. And so it goes, like a song I wouldn't be able to get out of my head for days. Once again Mom was the conductor and once again I just got played. Lawd have mercy!

The Edge of Reason

I was a moody bitch these days. I managed to contain myself while at work, but as soon as the 5:30 p.m. bell rang, I just couldn't seem to help myself. The bitch was back. Everyone noticed; everyone, of course, but the two people who should have. I thought I played it smart. I thought that it would take Veran less time than it took to shake a tail feather to figure out what's good. I had far less faith in Draia. You see, there was this one time, not at band camp, at school actually, where Draia and I met, some years ago that this situation already took place.

****

"Mom, quit arguing with me about the state of the house. I could care less. He's cheating on me. He's been cheating on me for months." I hurled the revelation at her like an open sack of flour, heavy and messy.

"How do you know?"

I shook my head while the corners of my mouth simultaneously turned south. The fact that she wasn't surprised sure surprised the hell out of me.

"I know. Besides playing the jackass for the better part of a year, he finally admitted it, only after she called me, of course."

And that's when my mom gave me the best and most unappreciated advice ever.

"Don't bother with him. Right now you should concentrate on improving yourself. Go back to school. Work on you."

And so I did. And that's when I met Draia.

She was brash, beautiful and bold. She was a complete misfit and badass. I liked her immediately. Her opening line was "females don't usually like me."

My response had been, "I'm not most females."

We've been inseparable ever since. The thing is, I could see back then why females didn't take to Draia. She had a way about her that managed to multiply any insecurity you might have. The reason we never had a problem is because I don't compete, not just with Draia, with any females. I always picked the guy who only had eyes for me. Disaster averted.

Life was complicated simplicity back then. I worked from 9:00 to 5:30, and then dashed across five blocks to report to school from 6:00 to 10:00 p.m. It was grueling but it beat being at home thinking about my absent husband. Gaia was not yet five. She spent most of her time at her grandma's house.

It was hard to adjust to her absence but I had to sacrifice the present for our future. By the time I took the train and bus home, it was practically midnight. I got home in time to kiss her peacefully sleeping baby face good night, study for an hour and hit the sack.

I cherished my mornings because that was the only time Gaia and I really had together—for the better part of eighteen months. I made her breakfast, got her dressed, chatted with her and saw her get on the school bus. It was hard to keep everything together, but I could see the silver lining, an end to the chaos. It helped me maintain focus. I had a plan. I had a goal, and I kept it pushing.

My friendship with Draia made school much easier to deal with. In fact, our friendship probably saved us both. She was escaping from an abusive baby daddy and I was escaping involuntary Big Love at home. It was crazy and yet one of the best times of my life. I couldn't believe how easy it was to get back into the swing of things at school. I missed the smell of number 2 pencils, taking notes, answering questions in the classroom and interacting with other students. You might say one in particular. Jordan Gonzales caught my eye in the worst way.

He was an absolute dish. Truth be told, he could have been Trey Song's twin. Yes, that kind of honey drip! For a while he didn't know I existed. In the six months of my invisibility, with the breakneck pace of home, work, study, I'd managed to drop quite a few pounds. I started to embrace my new body with fierceness and shopped accordingly. Crop tops and tight jeans started to become staples in my wardrobe.

Jordan began to notice me. I began to take notice of his notice. Soon there wasn't an evening that we weren't having one intellectual exchange or another. We played it cool. I wasn't concerned about my marriage. At that point it seemed more like a technicality.

My husband at the time was spending most of his time with his girlfriend. He was tired of hiding it. I didn't even care. He held no interest for me. We grew tired of each other. At this juncture we were living like the Odd Couple, roommates that could hardly stand each other but were cordial for cordial's sake.

Draia didn't seem interested in any guy at school. I observed both her and Jordan. They use to talk a lot in the beginning, but once I changed, Jordan didn't seem to notice anyone else. Since Draia never appeared to notice him, I started contemplating the possibility of dropping some gates and allowing Jordan entry. Take that as you will. We were all invited to a party a few weeks prior to graduation. Jordan made it a point to ask me if we were going, Draia and I. I hesitated not and confirmed our attendance, then immediately went shopping.

Draia and I arrived at the party early and mingled. Eventually we made our way to the makeshift bar, acquired a drink and parked pretty close to the DJ. I voiced my disappointment Jordan had yet to grace us with his presence. I was beginning to think he might have had more fascinating plans. I had a great view of the door and blessed be he made an appearance an hour later. I sucked in my breath.

He looked incredible. What's even more telling was that as soon as he crossed the threshold he immediately scanned the floor and broke into a wide grin when his eyes came to a rest on me. That little observation spoke volumes, and told me all that I needed to know. He didn't waste any time and made his way over to us in a hurry.

"Hey. Wow, you look amazing," he stated, giving me a very appreciative once-over.

"Thanks Jordan. You look really nice yourself," I said, returning the favor with a bit more subtlety. Always gotta leave 'em wanting more.

I rocked a form-fitting black spandex, spaghetti strap dress, ankle length with a thick, white stripe bordering both sides. The effect was worth triple my weight in gold. I wanted a departure from my usual style. It was a confection of perfection. Jordan was far from the only one who noticed but he was the only one that held any interest for me and that made all the difference.

"I'm going to mingle with the DJ for a bit. I'll catch ya later," Draia said, startling me. I'd almost forgotten she was standing there.

"Yeah, sure, no worries. Laters." I smiled at Draia and noticed she had been talking to me but looking at Jordan who hadn't so much as glanced in her direction. I got the impression it irked her, but I was too happily ensconced on cloud nine to draw any speculation.

After another round of drinks and about an hour later, Draia found Jordan and me giddy and happily entwined on the dance floor. She found some guy who was the guest appearance at the party. She introduced him but wrapped up as I was I could hardly be expected to pay the intro any attention. I was blissful, she seemed happy. We danced back to back sharing a laugh and our perceived good fortune.

She leaned back inquiring loud enough to sail over the music, "You kiss him yet?"

Jordan's eyebrows went up a fraction of an inch and his fingers splayed my waist in silent consent.

"No, but I'm working on it," I answered while Jordan and I both laughed. He pulled me closer and planted my lips with a fairy-tale kiss. I closed my eyes inhaling his cologne, feeling his body rock against me, and floated skyward. I wanted to live in this perfect moment forever.

Over the course of the next few weeks, whenever we were in school, Draia plied Jordan with nonstop attention. She dressed more provocatively and turned all of our conversations towards sex. Her focus on him was undeniable. Poor bastard never had a chance. And as much as I liked Jordan, once he started to bask in her attentions, I lost all interest.

I learned a few things during that time, some about myself, some about Draia. I could not comprehend why Draia acted the way she did on occasion. I never felt like she was jealous or envious. Maybe she did certain things just to see if she could. There have been plenty of men that have been interested in me and Draia never batted an eye.

However, there was no telling when she might get the itch. I was afraid that when she did, and decided to pull out all the stops, she would take what might have been mine. It was starting to make sense why she wasn't very popular with the ladies. I also learned that I wouldn't compete for a man. If he could be so easily taken, then was he ever mine to begin with? There was something about Draia that made me apt to give up the guy rather than confront her about her behavior. Given a choice, I'd much prefer to lose them than her. This mode of action had served me well then. What was it doing to me now?

Fraction of a Whole

By week three, living in New York with Nikki had become routine for Christian and me. C acquired a job with his cousin, transporting X-rays. It wasn't his dream job, but he was good at it and seemed to like it. I breathed a sigh of relief and said a silent prayer to Jesus.

Meanwhile, back at the crazy ranch, I went to and fro, running scenarios in my mind. The one I liked best? I could accept Draia's interest in Veran and allow it to burn out naturally. After all, where could it go? Unfortunately, the scenario that seemed to play out was the one where I sulked like a foolish tween while V and Draia grew closer. I was insanely jealous of their intimacy. He called her. He texted her. Clearly he was interested. I always called him. I always texted him. He answered, but that's hardly the same, is it?

I began to see the flaws in our relationship, V's and mine, Draia's and mine, and this irked me to no end. It haunted me in my dreams. I was on the edge. Christian became aware of my mood shifts, though he could not or would not attribute it to any particular cause. I always had a few flirts on the side, but I was never thus affected. My agitation was becoming transparent.

My separate lives were bleeding into each other. I used acidic tones whenever I called Veran, demanding all manner of updates between him and Draia's growing fancy. He indulged me and answered all of my questions, but not without hints of annoyance. This served to only water the seeds of jealousy, and they began to grow at an exponential rate.

When I wasn't plying him with questions, I was attempting to fetter details out of Draia. I wasn't even clever about camouflaging my insatiable curiosity. Perhaps that's why Draia, completely fed up with my antics, divulged information that V shared with her about my incessant calls to him prior to their meeting. This could only mean one of two things.

Either I really was a bugaboo and he had nothing better to do at the time than answer my calls and indulge my delusion of a relationship betwixt us or, now that he had a new interest, what better way to solidify the new than make light of the old? Either way, he had thrown me under the bus all too willingly. And I consumed all of my waking moments analyzing everything they said to each other. I was truly in a hell of my own making.

I still managed to hang out with C and maintain my "normal." We had these great dates on the weekend. We'd wake up, get dressed, have breakfast, leaving some for Nikki, and then split. Nikki dug it because she loved to sleep in and have her place to herself for most of the day and evening. This was just up C's alley! He loved to get up, get out and do stuff. Me, not so much. I preferred evening dinner dates and movies.

But NY had a transforming effect on me. I wanted to give Nikki some time to herself, and I wanted to please C. In the process I had a lot of fun on our dates and tried to push Veran and Draia to the back of my mind. I wasn't always successful. And when I was distracted and distressed, Christian would ask me what's wrong. I would lie and make up excuses about a work project or that I was tired. This whole thing was spiraling to an unfamiliar place, and I couldn't give my all to anyone, not even myself.

"So do you want to eat at the Cheesecake Factory or do you want to try something different?" C asked, just as we rounded the corner, passing Swarovski.

"Huh?"

"Babe, you're not paying attention to anything I'm saying. What's wrong?"

I sighed. Why couldn't I just be left alone with my own thoughts? I preferred to be alone and wallow in despair. I didn't want to be here, and yet I did. It was the distraction I needed. How incredulous! I now needed my real life to be a distraction from my fake life. I was completely out of control and still couldn't figure out how to reel any of it in.

I looked into my husband's handsome, worried face and felt stupid and guilty. I wanted to forget about everything else but him. I needed to start living in the moment rather than reliving past moments, moments with men who never belonged to me. What seemed like a fun harmless game was becoming too real.

I squeezed his hand and pressed myself against him.

"Nothing. I'm being silly and I'm putting an end to it right now." A determined smile spread across my features. "I could eat. You?"

C looked at me for a moment, and I swear he could see right through me, that he knew it all and was gonna' tell me off in no uncertain terms. Instead he squeezed my hand back and said, "Yeah, I could eat. Cheesecake all right?"

"Absolutely. I'm famished!" I swallowed my guilt, tucking my hair behind my ear.

"Dem big words, baby. Wha' dat mean? Big words, big, big, big."

I cracked up alongside my husband and we laughed the tension out of our bodies. There's nothing that puts a smile on my face quicker than when my hubby puts on his Trini accent and gets cute with me.

This week I was going to put this whole V and D thing to bed, all pun intended; it was festering in me like a disease. I wanted to get on with my life, my real life. Enough was enough.

Taking Out the Trash

I was making headway and for the most part was able to leave Veran and Draia on their own. I no longer called him. I no longer questioned her. I hardly spoke to him at all, and Draia hardly spoke to me. The tension between us was obvious to all of the teacups, but no one brought it to the forefront. I was grateful, but I knew sooner or later I was going to have to clear the air with Draia, come clean with my true feelings and apologize for convoluting the entire situation.

Gaia called me today. I hadn't seen her in a few days. She had been busy hanging out with her dad's side of the family and settling in. For the first time in years, I didn't feel the need to check up on her every second. Finally I could relax a little and shift focus. Gaia was happy, safe and sound and apparently overwhelmed.

"Gaia? Are you okay, little mama? What's wrong?"

"Hi, Mom. Yeah, I'm fine. Nothing really. It's just that Dad is kind of a slob and the house stinks and there's dishes in the sink and clothes everywhere and I just don't know what to do and where to start." Her hysteria tumbled out in words, reaching through the phone and slapped me in the face.

"Are you at home?" I looked up as Christian made eye contact, sliding off of the couch, a worried expression etching his face.

"Yeah."

"Where's your father?"

"I don't know."

I glanced at the wall clock. It was almost 10:00 p.m. I frowned into the phone, my eyes angry slits. I shrugged and shook my head at C mouthing the "what's wrong" question.

"Okay, I'm coming. Hang tight, I'll be there in ten minutes."

"Thanks, Mom. Love you."

"Love you too little mama." I ended the call and shook my head repeatedly.

"What happened?" Christian asked calmly.

"Apparently the house is in filth and he's not even home. She's all by herself."

"Well, babe, Gaia's not a baby. The man can go out once in a while," Christian reasoned.

I hitched my eyebrow up a couple notches and twisted my lip at one corner.

"Christian, Arjune's had years to himself. We've been parenting Gaia all of this time. Don't you think the one time she lives with him after all of these years that maybe he would want to spend as much time with her as possible? I mean, damn it—she just got there. Is it unreasonable to assume he would want to for at least the first few weeks until she gets a routine going or something?

Whatever C's opinion, he knew better than to come at me with any rebuttal. His mama didn't raise no fool. Instead

116

he grabbed the car keys off the side table, plopped down on the ottoman and started pulling on his boots.

I kissed his bald head and reached for my shoes.

****

The stench infiltrated my nostrils as soon as Gaia opened the door. I literally backed away from the aerial assault, tripping all over an already testy C directly behind me. It dawned on me that he wasn't terribly comfortable hanging out in my ex's domain. I recognized the angst slowly creeping across his face and into his clenching knuckles on the drive over. I pushed it to the back of my mind for further analysis down the road. Dealing with the problem at hand took precedence.

"Gaia where are the garbage bags?" I asked, hardly hugging her.

She fished them out of a pull-out drawer and handed them to me, clearly relieved that someone else was in charge.

While double bagging the garbage and fumigating the can with Lysol, I managed to do a quick once-over on half the joint. It was a complete disaster. There were at least a few days' worth of dishes piled in the sink, various pots decorated a messy stove, dishes and glasses were scattered on the dining room table along with grocery that should have been put away. I was disgusted. Gaia was not used to taking the helm on all of these projects at once.

It became clear to me that her dad had greater expectations than Gaia was capable of meeting. And I knew my daughter. She probably tried to keep a lid on things until she couldn't, forcing her to call for backup. I wonder what else I should have been up on and felt an almost physical pang of guilt. I was way too busy in my own soap opera to put my focus where it should have been. My punishment could wait. I had plenty of time later to kick my own ass.

"What are you doing?"

I turned to C who leaned against the arm of the couch with his hands folded across his chest defensively.

I took a deep breath. "What do you think I'm going to do, babe? I'm going to help her get this place in order."

"You're going to clean his house?" His voice dropped an octave.

I turned to Gaia and could see the fear in her eyes. She didn't need to hear any of this.

I took a breath and put my fake smile on. "Gaia, please start straightening your room. When I finish up here, I'll come see how far you've gotten."

She nodded and scampered off to do my bidding.

I took another breath. "Babe, I know this is probably a little uncomfortable for you. But yes, I'm going to clean the house that my daughter lives in. I don't plan on making it a habit, but right now this needs to be done. I'll call her dad tomorrow and we'll have a conversation about how unacceptable this is. For right now, I need to make sure Gaia is living in a clean and comfortable environment. This shouldn't take me longer than an hour or two max, okay?"

C clenched his jaw, turned around and reached for the TV remote. He didn't say anything, but I could see his controlled anger just beneath the surface. I'd have to find a way to make it up to him. This was a lot to ask, but there was nothing else to be done.

I turned around and started washing the dishes.

"You're not going to clean his room."

My head snapped up. Clearly, he wasn't asking a question. Before I could say a word, Gaia was running down the hall with some fast food wrappers in hand.

"Nope, I'm gonna' go do that now. My room was clean except for these." And she scampered off for the second time to complete another task she could comfortably manage.

"Would you like me to get you something to drink, babe?" I asked evenly.

"No. I just want you to hurry up," he snapped.

While I knew this was uncomfortable for him, it wasn't much of a picnic for me either. I was prepared to take only so much of his crap before I would dish out some of my own. Instead, I took a moment and had a word with my Jesus.

"Like I said, I realize this is uncomfortable for you; however, I don't have the luxury of ignoring what's going on and leaving Gaia to manage this mess on her own. I have to consider Gaia and put her before both of you, and that's exactly what I'm doing. So tuck your anger away for a minute and marinate on that. In the meantime, if you get thirsty, let me know. He's got that Starbucks Cappuccino thing you like in the fridge."

By the time I got to the stove, I glanced over at the couch and could see Christian's shoulders in a relaxed position. He was watching the X-games with genuine interest. I felt better. I could do what I had to do in peace.

A few minutes later Gaia opened the fridge and Christian asked her to get him the Starbucks drink. When she handed it to him, he grabbed her hand and tucked her into the couch beside him.

"I'm sorry I had to call you guys," Gaia said, handing him the drink.

I paused, my eyes glistening while I held my breath.

Then C grabbed her in a bear hug.

"Nah, Gaia, don't mind me. It's good that you called us. Your mom is going to talk to your dad tomorrow and hopefully he'll be straight after that. But you call anytime you need us. We gots your back homie. Aight?" C smiled, bringing the Bronx lingo to the surface, easing the remaining tension.

Gaia nodded, clearly relieved.

That's the thing with C. As a child of divorce himself, he and Gaia share a unique perspective on our triangular relationship and all of its pitfalls. He can't help his feelings, but he finds a way to make sure Gaia doesn't take it personally. While I keep thinking that she can't handle the truth and do my best to shelter her by softening it up, C just gives it to her straight. And I suppose he must be on to something, because as Gaia skips past me she is back to her old self. No angst in sight.

After we cleaned up the joint, I sat Gaia down and asked her what her schedule was like now that she was living with her dad. It seemed that he was out a lot, both for work and for socializing. I suppose, to be fair, he'd been living the bachelor lifestyle for so long it probably didn't occur to him that he'd have to make some changes now that his daughter was home full time.

He never remarried, and I heard his new Miss-issippi masala split a few months before we came back to New York. That was ill timing. I counted on her to take the lead with Gaia more so than him. She always treated Gaia well.

Apparently Gaia's father thought she could handle the full duties of keeping house. While I had always given my lil mama a few household chores, I never expected her to do too much. I wanted her to enjoy her childhood. Plenty of housekeeping in her future, why rush it? Clearly she was not equipped for this. I glanced at my phone. It was damn near midnight and the man had not walked through the doors yet. Gaia wasn't surprised. She said she was usually in bed when he got home for the night. I did some quick math in my head. I planned to live with Nikki for a year and save money, pay all of our previous bills and get on our feet. We did have some debt we needed to clear.

But the way things were going, I'd have to speed up my plan. I needed to make this happen in maybe six months. I know my ex-husband. I had no control of him when we were married; I didn't expect much now that he seemed to be on the market again and exploring the single life. I had work to do. I had to laugh at myself. The soap opera between Draia, V and I seemed like such a joke right about now. God has a strange way of putting things in perspective.

On the drive home, C held my hand and I knew he had made peace with the situation. He would not readdress any of it with me later. Good, because I had bigger fish to fry. Tomorrow I would talk to Gaia's father Arjune and Draia. Tonight I would go over the situation in my mind repeatedly, my cerebral ass kicking, if you will. Until I planned exactly how I would resolve everything, I would not sleep. But I could feel it. Resolution was at hand.

To the Left, To the Left

I walked in Ticks with a purposeful gait. I was early.
Draia wasn't due for at least another fifteen minutes, and
she usually ran late, so I probably had about a half hour to
gather my thoughts. I would do it over a drink. I ordered
and stepped outside to have a smoke. The air smelled like
rain.

Today's forecast was a reflection of my mood, chilly and
grey. I lit up and inhaled deeply, fascinated by my own
smoke stream and the wish that my problems could
dissipate like vapor into the night. The door banged closed.
Another smoker joined me in the fray. I'd have recognized
him in the dark.

"Careful, people might talk." I chuckled while pointing
accusingly.

"Yeah, why's that?" Ray asked not so innocently.

I shook my head. "You do show up at the damnedest times
Raymond." I elongated his name. I wanted it to last longer
rolling off my tongue. I wanted him to differentiate me
from the rest. And I was sure there was a whole lot of "the
rest" to stand apart from. Old habits die hard. I was here to
extricate from one situation and already I wanted to place
myself in another.

"Can I steal a cigarette Catherine?"

I liked that he accepted my dub without question. "Sure. I
hope you don't mind Newport Menthols," I said, fishing
one out of my pack.

"Nope."

He accepted the cigarette and waited for me to light it a second time.

I was no closer to reading him now than before. He said so little but when he looked at me, I swore I could see all of the things he kept to himself. But what did I know? Perhaps I was finding what I sought and not what was actually present. Fresh scabs left me open, vulnerable and uncertain, abandoned by logic and confidence.

We smoked in silence for a minute. He looked comfortable. I attempted to imitate the same impression.

"You here by yourself?" he asked casually.

"I'm meeting my girl. She's running a little late so I figured I'd have a drink and a smoke while I waited.

As usual he said four words, I had a story. He nodded his head like he knew all about it.

"You here by yourself?" I asked, just as casually.

"Yeah."

"Oh." I smiled, taking my last drag and flicking the cigarette.

"I wanted a drink before heading home," he explained.

I smiled. "Hard day at the office?"

"I do duct work. It was a long day."

I almost rubbed my hands together in utter delight at the personal tidbit. Instead I steadied myself and smiled in response. I couldn't be trusted to formulate words.

"I wanted to tell you something." His face grew serious. His lips were wet. From the rain? I couldn't tell.

I snapped my eyes upward toward his. "Sure. What is it?" I blinked in surprise.

"I—Never mind. Nothing," he said evenly and ground his cig underfoot.

"Got somethin' on your mind, Raymond?" I asked in my best Mae West impression.

He smiled, his eyes bright with intensity. "Not just now."

His voice had a slight Guyanese lilt to it, melodic. I chose not to press. I wanted to cast an air of aloofness that he so obviously mastered.

"Okay."

He smiled as if he heard the questions I never asked. A confident smile that held all of the answers. He held the door open for me. It took me a minute to realize he hadn't come back in behind me. I was beginning to think that the man was something of a creation of mine, a form in shadows and a trick of light. He never said hello or good-bye. He appeared. He made an impression. He disappeared.

I was hooked. I had to remind myself I was getting rid of something trivial. I didn't need to get into anything else.

Still, his words whispered in my ear, "I want to tell you something."

****

I was mulling it all over when Draia showed. We kissed each other on the cheek but it was forced and awkward. I asked what she was having and ordered her a Corona. I waited until she had a healthy swig before I got down to it.

"Well sweetie, I think you know why I was hoping we could meet. I wanted to clear the air between us. Things have been a little weird with this whole you, me and Veran business."

Draia took another swig, her eyebrow up, a tell that she was annoyed.

"Yeah, I know."

I didn't even know what to make of those three words but I didn't care. I wanted this nonsense behind us. I took the last sip of my drink and ordered another before beginning my speech.

"Draia, first of all, I want to apologize for this whole mess. The only reason that this whole thing reached this ridiculous level is because I wasn't honest with you from the beginning. Veran was my flirt. I mean, we've been like that with each other for years. It's never been anything more than that, but you know how foolish and territorial we girls can be sometimes."

"Yeah but I didn't even know you guys were like that with each other. Didn't I ask you if it was cool to talk to him?"

126

Truthfully, I couldn't see how Draia could have missed it, but she was right. She asked, I answered, and the whole mess ended with us here. I'd made so many mistakes, my interest in V was down to zero and I wanted my best friend back. I also just wanted the situation to go away.

"Well, the truth is, I should have told you instead of pretending that I wasn't affected. I should have told you from the get what V meant to me and that would have been the end of it. Instead, I not only pretended it didn't affect me, but I encouraged you both to get closer knowing that it was killing me.

That was so incredibly stupid and childish I don't even know what to say. I'm disappointed in myself and the way that I handled this bullshit from beginning to end. I know I harassed you every day after I encouraged you to have a relationship with him, and I can't really tell you why I behaved so irrationally.

All I can do now is ask you to forgive me and swear to you that I will never do something like that ever again. If I have a problem, I will come to you and we will work it out. I don't want to lose my best friend over something so ridiculous and trivial and of my own making."

"Well I'm glad you finally told me. You know, after all the crazy that was going on between the three of us I just got fed up. I ended up calling him and telling him that it's not a good idea that we continue seeing each other. He didn't really understand what the problem was, but I told you weren't comfortable with the whole thing and that was it. So ever since then we haven't talked."

Oddly enough I wasn't happy or sad. Things had gone so far I simply felt indifferent. To try and give her my blessing now seemed moot.

"Draia, all I can say is that I'm really sorry. Please forgive me and rest assured that whatever decision you make regarding Veran, I will have nothing negative to say. If the status changes betwixt you two, you'll have no argument from me."

She swallowed everything I said, and it appeared that it went down a whole lot easier than she imagined.

I hugged my girl with sincerity and bought another round. It was going to take a while for us to put this entirely behind us, but we were well on our way. A few more awkward moments and we'd be straight. The important thing is we were both willing to move forward together. We loved each other for real, and there was hardly anything more important than that.

Getting It Together

Days were turning into weeks that were turning into months. Summer had come and gone and spring was in full swing. It was one of my favorite seasons. I could dress exactly how I wanted, not too hot, not too cold. I wasn't one to be bothered by the rain. In fact, I kind of dug it.

Spring was keeping me in focus. Between the grind and visiting Gaia every few days to make sure everything was copasetic at her dad's joint, the occasional girl's night out and date weekends with C, life was moving at a breakneck pace. Nearly two months had passed since the whole Draia, V and me business.

At first it was awkward between Draia and me, but after the first couple of outings, we were back to normal. It helped that Veran returned to his post and was out of visual range. I don't know if they still communicated, and I never asked. Truth is I didn't much care anymore. I shifted my focus back to Gaia, C and myself, which didn't leave time for much else.

Veran took longer to forgive me. Last week he sent me a short greeting, how are you doing type of text. It was enough. I kept it short and sweet and pushed on. I wasn't going back there. I preferred the way things were now between us. He never really valued me, and now that I knew, his stock plummeted. I would keep it friendly but frosty.

Ray crossed my mind every now and again. I hadn't seen him since that night at Tick's in the rain, but I could recall every moment in crystal clarity. I couldn't characterize him as a flirt. I couldn't characterize him as anything but an enigma. I also couldn't deny my reaction or attraction to him. This mattered not at all since I never saw him again. I had this feeling in my gut that I wouldn't be running into him anytime soon either.

Still, I couldn't entirely dismiss him. So I pushed him into a corner of my mind and yup, kept it pushing.

****

As I walked up the stairs I caught a whiff of something delicious.

"Wow sis, that smells gr—"

Nikki sat at the table with the phone propped up between her shoulder and ear, fanning her hand, motioning me over. I passed her and ducked into the kitchen to turn the stove down. She only had olive oil and some onions and minced garlic in the pot but I was afraid the oil would pitch. I quickly filled a glass with ice water and took the opposite seat.

Her eyes were widened while she spoke into the receiver. I could hear my mom's voice reply. She probably had news about my uncle's condition. I closed my eyes and said a small prayer. I couldn't tell how serious things were by Nikki's expression.

Sometimes she looked concerned and a tad dramatic over situations I didn't find very concerning or dramatic, so I sipped my water patiently and logged into my phone. A few minutes later I heard Nikki wrapping it up and saying good-bye. I clicked my phone off and gave her my full attention.

"You want any water or tea or anything?" I asked, half out of my seat.

"No, no I'm good," she shook her head.

"So what did Mom say?" I asked, leaning back into my seat.

Nikki did a deep sigh. "She said Uncle is gonna' be okay."

I let out a huge breath in a whoosh, wiping the imaginary sweat from my brow. "Thank God! So what's wrong with him? Nothing?"

"No, he's, umm, got lupus, but the mildest version of the disease. Thanks for turning off the pot. I totally forgot about it. I'm gonna' continue to cook while we chat, is that cool?"

"You wanna have a ciggie first?"

"You know I do. But I should get the chicken in the pot and let it simmer first, because I'm sure we're going to need more than one. In fact, lemme turn the kettle on."

I jumped up and followed her into the kitchen. "Let me make the coffee and tea and you get to the chicken. C should be home in like an hour and a half, so we don't have the world of time."

"Oh yeah, girl, I all but forgot about him." She laughed, stirring the seasoning in the oil.

I thought to myself, "wish I could," but I didn't want to address my marital issues with Nikki just yet. C was starting to sing the same old song when it came to his job.

There were days when I wanted to scream and shake him like Kit Marlowe did Millie in Old Acquaintance. I had come dangerously close on several occasions.

I'm sure if we were alone in our old apartment I would have lost it by now. But the fact of the matter was we were not. And I didn't want to bring our shit into the mix with Nikki. Things were going so well. The three of us were getting on famously, and between work and Gaia and our date nights, most of the time things were pretty spectacular.

We worked in our own personal silence for the next ten minutes. She covered the pot just as I finished stirring the milk in her teacup. I balanced the cups and slipped on my flats while she took the ciggies out of the freezer and the lighter out of the drawer. We were perfectly synchronized.

Neither one of us had changed out of our work gear. This morning I had chosen a form-fitting grey and pink sweater dress with matching, heavy grey tights while Nikki looked much more formal in navy wool slacks and a silk blouse. I put the cups on the stoop and brushed past her to grab our jackets. The temperature dipped too low for us to be comfortable sitting for any length of time dressed as we were.

"Thanks sis." Nikki smiled in gratitude, threading her arms through her jacket.

"Anytime pumpkin."

I waited for her to light us up. We took a few sips from our cups and sat in comfortable silence. I took a pull from my cig and wondered at the quiet before me. Her courtyard really was charming. A teenage Asian couple I recognized from the neighboring building snuggled together on the bench. With the lamppost above them, they looked straight out of a John O'Brien Parisian mural.

Soft, happy giggles floated past us light and weightless. I smiled inside. Steven Mendoza, eighth grade. He made me feel like that. He kissed me once and held my hand maybe twice. But we had it. That Edward and Bella shit. You get older and the world weighs you down with responsibility and bills and worries. Don't get me wrong. You do fall in love and it is grand.

But it's never the same as that teen thang. I turned to face my sister. She tore her eyes away from the couple long enough to smile at me and nod their way. Synchronized, or as Nikki would say, Sympatico.

"Damn, girl, that's that teenage shit right there," she giggled, taking a long drag.

"Yeah, girl, you caught that, huh?"

"Man, they make me wanna take a cold shower." She chuckled.

"It's like you said, Nikki. They kiss like one of them is going off to war. We can't compete with that, girl."

"Nah. We sure can't." She flicked the butt and lit another for us both.

"So about Uncs."

We spent the better part of the next twenty minutes discussing Uncle's condition. It sounded much more intense than it was. Bottom line was he had lupus. They could not determine how he acquired it. His immune system was compromised but not by leaps and bounds. He will need to take meds for an undetermined amount of time. He would need to monitor the situation with his doc every so often. However, he was not terminal or anything close. His quality of life for the most part would continue as it was. In other words, the man was aight.

The stress he underwent over the half-assed original diagnosis was probably more dangerous. My mother must have pointed that out several times, which must be why Nikki followed suit and emphasized it to me. I didn't blame Mom. She's been privy to my uncle's behavior a great deal, so she earned the right to gripe.

Men can be such babies. Uncs was no exception. You get to a point where you are grateful that they still have each other, because you simply have not acquired the patience and life skill necessary to deal with the yesteryear generation full time. Yet. Said a small prayer of thanks. Said another prayer for preparation of the inevitable time ahead. We're West Indian, we take care of our own.

"You want one more ciggie before we go up?" I paused, reaching for the lighter.

"Yeah, light me up," Nikki answered as she sipped the last of her tea.

I lit up and thought, I know why I need one but why do you little bunny? I'd been so wrapped up in daily life and my issues with C I hadn't really had much time to observe my sis. Lately she's been MIA and, dare I say, even a little secretive. She casually mentioned a few weeks back that she started seeing someone, but not a peep since.

My ears hadn't pricked skyward at the initial news; therefore, I hadn't given it much thought. But as I watched my little sis watching the young couple with an intensity I could not place, I pondered and wondered. I had been keeping things to myself. Perhaps I was not the only one.

The Hunt

"Hang on a sec, babe. Hi John, what's up?"

I put my hand over the telephone mouthpiece and smiled at my boss expectantly.

"Hey Cat, I got to run out to a black-tie thing in a few minutes but I just want to give you this to put on my expense report. I need this and this to go under the new account and everything else to go under the administrative fund," he explained, pointing items out before handing me the list with the coordinating receipts.

For some reason, my boss took to calling me Cat instead of Catherine. Some of the girls thought it was hysterical, but I rather dug it. I had a habit of rebranding everyone myself.

"Sure thing, JC, I'll have it done before I leave." I smiled, tucking the papers under my keyboard.

"Oh, that's great. And I should be in tomorrow around nine. I've got a breakfast meeting over at the Hilton."

"Sounds good. I'll leave it on your chair for you to sign before I pass it on to Lenny."

"Perfect. Can you tell Lenny I'm leaving, and I need to see him in my office for a minute?"

"Sure thing John. Babe, hang on, I'll be right back."

I put Christian on hold and walked quickly over to Lenny's office. He was our CFO and serious eye candy. It was nice to have at least one in the office. We had run of the entire seventeenth floor. The box within a box was a simple yet refined design; the admin staff in the middle, small conference room and my desk at the front. The outer lining space contained all of the big wig offices as well as the large conference room.

I ducked my head into Len's office. He was staring out of his window absently twisting the ends of his hair. If he had a red smoking jacket and a black and gold walking stick, this could have been a scene from The Count of Monte Cristo.

"Hey Len."

"Oh, hey Catherine." He smiled, a little embarrassed, clearly startled out of his thoughts.

"John's leaving in a minute and wanted to see you before he goes."

"Sure." He fiddled with the mouse for a few seconds before following me out.

I hurried back to my desk and picked up the receiver.

"Babe?"

"Yeah babe."

"Sorry, I had to do something for my boss."

"Sure, no problem. I'm just waiting for them to take these X-rays from me then I can leave."

"Can you pick me up from the train station? I should be leaving on time."

"Yeah, I can do that. We should be getting there around the same time anyway. You tired?"

"Not really. But I came across another apartment ad and called the people. They said we can see it tonight, around 7:30."

"Oh man, tonight?"

"Yeah babe, tonight. What's the problem?" I couldn't keep the irritation from my voice. Did everything have to be so difficult?

"Nothing, I'm just tired. I didn't want to do anything but pick up some food and relax."

"Babe, I understand how you feel but it's time. We got to get out of Nikki's joint and the only way to do that is to find our own place, you know what I'm saying?"

"I know. I just wish it wasn't tonight."

I grit my teeth and took a silent, slow breath. This was far from an opportune moment for me either. I was already riding the crimson wave this week. Based on the last few apartments, and I use the term loosely, I could hardly blame him but for once I wish it wasn't my job to always be the practical let's do what we gotta do cheerleader. I wish for once I didn't have to spin this routine and he could just say, yes, sure, I'll be there. Let's get it done.

My boss's office door propped open and I could hear that he and Len were wrapping up their conversation.

"Hold on a sec babe." I put the call on hold and pulled up the Excel expense report spreadsheet.

138

"All right Cat. I'll see you tomorrow. Lenny, you'll take care of that thing we talked about, right?"

"Will do," Len replied, propping his elbow on my desk ledge, arching an amused eyebrow in my direction.

"Good night, John. See you tomorrow."

After JC stepped into the elevator, Len turned to me.

"So John said he gave you his expense report?"

"Yes. I'm actually working on it right now. But I'm going to have to leave it on his chair for him to sign when he gets back tomorrow morning before I can pass it on to you."

"Oh right. So what are you doing tonight? Any special plans?" He smiled.

"Well, we're going to look at another apartment tonight. Oh joy!" I feigned utter delight.

"Oh right, right. Haven't found anything suitable yet, I take it."

"I take it light and sweet. But no. Not even close." I smiled with just a hint of wickedness.

"You're funny." He emphasized, angling his head in my direction.

"And just think, I'm here all week." I laughed.

He chuckled, lingering for a few more seconds. He tended to relax a bit more when JC left the office. He wasn't alone, but I loved John. He might have been the boss, but he was cool peoples. Everyone here had their quirks but I dug them all. Some of the previous jobs I've had, people treated me little better than a housemaid. But here, they were good to me, some more than others.

"Well, all right," he announced, drumming his fingers on the ledge. "I guess I'll wait for him to sign it."

"Yup." I bedazzled him with a professional smile and inclined my head in his direction.

He smiled shyly once more before strolling back to his glass cube.

Oh shit. I snatched the phone and released the hold button.

"Babe?"

"Yeah."

"Sorry, boss again."

"It's fine. I'll pick you up from the train around seven. Where's this place? How'd you find out about it?"

"From a sign that Gaia's father saw. He called, told me about it and passed me the number. I called the landlord, his name is Marcas. He said that we could come tonight."

He sighed long and loud. "All right. I guess we'll go see it then."

"Okay, let me go. I gotta finish this report. I'll see you soon."

"Okay. Love you."

"Love you too."

I hung up and started separating the receipts JC handed me. Thank God I didn't tell him that Arjune said the front of the house looked practically abandoned. When I called the landlord, I did ask him if we could see the apartment tomorrow but he stressed that we should see it as soon as possible. He even went so far as to say it's possible that tomorrow might be too late because it might be rented by that time.

I wanted to tell him never mind, to forget about it but a strange feeling came over me. I knew from prior experience to ignore that feeling never served me well. So against all odds we were going, tonight. I had two bosses both with JC as their initials, though I would hardly classify them in the same league. No siree Billy Bob Joe!

****

"Well hot damn, this place does look abandoned," I whispered as we pulled up to the address I jotted down in my iPhone.

"What babe?" Christian asked irritatingly, switching off the car.

"Nothing. Nothing. Well, we're here already. We might as well go inside and see it."

"Which house is it?"

I almost didn't want to tell him. I knew he would voice exactly what I was thinking, that this was a huge waste of time.

141

"It's the one on the left-hand side on the corner," I said casually, as if he wouldn't notice.

"WHAT? That place looks decrepit."

Seriously! The one time the man uses big words and it's in this context?

"Yeah, I got that memo. Let's just go inside boy. We're already here. There's no point in being here and not doing the whole nine."

He slammed the car door with extra umph and followed up the steps. There were two old lion statues flanking the stone steps giving the air that once upon a time this property might have been grand. C was behind me, sucking his teeth. Instead of finding it ridiculous I actually found it comforting. It kind of reminded me of one of my favorite places to walk past, the Public Library on Fifth, flanked by the two grand stone lions, Patience and Fortitude. Awesome, 'cause we're gonna' need both just to walk through these doors.

There was an open windowpane door at the top of the stairs that led to a small entranceway containing the apartment mailboxes and separate doorbells. There were four apartments in the building from what we could gather. The heavier interior locked door had a peephole and a bell. We pressed once. I took the time to peruse our surroundings while we were waiting. The block seemed pretty quiet. It was 8:00 p.m., dinnertime.

Many front lights were on in the homes lining the street. There was adequate parking. There was a tiny park across the street, with some stone benches, a bus stop and a stone cross. Did I mention the landlord's name was Marcas, like

Marcas my best boy? I smiled. So far everything pointed to being in the wrong place, yet somehow surrounded by all of the right signs. Odd. No one answered the door.

"I don't think there's anyone here babe. This place looks crazy. We should just go."

I ground my teeth and turned to look at Christian. If I pushed my anger aside, I found that I agreed with him. The place did look exactly how he so colorfully described, decrepit. But something planted me firmly in my place. I sighed loudly and rang the doorbell once again. After another minute, I pulled my phone from my bag.

"Maybe he can't hear us. Let me try one last thing and call the man."

C shrugged like he thought it was completely unnecessary, but he didn't elaborate with words. Thank God.

"Hi Marcas. This is Catherine. We spoke a few hours ago on the phone. Yes, we're actually in front of the door ringing the doorbell but maybe you can't hear us. Okay, great. Thanks so much."

I hung up the phone and smiled at C. "Well, he's here. He'll open the door in a minute."

C rolled his eyes just as the door opened.

And older, handsome Guyanese gentleman in dark jeans, old boots and a plaid shirt greeted us warmly.

"You must be Catherine." He smiled, extending his hand.

"Yes, and you must be Marcas. Thanks for letting us see the place this late in the evening," I replied, shaking his hand.

"This is my husband Christian."

Christian smiled and shook his hand. Whatever he was feeling, he tucked back and pushed his warm side to the forefront.

"Sure. I'm very glad you could make it, because I just showed it to another couple and they're very interested and will come back tomorrow with the form filled out and their references. So it's not going to last long on the market."

As we followed closely behind Marcas, C and I exchanged a yeah right look.

The small hallway displayed the same winning personality as the front. On the bright side, however, it was well lit. Silver linings. Silver linings.

"There are two apartments on the first floor," Marcas said, pointing to the big white doors on both the right and left. "And there are two apartments upstairs. They all have the same kind of layout. The tenant that I had unfortunately went through a divorce. After a while he couldn't afford the place by himself and had to move out."

"Aww. That's so sad."

"Yeah. They looked so happy. I don't know what happened. Anyway. Here it is."

He turned the key and unlocked the door on the left-hand side. When the door swung open, my jaw quite literally hit the floor.

Marcas held the door open and ushered us inside.

"Everything is brand new. Brand new floors, brand new bathroom, brand new carpet. We gutted the whole kitchen and bathroom and rewired all the electric. I'm an electrician by trade, you know. I work for NYU, and I do my own thing sometime too, you know?"

I was hardly paying attention to what Marcas was saying. I had my back to him. C was facing me and had the same look of wonder on his face that I must have had on mine. I mouthed I want this place, and he nodded almost imperceptibly.

"I'm finishing up some work in the basement. You guys take a look around. I'm gonna' leave the application with you. I'll be back in a few minutes and we can talk, okay?"

"Yes, thank you," I barely managed.

As soon as he left the apartment, I crushed C with a hearty hug.

"Babe, this is it. This is freakin' it!"

"Yeah, yeah, calm down. Let's look at the whole place before we decide."

"Don't bring me down with your practicality. We've been looking at hole in the wall joints for weeks. This is an oasis in the desert!"

"Let's see what the rest of this place looks like before we get too excited, thank you very much."

Walking into the joint, you had a tiny entranceway flanked by two doors, one on the left and one on the right. The one on the right led to a three-piece washroom. It was pretty standard in size, nice big tub with a deep windowed ledge, perfect for all of the shampoos and conditioners.

The door on the left led to a huge bedroom with some built-in shelves, two huge windows and one closet. The shelves were an oddity, but it was nothing that I couldn't work with. Farther in, you found yourself in a huge kitchen. There was a lot of square footage but not a whole lot of countertop space. I could work in a seating area easily. And with my HGTV skills that I'd been acquiring for years, I was sure I could find a way to maximize the counter space that was available.

Past the kitchen there was a square arch that led to a very cozy living room. It wasn't huge, but you could see there was more than enough space for a couch, some chairs, the TV and a few other must haves. Again there were two huge windows, and a lovely, high picture window which gave the room a great deal of natural light. Then off of the living room to the right was a small door that led to a tiny bedroom with a deep closet. That was a bit daunting.

"Babe, you really think that's enough room for Gaia?" Christian arched an eyebrow in question.

"No. That really sucks actually, but I can make it work. It will have to do. There's nothing we've seen that comes remotely close to this joint."

C sighed, tucking his hands in the pockets of his jeans and rocking on his heels. "Yeah. That's true."
We heard some keys jangling. The landlord was back in the apartment. We made our way over to the kitchen.

"Wow Marcas. This place is really beautiful. I'm so glad you convinced me to come see it tonight. Umm, so how much is the rent? Is there anything included with that?"

"Thank you. Yeah we put a lot of work in this place man. I wanted to make it perfect, you know. I like to treat my tenants good. I'm good to them and they're good to me."

"That's so nice. Do you live upstairs?"

"No, no, I don't live here. I live in Queens Village."

I turned around and eyed C with a silent winner look.

"So the rent is $1,200.00. That includes water. Every tenant has a separate Con Edison bill and a separate gas bill. I have everything wired separately for each apartment so you only pay for what you use, you know."

I turned around and checked with C.

He gave nothing away but inside I'm sure he was doing somersaults; $1,200.00! Holy cost effective, Batman. Seriously! That was practically dirt cheap. I know why of course, because essentially with that tiny bedroom it really wasn't a true two-bedroom apartment, but with all of the upgrades, the immaculate condition of the apartment, the two-door fridge with built-in icemaker and water, this practically felt like an episode of cribs.

C knew I couldn't be trusted once he saw my face and took over at this point.

"Okay, that sounds reasonable. We're very interested, Marcas. What can we do to make this apartment ours?"

"I'm very glad you like it. You mind if I ask you some questions?"

"Oh no. Of course," I chimed in.

"Is this apartment just for the two of you?"

Christian passed this one onto me. "No. We have a daughter, but she's fifteen. And we have one cat. She's very small."

C's eyes went wide. Damn. I probably should have left that out.

"You think the small room is gonna' be big enough for her?"

"Oh yeah. I specialize in design. We can make it work." I smiled confidently.

"I don't like cats. I'm from Guyana, we're scared of them things. But one small cat is not gonna' be a problem. You're from Guyana?"

"Oh, thank you. She's really small. No, actually I was born here but my parents are from Guyana. And my husband is from Trinidad."

"Oh Trinidad. I went on vacation there. That place is sweet man. Nice water and beaches and the people are very friendly."

"Yeah man, dat is how we do," Christian replied, busting out his Trini accent.

"Which part of Guyana are your parents from?"

"Berbice. Tain Settlement, I think." I was never really confident about these stats. Nikki had the 411 on such knowledge.

"Oh yeah. I'm from Georgetown. What's your father's name?"

"Akshay. Akshay Persaud. Do you know him?"

"No. No, I don't know him," Marcas said, disappointed.

It's a common practice among all old school Guyanese people to ask where you or your parents hail from fully expecting to know someone who knows someone who knows someone. It's like the six degrees from Kevin Bacon connection.

"Well, anyway I'm glad you guys are interested in the place. The couple that was just here said they want to rent the place but to be honest with you, I prefer for you guys to have it."

"Aww, that's so sweet of you. Thank you so much," I gushed. Silent thank you to my Jesus. I would get into more detail with you boss-man, later. My knees and you got a date!

"So what are your requirements, Marcas? Fill out the form, of course, would two references do?"

"Yes. Sure. Yes, fill out the form, I would need two references, people that are not related to you. I need to see a credit report from both of you. And all I need is one month's rent and one month's security. And since we're in the last week of the month, after we get through all the paperwork, you can start to move right away. I'm not bothered about the few days left on this month."

"Oh, that's so generous of you. Really appreciate that, thank you. Okay, so what we'll do is have this back to you by tomorrow or the next day and also the money and we can move on forward."

"Okay, good. The sooner the better, right? Catherine, I have your number and you have mine, so if anything should happen you'll call and let me know." He smiled, extending his hand.

I gripped it firmly. "You will definitely be hearing from me tomorrow to make arrangements as to when we can drop the paperwork and rent over to you."

"Sounds good. Thank you."

He shook C's hand.

"Okay, thank you. Good night."

"Good night. Thank you," C said, smiling warmly.

When we got in the car, I grabbed C and peppered his face with kisses. "Schmoops"—(that's my pet name for my baby)—"can you freakin believe that?"

"Wow. I would have never believed that place looks like that from the inside."
"I never had a doubt!" I smiled impishly.

"Hmph. Sure ya lie." Christian guffawed in his Trini accent, pinching my side.

I burst into giggles, pulling away from him.

"Eh, Triniman, I can't wait to move in! We're gettin' on our knees tonight. Thank you, Jesus!"

Walmart Woes

The next few days were a whirlwind of maddening proportions. Obtaining the apartment was the easy part, but time doesn't stand still simply because your cup runneth over. After acquiring the keys, Christian and I, well mostly C, bombed the joint to annihilate any leftover critters. The apartment was small and two fog cans for each room was a bit of overkill, nonetheless, C set them off like sticks of dynamite, one by one. I waited outside in safety while he completed the task.

We spent the next few days concentrating on work and our evenings sitting over a hot plate planning and preparing for the move. I thought that Friday would be an ideal time to give the apartment a thorough cleaning and on Saturday we would get what little furniture and knickknacks we had out of storage and officially move in.

Christian's cousins were a Godsend and agreed to help. It was a two-part job. C and I were able to move everything out of Nikki's place to our new joint on our own. Then we met up with his cousins and rented a small U-Haul truck to get the rest of our stuff out of storage. With promises of a hearty meal complete with dessert, the fellas were eager to get the show on the road.

As they moved stuff in, I unpacked and put away. By the time we were finished, our clothes were hung in the closet, shower curtain was up and things were looking fairly homey. Nikki and I went shopping a few weeks prior for necessities.

We wanted to be prepared when we finally did discover the apartment of our dreams. We purchased a new set of dishes, coffee mugs, an electric kettle, utensils, shower curtain, bathroom essentials and rugs for the bathroom and kitchen. My sister was exceptionally generous and paid for everything. I think she felt a little sad that we were moving after spending only eight months out of the expected year, but the timing was right for all involved. I even managed to talk Christian into doing a Target run one night after work to purchase a toaster and a microwave.

In the last month, I could tell that Nikki and her mystery boyfriend were getting serious. And even though she wasn't in her own home very much, there were telltale signs she was starting to get a little annoyed at our ever present invasion of her space.

Winter was coming on, and C and I spent a great deal more time in the apartment. While we were barely home during the summer and most of spring, we tended to hibernate during winter.

Being in such close proximity for so many hours was taking its toll on all three of us. I was starting to feel like the monkey in the middle, in a state of tension trying to keep an even keel between Nikki and C. They both had personalities that were used to being large and in charge and were clashing silently. I didn't like it. I don't think anyone did but we took it day by day and kept pressing on.

C's attitude about work increased in volatility. He complained all of the time and was a pill to be around. The way he was going I was sure they were going to either fire him or he was going to quit any day. I was sick of trying to figure out how I should deal with him and made my escape by grabbing a few drinks after work with my boy Marcas.

This placed Nikki in the awkward position of being home alone with C, which only served to make matters worse between all three of us. I pretended I was hanging out with my work mates so C wouldn't give me grief but it wasn't long before I started slipping.

One Friday night I hung out 'til the wee hours of the morn' and came home damn near completely soused. The more C's attitude about work worsened, the more frequently I hung out with Marcas. I didn't care, my anger was taking over and Marcas was my only sense of relief. My behavior fed C's nasty attitude and his nasty attitude fed my selfish need for escape. We were in a dangerous catch-22 and neither of us seemed to be able to turn from the path we set.

It was only a few weeks ago when we were finally in a good place financially, paid off our debts and obtained a little nest egg that we decided it was time to seek our own shelter. It's amazing how things keep on moving even though inside you feel like you've shut down. Thank God for my job.

Having a position that made me happy and feel important and needed saw me through the insanity that was going on at home. Finding an apartment became the catalyst for change. Once we started looking, I put Marcas on ice and hoped that this would be our new beginning. When you're down there's just one way to go.

Gaia couldn't wait to leave her huge bedroom in her father's house for the closet-like room in our new place. Before I was done unpacking, she texted me that she was heading over with clothes. I thought I would have a few days to prepare for her arrival but since that wasn't going to be the case, I set to work on creating a temporary space she could be comfortable in for the time being.

We hadn't yet purchased a twin bed, so I used the airbed from Nikki's apartment. It was pretty decent, an Aerobed, so at least because of its height it had the look and somewhat feel of a solid bed. I grabbed one of the three-drawer plastic mini-dressers to hold her night clothes and underwear and such. It would serve double duty and would also hold her TV on top.

Thank goodness we still had her twin sheets, pillowcases and pillows from storage. I was able to accommodate her in record time. Her dad dropped her off with her clothes and her TV. We'd return the TV once we purchased another for Gaia.

The first time we took her to see the apartment she was disappointed about the size of her room. She, much like us, was hoping that it would be larger. She was in high school now and planned to have friends over from time to time. I promised Gaia her that she could use the living room right next door when she was entertaining, and that Christian and I would stick to the kitchen and our bedroom in such cases.

She mumbled something about being able to manage. It broke my heart that I couldn't give her something better. But when Gaia came home after I worked my magic and saw the bed made and the drawers in place, she sighed with relief. It was only then I realized just how badly she wanted to get out of her dad's house.

It's funny, when Nikki and I were kids, we couldn't wait for our parents to leave the house so we could have a bit of freedom. Gaia's father was hardly home. Apparently she had more freedom than she knew what to do with. C and I had become the stable foundation she had grown accustomed to, and I guess she didn't feel we were oppressive to be around. (Insert pat on back here).

155

Even though her dad had a big house and beautiful furniture and luxuries we did not, what we did have the kid needed desperately. We all sacrificed something to get back home to NY. I was thankful that it was necessary for only eight months and not longer.

Sunday, C and I woke early. There were a few items we needed to purchase before the apartment was really comfortable enough to abide a hassle-free workweek. After we had breakfast, we drove to Walmart for a few grocery items.

I also wanted to check out some cheap, temporary seating options, maybe a few folding chairs and a set of tray tables. Gaia would sleep in and at some point go back to her dad's house to gather more of her necessities.

****

We had the shopping cart half full when we rolled into the paper towel aisle. I checked the sale prices and was happy to note Viva, my preferred paper towel, was on sale and tossed the twin pack into our cart. I moved on to check the bathroom toilet tissue when I noticed that Christian replaced the Viva towels with Bounty. And that, ladies and gents, is how the fight started.

"Babe, why are you changing out my towels? I prefer the Viva." I spoke calmly, though my voice carried a distinct edge.

"Yeah but the Bounty is better," C replied, matching my tone.

"Babe, it is not better. The Viva is way better, plus I prefer it because you know my nose runs nine times outta ten.

The Viva is way softer. It's cloth-like so it's a necessity for me." I shelved the Bounty and tossed the Viva back into the cart.

"No. It's not. The Bounty is a way better brand," C stated abruptly, fishing out the Viva towels and again replacing them with the Bounty.

I looked around me like I was sure that I was on the set of the Twilight Zone. Unfortunately I was still in the Walmart paper towel aisle. A little Black boy around seven years old was looking at C and me like we were aliens. I didn't blame him. I wasn't sure myself. His mom was farther down the aisle and wasn't paying attention to the scene that was about to unfold. Boy, was she in for a rude awakening.

"Dude, are you freakin' for real? I'm actually taking the time to explain to you the reason, the logic behind why I chose the item I chose, and you're here givin' me the 'it's a better brand' bullshit. Have you lost your damn mind?"

"It is a better brand. We always buy Bounty. I don't know why you're being so stubborn about it," C yelled.

At this point both mother and son are watching us in absolute horror. I didn't care. I was past the point of no return.

"Are you fucking kidding me right now? My fucking nose is soar as fuck and you are sitting here trying to tell me to buy the paper towel that's going to make it worse rather than be sympathetic to my situation and let me have the brand I need? What the fuck do you care about the paper towels, anyway? You don't even use the fucking things. I'm the one who cooks, cleans and uses them to wipe my fucking nose, and you're pulling this fucking bullshit?"

157

"Stop cursing like an idiot. Yes, I'm telling you to buy the better brand, the brand that we damn well use all of the time!"

"Don't you pull this shit with me. I can lose my fucking mind just like you. I ain't down with people looking at me like poor little Indian girl, this is what happens when you marry the big Black man. Fuck that. If they're gonna' feel sorry for someone in this fucking relationship, it's damn well gonna' be you."

It is precisely at this point when the mother grabs her young son's hand and runs down the aisle as if it's on fire. I'm so damn angry I don't care if security is on their way. I'm seriously contemplating running this man down with the cart. C just looks at me and throws his hands up in the air.

"Fine, buy whatever friggin' paper towel you want," he screams before shoving his hands in his pocket angrily and marching past me.

I spend the next five minutes hauling the cart from aisle to aisle like a wayward child, silently talking to JC and going through all of the reasons that made this man a complete freakin' moron. The last thing I want to do is continue shopping, but I have little choice as shit has got to get done. We need some groceries! I need to make my way to the furniture aisle to check out seating and dining options.

Walmart does seem to have everything, Lord, why not an express aisle for divorce? Seriously, Lord. I mean, am I crazy or did we just have a fight about paper freakin' towels???? I know he's a good man in general, but between his job woes and now this, I'm really starting to rethink the validity of our union, Lord. By the time I finish the groceries and make my way over to furniture, my storm is winding down. All I feel now is sad and hopeless.

I know that I'm contributing to the problem with my interaction with Marcas, JC, but seriously, how many times is this man gonna' put me through his job bullshit? Any escape I can make for myself is absolutely justified, wouldn't you say? And as I'm reasoning with my Jesus and trying to assess the assortment of tray tables, C strolls down my aisle.

He says nothing but clings to me as if his life depends upon it. I feel all of the tension leave my body and immediately feel like everything's gonna' be all right. He releases me, whispers "I'm sorry" and replaces the Bounty with the Viva.

I wipe the tears streaming down my face and take a deep breath.

"Let's go check out the folding chairs."

I didn't feel like scaring any more children that night. It was time to whip out the Band-Aid and keep it pushin'.

The Other Shoe

I knew I was getting on the man's last nerve, but my excitement was exponential. Our new place had the potential to serve out every single one of my HGTV fantasies. We were given the green light by Marcas our landlord to do whatever we desired. I was certain he had no clue as to the weight those words held with me, but he was about to find out.

The Internet became my best friend. Every spare moment of down time I had at work was spent hunting, shopping and printing out several different options of furniture and lighting. Cabinet options, dining table options, home bar options, baker's rack options, you name it and I had a binder with a section of options. I took organizing to new heights. I am a Capricorn, after all. This was my world.

Christian noticed the immediate change in my disposition. I was never out unless I was with him. I shelved Marcas. I shelved the girls. I only had time for work, family and furniture. He in turn stopped grumbling about his job. Whatever was going on, he was either dealing with it better or keeping it to himself.

Either way, with furnishing the apartment as my number one salvation and distraction, I let it rock. I wasn't in the mood to ask questions. I just silently prayed that he was working on handling things better and that his job wasn't in jeopardy.

Before we acquired the apartment, I prayed for a few specifics. I asked JC for a joint without stairs, a landlord that did not live on the premises and that the rent was below one of my biweekly paychecks. I was trying to prepare for the worst case scenario. Jesus gave me all that I asked for and more. I wasn't about to spit on the blessings. I figured if I was good and kept my head focused on what I needed to do, we'd be all right.

I was maniacal about furnishing the joint in a timely manner, which to me meant I wouldn't stop until all was done. We discovered stores like Pier 1, Home Goods, Ikea and Bob's Discount Furniture. Don't let the name fool you, my friends. The only thing discount about Bob's were the prices.

For the next three months I was consumed with creating a unique, stylish and comfortable space that I could be proud of. Every single time I opened or closed my door I thanked JC for giving us the place of our dreams. Yes it was small, it was only an apartment but I felt like we struck gold. I felt blessed beyond all measure.

When all was said and done, I invited my teacups for a little dinner party slash housewarming. I know most people have housewarmings as a way of helping them acquire some of the things they need for their empty apartment but West Indians are a little different. We like throwing a jam when we've got everything together, sort of like, Hey, we did well for ourselves. What do you guys think about the new digs? Here, sit, eat, gyaff nah man.

"Ladies, what ya'll think? You like?" I asked Princess, Draia and Ashley, the first to arrive. I took their coats and hung them up on the Command hooks I put up above the umbrella stand to create a small entryway.

"Oh my gosh, I love your kitchen. It's so big," Princess exclaimed.

"Yeah girl. I see you've been busy during all this MIA time," Ash chimed in. She wasn't gonna' let me escape ditching them for so long unscathed.

"Is that your bedroom?" Draia asked, peeking into our bedroom.

"Oh, I'm so glad you guys like it. Yes, that's the boudoir. Lemme get your shoes and I'll give you the ten-cent tour, ladies," I said excitedly.

"Girl, what is that? I love that. Where did you get that?" Princess asked pointing to the folding shelves I was using as a temporary shoe rack.

"Girl, I got this online at Stacks and Stacks. This is a folding shelf thingamajig. I take it out when I have guests so they have some place to put their shoes and bags and stuff. But usually I fold it up and tuck it behind here," I said, pointing to the baker's rack by the kitchen window.

"Cat that is so nice. We need one of those. Can you e-mail me the site?"

"Of course Princess. I'll send it to your Facebook."

"Okay, good. My mom is gonna' be so happy. She hates having our shoes spread out all over the front of the house."

"Girl you know how I do. I'll be glad to send it. Okay, ladies lemme' give you the tour."

The girls saw and loved just about everything, and believe me, there was quite a lot to see. C and I purchased a mural of a French bakery nestled on a quiet Parisian street which hung like wallpaper in our kitchen. Instead of having a

162

traditional banquette we decided on a beautiful marble pub table and four luxuriously comfortable high chairs in the spacious kitchen.

Since we didn't have a dining room, I thought it would be practical and fun to create one in the kitchen, where we had ample room. We purchased a white, beautifully crafted bar cabinet from Crate & Barrel. I had a thing for white cabinets, which is why you'll find them sprinkled throughout the apartment, illuminating a few dark corners.

The rest of the joint we decorated in earth tones with bits of sparkle here and there to give the entire space a warm but very Manhattan tres chic feel. Every single piece that we chose met the three definitions of good design, SFF, style, form and function. Candace Olsen and Sarah Richardson are friends in my head, can't you tell?

Nikki and Charmy dropped in about an hour later and I repeated the process, pointing out this and that, noting where I purchased what. C was out with his cousins, so it was nice to have this time alone with the girls. Gaia popped in the kitchen, dished out her food, said her hellos and closeted herself back in her sanctuary.

She gave me full rein to get creative with her room design and I went to town. We spent a bit more money on furniture and accessories than our usual budget. Charmy saved me some coins by gifting me a gorgeous wrought iron daybed she just happened to be storing and didn't have a use for.

We splurged on beautiful drapery from this amazing online store called Swags Galore, creating quite an effect, and a much larger feel in the space. We hung a black and white toile valance with billowing, soft white, long curtains that I wrapped around holdbacks to create a balloon affect. To keep the walls from appearing too plain I dropped a large, black, whimsical fairy tree decal on the wall behind her door.

I spent an hour filling a few of the leaves with Swarovski crystals I acquired from M&M Trimming in the city to add some sparkle. I used all of my powers of creativity to design a space that Gaia would feel warm and cozy in, which paid off in spades. In fact, perhaps it worked too well. She hardly ever left her room.

After the tour, the girls and I sat down around the dining table to chow down and bare our souls. It had been far too long. Having them before me now made me realize how much I missed them and how I desperately wanted to catch up on what was going on in their lives and unburden some of my own troubles.

I grabbed two dark brown mahogany folding chairs and set them down at the table in order to accommodate all six of us. I cooked something special for the girls, chicken royale with apricot glazed baby carrots and homemade mashed potatoes. I set the wine glasses out and poured everyone some Martinelli sparkling cider. If you ain't know about Martinelli, ya better ask somebody – it is the quintessential West Indian non spirited, spirt of choice. I was one who appreciated the access to excess at all times. Here today, gone tomorrow, no need to wait for a special occasion. Besides, what could be more special than sharing our new digs with my teacups?

After I said grace and we dug in, I sat back and listened to my girls amiably chatting and sharing with one and all. Christian affectionately dubbed our chats the "clucking of the hens". Taking in the scene before me, I had to laugh to myself as he did have a certain point.

One by one the girls filled me in on what I'd been missing during the last few months. Charmy had us in stitches as she performed complete skits about her job and a certain coworker, Mrs. Bongiacamo. We laughed so much that I'm certain any weight we might have acquired during the meal, we, for sure worked off.

Princess, Ashley and Draia revealed some issues with their men. It wasn't anything we hadn't all discussed before, and none of us really had the answers. But there was a sense of relief just to be able to talk about it with your girls.

Nikki was still fairly silent on the new boyfriend but it was out in the open that she was dating someone she felt had the potential to maybe be the one. We all listened to her brief announcement, and then she abruptly changed topic.

None of us pressed. It was not in our nature. When she was ready to talk, we would be there to listen. We all relayed as much and then it seemed as if all eyes were on me. I had much to say but I preferred to do it over dessert.

I hit the electric kettle and starting taking tea and coffee orders. As per our usual custom, Nikki and Draia wanted tea while the rest of us preferred coffee.

"What the heck is that girl?" Ashley's eyes went wide as I brought out a cake from the fridge.

"Oh my gosh, that looks yummmm," Nikki exclaimed.

"I see you've outdone yourself, bestie," Draia smiled.

"What kind of cake is that?" Princess asked.

"Yeah Cat, what kind of cake is that?" Charmy mimicked Draia.

"Well ladies, after hearing what you bitches were just saying, I'm sure I made the right cake. It's called Better Than Sex." I giggled.

"Well, we gonna' find out!" My sister smiled, getting up and heading to the bathroom.

The rest of the girls agreed with the sentiment in one form or another.

After serving the beverages and letting Nikki do the honors of carving up the cake, I sat down and began my story.

"Well girls, I really appreciate ya'll coming over. I missed the hell out of all of you even though, as you can tell, setting up this joint took every spare minute, and money I might add, that I had. However I'm definitely gonna' ask you ladies to clear your calendar about once a month, 'cause this ain't no one-time thang, ya know what I'm sayin! Seriously though, sitting here, chatting with you guys, I realize just how necessary this is to clear my mind, free my heart and quiet my soul."

The girls all nodded in between sips of tea, coffee, and bites of cake.

"The older I get the more I'm starting to realize how much we need each other. One time I was chatting with mom, complaining about Christian's lack of understanding when I was trying to express to him some of the pressures I was feeling. I was really upset that he wasn't able to say the

166

right thing to comfort me. You know that woman said something absolutely profound that hit me like a ton of bricks."

"What's that Cat?" Charmy asked.

"She said, Catherine, aside from God, who is the only one who can give you everything, don't depend on men for everything you need. For the things they can't give you, you have to look to women, your sister, your mother, your girlfriends. Men are not equipped to fulfill every part of you."

"She right." Charmy nodded emphatically.

"Umhmm," Ashley agreed.

"Yup," Draia pointed her fork at me.

"You know Mom be saying some good things every now and again," Nikki chimed in.

"I know, right?" I said, looking at all my girls.

"Well, I knew that," Princess said, waving her hand dismissively.

We all pinned her down with our Care Bear Stare.

"Shut the hell up bitch." I laughed good-naturedly.

"Of course, the princess over here dripping in diamonds would say some shit like that," Ash chimed in, pretending to hate.

"I told you we should kill this pretty know-it-all bitch in the bathroom. Bitch, if you weren't so pretty and gettin' us all free drinks every time we hang, we would have killed you a long time ago," Nikki said, reaching for her second piece of cake.

"Aww you bitches always make me feel special." Princess laughed at us all.

"Yeah you special all right. Only you would think a bunch of bitches telling you we're gonna' murder your ass on a daily is awesome." Ashly retorted sending a new wave of hysterical guffawing throughout our small party.

"Seriously though, I feel blessed to have you ladies in my life. Now how about this cake? Does it live up to its name or what?" I expressed sincerely.

"Hell yes," my sister said. "Next time you better make two."

I laughed. "Next time I will."

"So what's up with you Cat? How's everything with you?" Draia asked, getting up, collecting the empty plates on the table and slyly making her way over to the sink.

"Bitch, you're a guest in my home; you better leave them damn dishes alone."

Draia laughed. "How'd you know what I was gonna' do?"

"I know how you stay. Now sit your ass down."

Draia chuckled, resuming her seat.

168

"So I don't know how much ya'll know or whatever, so lemme just tell ya'll. Since C and moved into our joint, I basically stopped chillin' with Marcas."

"Wow for real? He cool with that?" Nikki asked.

"Well, not at first, but he got cool with it. You know I love that boy. I've known him for forever and he's so much fun to chill with, but I started to lose my mind and just act the fool. That shit started to interfere with me and C, so I had to let it go." I waved my hand for emphasis.

"Yeah, I hear that," Charmy said.

"So what's goin' on now? Things straight between you and C?"

"Well, since I put Marcas on the ice, C and I have been good. He hasn't bitched much about work these past couple of weeks, thank God. Girl, I just hope that he stops being such a punk ass and finally gets his priorities straight."

"I hear that," Draia said.

"What's the issue? What's C's problem with work?" Princess asked.

"Yeah?" Charmy and Ash asked in unison.

"Well Nikki and Draia know more about this 'cause, of course, I was living with Nikki, and me and Draia are kind of married to the same type of Trini man so we commiserate together. Well, anyways, lemme' give the rest of ya'll the 411."

"Okay. Let's hear it," Charmy said, sitting back and giving me her full attention.

"Yo, before we get into all of that, can I just tell you how comfortable these chairs are?" Ash pointed out.

"Aw, thanks honey. Girl, I knew we would be in the kitchen for hours, so I picked these out in particular for just that purpose."

"Good job!" Ash said. "Okay, I'm done. Carry on."

"Thanks, bitch." I laughed.

"No, seriously though, you guys don't know this about C but he's not that great with jobs. I mean, ya'll know he's a good guy and he's got great characteristics. I don't know any other dude that has the great qualities that he has. He's not jealous, he's not argumentative, we love to do the same things, blah blah blah."

"Yeah, we know all that, bitch, cut to the chase." Ash laughed.

"Bitch, shut the fuck up and let her talk," Charmy said, threatening Ash with her fork.

"What? Okay, sorry. Please, carry on." Ash replied without sarcasm.

"Aren't you so bloody generous? Thanks bitch. Anyways!" I retorted, flicking my hair like Cher and trying hard not to crack up.

"As I was sayin, when C gets a job, at first he's doing great, then he starts to complain about it now and again. Then he complains all of the time and eventually he wants to quit. I just can't stand his lack of work ethic sometimes you know."

"Hmm, well that ain't good," Nikki said.

"Nah, that ain't," Charmy agreed.

"So what's going on now? He's still at this job with his cousin, right?"

"Yeah, he's still there, and like I said, since we moved here I haven't heard much complaining from him about his job. So I'm kind of hoping that since I've done a drastic 180—I don't be hanging out anywhere, I hardly text Marcas or anyone else for that matter, I barely see you girls—well, I'm hoping that will give him some incentive to change his ways too.

You know, if we both come around, I think he and I will get to that next level and kind-a like grind hard, play harder. I mean, I ain't askin' him to be no Rockefeller. I just want him to maintain a job so we can just keep on keepin' on, ya know what I'm sayin'?"

"Hells yeah girl. These men don't know how hard it is to work and come home and cook and clean and take care of the kids and be under all this pressure trying to stretch that 50 cent into two dollars. They need to take care of themselves and start taking some of this damn stress off of us," Draia explained.

"For real," Charmy agreed.

"Well, hopefully now that you guys have this new place he'll realize that you need two paychecks to maintain, and he'll, like, come correct, you know?" Princess said. "Yeah, girl, I sure hope he keeps takin' them act right pills and push forward. Thanks for listening ladies, much appreciated."

"Of course girl," the girls chimed in unison.

"So who's up for some more coffee or tea and another slice?" I asked, getting up and refilling the kettle.

"That would be my third slice, thank you very much," Nikki said reaching for her plate.

The girls and I chatted while I washed the dishes, made more coffee and sliced more cake. Later that evening after they left and I was folding away the shoe shelf, I took a moment to revel in my blessings. To have JC, a happy kid, a good man, beautiful apartment and the financial means to be stable, plus these amazing teacups to share my laughter and tears filled my heart with more happiness than I thought possible to contain. Whatever happens, I would be able.

Just as I was turning down the bed, C came home.

"Hey baby, how was your day? You had fun?" I asked, pulling back the blanket.

"Yeah, we had a nice time," he said sadly.

"What's a matter? Your cousins okay?"

"Babe, I got something to tell you."

"What is it?" I asked nervously, sitting at the edge of the bed fearing what I already knew.

"Robert told me that our supervisor didn't have enough work to go around and so he's letting the new guys, which includes me, umm, go," he revealed quietly, hanging his head.

"Say what now?" I countered.

And That, Ladies and Gentlemen, Is Precisely How the Fight Started

"Dammit, I knew this was gonna' happen!" I snapped.

"Babe, you know how it is. Last one in is usually the first one out. Come on, there's nothing I could do about that." C hooked his thumbs in his belt loops and squared his shoulders, his usual battle preparation stance.

"You really gonna' try and feed me that line of bull after I predicted this months ago?" I folded my hands across my chest, my own countermove.

"What line? I'm telling you what Robert told me."

I took a deep breath but it did nothing to quell my anger. Somewhere in the back of my mind, JC tried to reason with me, but I pushed him aside for the moment. I intended to have my say.

"Didn't I tell you months ago that if you keep up with your attitude they would fire you?"

"Babe, them letting me go had nothing to do with my attitude."

"Why are you so full of shit? It had everything to do with your attitude!" I roared, jumping off of the bed.

C grinded his teeth and backed away, making room for my escape. He should be so lucky. I just needed to do something with my hands, or I would wring his neck. I stomped to the other side of the bed, yanking off the decorative pillows and stuffing them into the pop-up hamper so I could turn the bed down. I needed some distance from this man and his betrayal.

"You promised me that when we got here you would work like a dog to get us where we should be. Do you remember that?" I stared holes into his eyes accusingly.

"Yeah, and I did. But they wanted me to work overtime like every day. I wish you could have seen how they treated us, then you wouldn't be saying this to me."

"The hell I wouldn't. I don't care how they treated you!"

"Of course you don't! You weren't there, you didn't see."

"Who bloody well cares how they treated you? You think when I was working in the dungeon they treated me like a princess?"

He rolled his eyes, let them hit the ceiling before climbing down the wall and settling back on me.

"You know I hated every minute of working in that place! And for $10 an hour. I don't think I made that little except when I was sixteen and working at McDonald's, but I sucked it up, didn't I? Why did I do that C?"

"Where's Gaia?"

"She's in her room. What difference does that make?"

"Lower your voice," he stated with quiet steel.

I couldn't believe this motherfrigger was actually angry. Oh, so now he wanna be wrong and strong. Nonetheless, I did lower my voice a few octaves. Gaia didn't need to hear anything about our future in this manner. It might freak her out and make her worry. It was the last thing I wanted or needed.

"I told you that if you didn't change your attitude, they would fire you. Robert and Trey work extremely hard. You knew this. They recommended you and you made them look bad. The only reason the company hired you was on the strength of your cousins. You completely changed everything you said to me from day one. How the hell do you feel like you have the balls to tell me that I better get a good job when I suggested this move and yet you feel like it's okay for you to do this? Why is it that I always have to be the one to put our family first while you always put yourself first?"

"Listen, babe, I'm sorry that this happened, but you're wrong. Nothing I did or didn't do made them let me go. They just didn't have enough work for all of us."

"That's the bullshit story you're stickin' to, huh?"

He shot me a pained look, sighed and walked out of the room. I didn't have the strength to follow. I heard him grab his car keys and slam the door. That made me grind my teeth. I thought the damn fool wanted us to be quiet!

My ADD did not allow me to rest. I left the room to check the front door. I guessed right. He hadn't bothered to lock both locks. I secured the top lock, went back in the room, closed the door and sat on the bed to have a good cry, if there was such a thing. Afterwards, I would be ready to listen to what JC had to tell me.

I Can Fix This

When he rolled in two and a half hours later, I already had things worked out. I had a good long talk with my Jesus and knew what had to be done. It's amazing how laying my burdens on his feet frees me. JC and me, we were developing strategies. I let him know, then I let it go. After that, I was primed for reception. The answer didn't always come quickly but when it did, it was crystal clear. However, I was still me. My anger subsided, but it hadn't disappeared.

I was sitting at the kitchen table, a cup a joe on a coaster by my right wrist, my laptop open, my fingers sprinting across the keys when he finally waltzed in. He seemed surprised, but I could tell by his eyes he still had too much fight in him. He wasn't going to apologize or take responsibility. Not yet. I left that between him and JC. We both knew what really went on. Doing the accusing and denial dance wasn't gonna' do shit for me right now.

"Sit down. I want to talk to you." I was calm but I didn't feel like breaking out the sunshine.

"I'm tired. Can't we talk in the morning? I just want to go to bed."

"Christian, if I have to ask you again, it's gonna' be on and poppin' up in this piece. We have some things that need discussing right now, and in case you forgot, I've got work tomorrow, and by the time we're through, so will you. Now sit down. Please." That last word almost took it out of me. Thank God we had no loaded weapons in the house.

He sat in a huff, with his shoes and jacket still on. This irked me to no one end. It reminded me of his unreliability and gave me the distinct impression that he could just get up and bounce anytime he wanted. I knew he wouldn't, but sometimes I doubted everything about him, about us. If it were up to me, I would cuss him out and cut and run. JC fixed it so that I could handle this joint on my own. I could swing the rent and bills. I might have to give up the car if it got to be more trouble than it was worth but in the grand scheme of things, who gives a shit? Did I really need this bullshit?

But when I had my chat with JC, he worked on me, softened me, put my feet in a new direction and said try this. It was that uncomplicated. Despite all of my fears and doubts and issues, JC said try this, work it out and that was the choice I made. Notice I didn't say happily made. My choice didn't make me Snow White, singing with the birds and mice and shit. I was still an angry bitch but I checked myself.

"So I've been discussing things with JC since you felt the need to drop the bomb on me and then go MIA."

He folded his hands across his chest and sunk back into the seat wearing an annoyed expression.

"Good, I don't need you to say shit, just listen. I've looked up the unemployment and what not. I saved the website under favorites. Tomorrow, file a claim. You should receive it for about a year but God willing we'll find something for you before that."

"Lemme' see the laptop."

I spun it around so he could view the screen and then got up to drain the rest of my coffee and put my cup in the sink.

"You want some tea or anything?"

"No, I'm good."

"All right."

"So what's the rest of your plan?" he asked, fiddling with the keys.

"Well, I saved a couple of other websites like Monster and the Daily News and a few others. It's important that you develop a routine as if you were still working. Get up, have your tea and some breakfast and look for a job through these sites and the paper. Anything you see that looks like a good candidate, put the fax number or e-mail and person to whom I should attention it to and put all of the info in a Word document.

Every day you e-mail me the Word document and I can fax it from my job. You can send the e-mails on your own, but keep a record so when you get a response we know the particulars. If you're diligent, I'm sure you'll find something, hopefully that's a better fit for you, maybe in an office environment, like in Jersey."

He sighed. "Yeah that sounds like a good plan."

"In the meantime, you have to keep on top of the unemployment. Make sure you file your claims every week. I worked the numbers. We should be okay even without the majority of your income, thank God."

He breathed a sigh of relief, and I could see the tension ease when he sloped his shoulders. I don't know why I felt better about that, but I did.

He pushed the chair back and walked over to me, enfolding me in a bear hug.

"I'm sorry, babe. I didn't mean for it to go like this."

That was as close to a confession as I was likely to ever get. It had to be enough.

I sighed and held him tight.

"I know. Hopefully this will just be temporary and you can find something better."

I felt him nod and hug me tighter.

"I spoke to Gaia, so she knows the deal."

"Okay. Babe, let's go to bed."

"Okay."

His kiss felt like a promise, like he was determined to do better.

Later that night, when he was asleep and I wasn't, I felt the old doubts creeping in. Was I being a fool, or was I doing the right thing? Was I listening to JC or deluding myself? I thought about that for a while. I ran down our history. Before I met C, my heart had been broken, shattered. I got down on my knees and asked God to keep me away from all men unless he was going to give me the one he designed just for me. Then along came C. I knew he was the one. I knew then, and I know now.

But why, Lord, did it have to be this hard? Why did he have to come with so much baggage and bullshit? A nagging little voice reminded me that I was no picnic either, and that maybe my extracurricular activities might have contributed to some of the circumstances that led here. NO! I pushed those thoughts aside.

I knew I wasn't perfect, but dammit, I hung in there with this dude and gave him my all. I'm not one of those princess girls that sit on the sidelines and demand that my man figure it out. Hell, most of the time, he's the one on the sidelines while I'm the one working all the angles. Didn't I deserve some kind of reward and space of my own?

****

The next morning, C was still sleeping when I got out of the shower. It was only 7:30 a.m. He probably was going to get going around 9:00 a.m. That was reasonable, I imagined. I maintained hope, but thus far I wasn't impressed. I was hoping for a little more get up and go but I second-guessed my own attitude. A part of me felt I was being harsh and unreasonable and not giving him much of a chance; after all, it was only the first day.

By 8:20 a.m., Gaia and I were ready to leave for the bus when C popped out of the bathroom fully dressed and all smiles.

"Babe, I thought you were just using the bathroom and then going back to bed. Whatcha doing?" I asked, completely shocked.

"It's time to get up. I'm taking Gaia to school and then dropping you off at the train station. On my way back I'm going to pick up the paper and get started on my routine."

I was clearly astonished, hell, by the look on Gaia's face I was not alone. I silently chastised myself for my earlier

181

thoughts. The man clearly had initiative. With this attitude and determination, he's likely to find a gig in no time. Despite everything, I was impressed.
"Wow, babe, thanks. Lemme just grab my bag."

"Cool. Thanks Christian," Gaia practically sang.

Christian affectionately mussed her hair as she tried to duck away.

"Cool. Gaia and I will warm up the car."

I made the bed up in record time, did a once-over, checked the stove and locked up. It certainly felt like we were on the right path.

One Step Forward, Two Steps Back

What started off promising tapered off into stoic obligation. The first couple of months of unemployment C took well. He maintained a great attitude and stuck to his routine. He even found ways to improve his job search and managed a few phone interviews, following up on every favorable lead. So far, nothing panned out but that's the game. You got to work the numbers just like in sales. What do they say? For every hundred calls, you may get anywhere from one to ten responses.

Six months into it and I could see him waning. His self-esteem was hitting the crapper, and I was getting tired of propping him up. Another month into it and his routine was shot all to hell. He no longer woke up early and took Gaia to school or me to the train station. He never got the paper anymore.

When I asked him about it, he snapped at me and told me that they never had any new leads to follow. I thought maybe he needed to get the paper once a week or once every two weeks instead of every other day. He resented the fact that I had an answer for everything, and I resented that he always had a problem that he couldn't seem to solve himself. I always tended to focus on the solution, while he kept turning over the problem. One day I said as much. This revelation only led to a lot more eye rolling and teeth sucking on his part and an old itch on mine.

I held on for another two months before I stopped focusing on him altogether. Our routine became a once a week exercise in volatility. I questioned him about job searching like a parole officer, and he answered half my questions like a sullen ex-con. During the other half of our exchange, he either left the house and took a walk or busied himself in his phone or computer.

I needed a change of pace. I desperately wanted to have a girls' night out or call my boy Marcas and have a drink fest, but I was afraid that it would only make things worse. I wasn't past the point of caring just yet. That soon changed.

One Saturday evening, I was taking a load off, chilling on the living room couch watching an old film noir, enjoying some alone time, when Gaia strode past on the way to her room. She stopped short of her door before turning to me.

"Mom?"

"Hmm." I was still fairly engrossed in Bogie and Bacall's conversation. He just kissed her. She said, I like that. I'd like some more. They don't make them like that anymore.

"Mom, when Christian says he's out somewhere, how do you know he's actually where he says he is?"

My first instinct was to dismiss what she said. But I recognized that old defense mechanism from my first marriage. I didn't need to bury BS for three years before I faced my demons. Instead, I thought about the answer to her question. Growth, ain't it grand?

"Well, I call him all of the time. I've never caught him in a lie or anything."

"Oh okay. That's good." She smiled, perking up. She gave me a quick peck on the cheek and dashed into her room.

Needless to say, I couldn't focus on the flick anymore. My answer made Gaia go into protection cover-up mode. She saw a denial in my response and she reacted accordingly, protectively. She wasn't going to uncover anything I wasn't ready to deal with. I lowered the volume on the tele and knocked on her door.

"Come in," she chirped forcefully.

"Gaia?"

"Yeah, Mom." She smiled, eyeing me while nervously fiddling with her phone charger.

"Why'd you ask me that question, lil mama? Did you see or hear something that would make you think that C wasn't where he should be?"

"Well, no, not exactly. But I just notice that he's always on his phone when he's home. And he's hardly ever home anymore."

"Yeah, that's true," I reasoned. "But this unemployment thing has really got him down, so he's chilling with his cousins a lot now for some stress relief."

"Okay, cool. It's just weird, you know."

"Yeah. We seem to be going through a weird time. But are you okay, lil mama?"

"Yup yup yup."

I kissed Gaia on her forehead and left the room. I sat down on the couch in a daze. I ran playback through my mind of the last time I called him when he was out with his cousins and couldn't remember. I trusted him so completely. There was never much reason to call him when he was with the fellas. He often hung out at Trey's house and played X-Box or PlayStation games along with Robert and Vernon. They all went out to eat or ordered pizza. It was practically systematic. But Gaia was correct. The frequency increased a great deal during the last two months. And he was on his phone more than he ever was before, but I just assumed he was checking job e-mails or playing games. Well, this was easily solved. I should just call him now.

What surprised me was the split second fear right after that thought. I can't believe I actually have a fear of calling this man. Right then and there I knew I had to call him, and so I did. He answered on the third ring.

"Hey babe."

"Hi. Where are you?" I wasn't about to pussyfoot around my issue.

"I'm with the fellas. What are you up to?" Was that nervousness?

"I'm watching a movie. Christian?"

"Yeah babe?"

"Where are the fellas?"

"They're in the living room playing games."

"Where are you? How come I can't hear them?"

"I'm in the bedroom. I came in here to answer your call. You know it's too noisy in there."

Right here, this juncture, this intersection, I had two options. I could have accepted this explanation and said see ya later, but of course I went left. I'm a hard-ass. If it's gonna' go down then it's gonna' go down.

"Well I can't hear anything. Walk back over to the fellas. I want to talk to Trey for a quick sec."

Dial tone. Motherfucker. Did he actually just hang up on me? Yes, he sure did. Well I didn't need to go much further, did I?

I called him back three times. He let it go to voice mail. I left a message. "Christian, you better get your ass home right now and explain to me just what the hell you're doing. Right now." My voice was deadly calm.

I texted him. The jig is up. Come home right now.

I was fuming. My phone beeped. He actually sent me a text.

"I'll be home in an hour. I'm on my way."

Wow. He was full of surprises. I was a bit shaken that he hadn't taken the lie further. What did that mean? Was he in love with someone else? I didn't know what to think. I was angry that his unemployed ass could find time to fuck around. I was hurt that he lied to me. I was mad as hell that I stuck by him through all his bullshit only to end up here.

I didn't want to talk to JC right now. Part of me was angry at my Lord. Part of me was even afraid to admit I was angry at my Lord, because I knew deep down inside my Lord has never led me down a wrong path. However, this sure was not what I expected. Did I cause this upon myself? Was I responsible? Did I read his signs wrong? Did I choose my own way and here was the penalty? I would chat with JC later. Right now I was just trying to figure out how C and I got here and what was really going on. Almost an hour later, I heard his key in the door. I hope he poured himself a drink, because I wasn't going to stop until I got all of my answers.

Revelations

I could hear him dropping his keys into the key bowl and plopping down on the ottoman in the kitchen. He must be unlacing his boots. A few minutes later, he came into the living room and sat down on a chair opposite the couch hanging a wary expression. I almost felt sorry for him. Almost.

"So what's the story?"

"Nothing. I was just out."

"Christian, please do not lie to me anymore and don't try my nerve. Where were you?"

"I went to the mall." He sighed heavily.

Dammit. This was gonna' be like pulling teeth. I would get nothing more than what I asked for. So I took a moment to think about my questions before firing away.

"Who were you with?"

"A friend." He averted his eyes to the floor.

What are we, a virgin now? I nearly throttled him where he sat.

"Which friend, Christian? Stop making me ask you all of this bullshit and just come clean with me. You're already busted. What the fuck is going on?"

"You don't need to curse."

"Are you for real right now? You're lucky I didn't shoot you as soon as you walked through the door. You've been lying to me about your whereabouts for God knows how long, and your married ass is what, dating? You better start telling me what the hell is going on."

He leaned forward and propped his elbows on his thighs, took a moment to rub his head, his signature gesture exposing his comfortability. If I was a man, I think I would have socked him in the jaw. Instead I remained rigid, waiting for my answers.

"What do you want to know?"

I almost lost it and cracked him one. But I could see that I wasn't going to get any answers that way. And right now it was more important to find out the truth. There was plenty of time to blow up on him later.

"Who were you with?"

"A friend of mine that I used to go to high school with."

"Christian, don't answer questions halfway. Who is this friend? Obviously it's a girl or you wouldn't be doing this dance."

"Her name is Lisa."

"What is she?"

"What do you mean?"

"Don't make me run up on you. What is she, Black, white, Spanish, coolie, what the fuck is she?"

"She's Spanish."

We could both hear Gaia turn up the volume on her tele. He was surprised, and then gave me a look as if I was the one subjecting Gaia to this bullshit. I was becoming more and more enraged with each passing minute.

"What did you think, homie? You thought that I could stash Gaia somewhere while we hash this out? Does this look like the set of The Real Housewives of Queens to you? What's a matter? You feel ashamed and you don't want her to know what you've done? I've got news for you, she figured you out before I did because I apparently trusted you."

"Can we discuss the rest of this in the room?"

The truth is I wish I didn't have to subject Gaia to any of this. She had already been through it once with her dad and me. C, Gaia and I had been together for seven years. She grew up with him. She trusted him. He had been a good stepdad. This was coming out of left field for both of us.

I dusted myself off, fluffed the pillows and walked into the kitchen. I spied the Johnny Walker Black and thought about fixing myself a tall boy but I was pretty sure that would send me into a murderous rage. So I kept pace to the bedroom and shut the door after C followed me in. He took a seat at the edge of the bed and tucked his hands under his armpits. It's just like a man to cause all kinds of trouble and then appear to be the vulnerable victim in the midst of the storm.

"So when did you start talking to Lisa? I never heard of her before."

"A couple of months ago she found me on FB and we started chatting. And once in a while we'd hang out. That's all."

"If that's all, then why didn't you tell me about her?"

He shrugged his shoulders. "I don't know."

"Do you have feelings for this girl Christian?"

"No. We're just friends. We just talk, that's all."

That almost took it out of me. They talk? Something we never do anymore. We fight. We argue. We're stoically silent. In my heart I knew it was just a matter of time. I had already lost him. I'd been down this path. I knew what was coming.

"Christian, do you want to be married to me anymore?" I sat down on the bed facing the window. I couldn't bear to look at him as he answered.

"I don't know."

The tears came and I despised every droplet. This is not how I wanted to go out. A line from G.I. Jane hit me like a silver lining in a black cloud. I wiped my tears, gritted my teeth and left sadness and grief to their own for a minute. I wanted to walk with anger for a few.

"I'm gonna' give you what you want. We're gonna' see how much you want what you get. Call your brother Christian, and tell him to come and get you. Until you know that there's nowhere you'd rather be than home here with Gaia and me, I don't want you home. I'm gonna' give you some time to work out whatever the hell it is you're

192

going through. But you better remember you're on the clock. Tick, Tick. Because once I decide that I don't want you anymore, it's done. There is no coming back."

"Okay. You want me to call him now?"

"Yes. Call him now."

He got up and went to the kitchen to make the call and I nearly crumpled into myself. My God, he didn't even put up a fight. I could hold on a little longer. I stiffened my spine. I'd been here before. Chin up bitch, you will not fall apart in front of him. I swiped at my tears and took a deep breath before going into the kitchen and hitting the kettle. I could use a cup o' joe or rather Marcas in more ways than one.

"He'll be here soon."

"Did you tell him what happened?" I asked curiously.

"No. I'll tell him later. I'm gonna' get my stuff together before he comes."

"Okay." I quickly turned from him and busied myself with the coffee.

A half hour later while I was standing at the counter I heard a car horn.

Christian came out of the room with his overnight bag jam packed. He dropped it by the front door and came over to me. He hugged me and I allowed it.

"I'm sorry," he said for the first time, tears streaming down his handsome face.

"No. You're not. But you will be," I said softly, kissing his cheek and turning away from him.

After he left, I calmly washed my coffee cup, straightened the kitchen and went in my room, locking the door behind me before hurling myself onto my bed and bawling like a baby.

One Foot In Front of the Other

The next morning I managed to get up, smile at Gaia, make her breakfast and see her off to school. I somehow was also able to get myself dressed and head to work. Will wonders never cease? I sat on the bus in a daze. I studied the trees from my window seat. I glanced at my fellow passengers and thought to myself am I in shock? I am doing everything that I am supposed to be doing, but my life has been altered beyond all understanding. My man is gone. Gone. There is an interloper in my midst.

I curiously checked her FB and scoured through Christian's as well for good measure. I couldn't believe all of the signs I missed. Obvious signs that something might have been going on betwixt the two. They were just a tad overfriendly with each other. They left a lot of comments on each other's page and right about the time she popped up his public messages to me dwindled down to an almost arctic chill.

It was like looking at a trail of bread crumbs. They weren't especially smart in as much as I was especially dumb. Of course, if I would have noticed it sooner, then what? Then we'd be where we are today.

I got off the bus and headed downstairs to the train. Everything looked the same and yet nothing felt remotely familiar. I took my usual position with my back against the door and observed the passengers before me. A handsome man sitting a few feet from me smiled in my direction. I returned a blank stare. I turned my back to face the outside, turned up the volume on my iPhone tucking my earbuds in further to ensure I heard little if anything other than the pounding rhythm of Daft Punk's Tron soundtrack.

At work I answered the phones, chatted amiably with my coworkers, did my job. If you looked too closely you could see the cracks but people were busy with their own lives and no one made a study of me, thank God. I wasn't ready to talk about anything to anyone. I still had a great deal of processing to do. Once I figured out what had been going on, then I could plan what I could do about it. Right now all I could do was piece together what happened and not fall apart in the process.

I was surprised at how relatively well I was handling matters. Perhaps it was because I'd been here before. No. I think it was because he hadn't put me through the works by dragging out the lies. I wanted to kill him. I was mad as hell. But the fact remained; when he got busted he came clean. He answered my questions and then he did as I asked. He left.

Usually through all of this I would talk to my Jesus, but I was purposefully leaving him out of it. I wanted to sit with my own feelings for a minute. I didn't want him to change my perspective until I figured out just what my perspective was. And yes, I knew he had the power to do that. He always does. So, I locked him out. For now.

I got through work one task at a time. I got back on the train and then sat on the bus. I walked the two blocks to my apartment and immediately felt better once my key was in the door. My Jewel Box Joint was my sanctuary and despite all, it was good to be home. I was grateful.

I changed into my comfy clothes and sat down on the couch with a cup of tea. Soon after I heard Gaia's key in the door. She was visiting her grandma and her dad just dropped her back home. I put the teacup down and steeled myself. It was time for another hard conversation.

You Broke It, Now Fix It

"Mom?" Gaia called to me from the kitchen as she dropped her keys into the bowl.

"Yeah honey, I'm in the living room."

"Okay, coming."

I smiled to myself. I could tell by her voice that the kid was worried about me. Her usual routine was to drop her keys and hightail it to her room, mumbling hello and planting a hurried kiss on my forehead. But now that she knew we were on our own again, her concern was evident in all of her words.

She sat down next to me and gave me a hearty hug.

"Lil mama, I want to talk to you about a few things that are obviously going on between C and me." I squeezed her hand and smiled in what I hoped was the picture of reassurance.

"I figured," she said, letting go of me and folding her legs Indian chief style opposite me steadying herself for my news.

I took a deep breath and began.

"Well you know after you and I talked yesterday I gave C a call. And as you know he wasn't where he was supposed to be after all. He was with a friend of his, some girl he knew from high school apparently." I tried to keep the bitterness out of my voice. I don't think I was vastly successful.

197

Gaia rolled her eyes and sighed.

"Anyway, we talked a lot last night and I don't think he's done anything beyond hanging out with this girl for a while but I think he really likes her and is now questioning whether he wants to basically remain here with us or start something new with her." I shrugged. Better words failed me. Gaia was not your average kid and putting sugar in the medicine would be an insult to her intelligence and senses. She had already been through the divorce of her father and me. And it was volatile. We both said and did things we were not especially proud of, and the kid had a front row seat to it all. Hiding any of this was not an option.

"So what happens now?"

"Well, really not too much. We can afford our apartment so we're fine. I don't want you to worry about anything like that. When I started looking for a place, I made sure I was able to afford it on my own. We can comfortably live here and take care of our rent and our bills just fine, thank God."

Gaia mulled this over and nodded. "I just don't want things to happen like last time."

I was a bit taken aback by her statement and unsure of her meaning. "What do you mean 'like last time,' Gaia?"

"Well last time when you and Dad were getting a divorce you had boyfriends over and you were basically a mess. I just don't want to go through that again."

I had a sick feeling in the pit of my stomach and my mouth dried up like an African riverbed. I had flashbacks of some of the things I had done and shame literally cowered me for a few minutes. After my brief stint of shame, I was nearly overcome with anger.

I was so resentful that my husband, Gaia's father, cheated on me, ruined what we had and then proceeded to live his life as a single man while I had to figure everything out with child in tow. I swallowed it back. It had no place in the present. That was a long time ago. Today was a different story and it was my job to make Gaia understand that.

I picked up her hand and held it firmly in mine. "Gaia, the things that happened when your dad and I were going through our divorce, the things that I said and did, well, you know I'm not proud of them. I made my mistakes but when I regained my senses I promised you that I would never act like that again and that I would spend however long it took to prove to you that I meant every word I said. And I have. And I will continue to do so."

"You don't plan on having anyone over here?" Gaia asked skeptically.

"Gaia, listen, you were just a little kid when your dad and I split up. You're not anymore. I've grown and so have you. I don't plan on having any stranger in our home. I respect myself and I respect you and I am not going to put either one of us in any crazy situation just because of what Christian is going through."

As much as I wanted to reassure Gaia of what I already knew, I didn't want to put myself in a position where she believed I had to answer to her. It is my job, however, to be truthful. When you screw up, even and maybe especially as a parent, you've got to honestly own it and then take all of the steps to move in the opposite direction. Transparency is an absolute must. Submission is a mistake.

"Are you guys getting a divorce?"

"I sure hope not. Personally, Gaia, I think Christian is just going through a phase. He's unemployed, he's down in the dumps and this girl is probably making him feel good about himself right now. I think this is temporary but I can't say for certain. Hopefully he'll figure things out and want to come home but if he doesn't you need to know that we're gonna' be all right."

She sighed. "Okay. Well I'm gonna' get to my homework now. Thanks for telling me what's going on."

I smiled. "You're welcome. Did you eat?"

"Yeah, at Grandma's." She threw back over her shoulder before closing her door behind her.

I swallowed hard, but the lump in my throat wouldn't go down. I knew Gaia was still worried but I could do nothing to reassure her. I could only complete one day at a time responsibly and eventually she would see things were straight. And as time went on, she would start to trust. It broke my heart that she still held me accountable today for mistakes I made so long ago.

No, it wasn't fair. That's the burden of being a parent I suppose. I was hurt. I was a bit angry. I was still ashamed. I walked into my room, closing the door behind me. I plucked one of the pillows from my bed and put it on the floor. I dropped to my knees and clasped my hands together.

The guilt I was feeling now from things I had done in the past might lead me left instead of right. I needed him to release me from it once and for all. I needed his guidance, presence and reassurance. I would be no good to Gaia without it. I needed to let him back in. I closed my eyes and prayed. "Help me, Jesus. Help me."

You're In and You're Out, You're Up and You're Down

The next week was something out of the Twilight Zone. Christian never called me. In fact, he forgot us. I believe the technical term is called abandonment. Yet life rolled along. I worked, cleaned, prayed and avoided everyone but Gaia. Thank God she had a full life and wasn't home long enough to take too much notice of my mood.

Although I wasn't sure if it would have mattered much since I had no real reaction to speak of. I felt unbelievably calm. Christian wasn't in love with this girl. I knew he was going through a rough time and that someone was making him feel good about himself; someone who didn't know him at all and could afford to do so.

Don't give me that look. I'm not one of those women who want their man so desperately that they're willing to not just overlook a betrayal but excuse and dismiss as if it never happened. No. That's not what I'm saying. But I do know a great deal about my man. I know the difference between him and my ex, and believe you, me, there is an innate difference betwixt the two.

My ex craved variety. He was like an addict. He had the attention span of a gnat. One woman would never be enough for him. Christian was different. He was solid when it came to that. His head was never turned before. He was dependable. In my heart of hearts, I believe he's a good man that took a wrong turn. Nobody made him do it. I don't blame the other woman. I blame my man. He betrayed me. He got caught up. But who better than me understands how easily that can happen?

Could I see his side so easily because I always had my own BS on the side? One had to be real with it. Maybe. Could be. I had a million male friends, didn't I? I spent time with some of them now and again. I flirted, I danced, I conversed, I drank. Was that vastly different than what he was involved in? Not especially. However, even though I did my dirt, let's just say, whatever I felt and whoever I felt it for, my extracurricular activities never shifted focus away from my man beyond the brief moment I was in another's presence.

No one ever made me question the validity of my marriage. No one ever made me question my choice of husband, made me second-guess that or made me want to better deal him. That's what angered me the most. That's what hurt the most. You mean to tell me that some fool could come along that made him feel good for ten seconds and in return he starts to question us, our family, our marriage.

I hadn't expected my man to be so damn dumb. He should have been able to take that confidence that she was giving him and use it as a catalyst for action, put some pep in his step and carry him through the wretched part of his day. It has a place and it serves a purpose. I found myself disappointed in the way that this bullshit had affected him. I simply couldn't believe that this was all it took to get him caught up. On one hand, it really spoke to how innocent the man was. This was his first brush with genuine flirtation and his reaction made it painfully obvious it was so.

On the other hand, it really made one (me in particular) question how smart was the man I married? I always thought if this type of situation came up, he would be able to easily brush it off, to see it for what it really was and act accordingly. His actions made me feel vulnerable and foolish. He made me feel like any trifling bitch could bat some eyelashes and he'd be gone. What remained to be seen was how long it would take him to regain his senses and the possibility that he might never do so. Of course, it could be even worse depending on your viewpoint. He could be a day late and a dollar short.

For now I would remain calm and play my position. I was his wife and I was waiting for him to regain control of himself and the situation. It might seem odd, but I was fairly confident that he would. I couldn't believe the man I was intimately acquainted with for the better part of nine years simply disappeared. I thought I knew him better than he knew himself.

When I thought about it, this was a predictable situation with a predictable outcome. She stroked his ego, and just like any fool, it caught his attention. But it wouldn't be enough to sustain it. If he had outgrown me, gotten bored with me, simply fallen out of love with me, then I would lose him. All these things are relationship killers. I'd have to accept it and move on without him. I didn't think that was the case.

My assessment: my man is going through a slump, he can't get a job and his self-esteem has taken a nosedive. The fact that I know he's not working hard enough to get a job and is verbal about it, while I'm accurate, serves to only plummet his self-esteem at an even more alarming rate. Do I blame myself for this? Ya mad? Of course not! I can't pretend my man is doing what he's supposed to be doing and reward him for being a lazy ass.

Short term, I might get some kudos but long term I'm only showing him that I'm cool with irresponsibility and somehow it's much more important to protect his fragile ego. So I did what I had to do, the only thing I could do. I walked softly but carried a big stick. And after months of his increasing foolishness, I smacked him with it.

Anyhoo, what he should have done was come correct. Take some damn act right pills and step up his game. What he chose to do was allow some foolish girl who had no idea what was really going on show him some appreciation, and he ran with it. He allowed that unearned inflation of ego (if you will) to turn our family inside out, and why do you suppose, ladies?

Hang on to your Hanes 'cause I'mma tell ya, because he simply wanted more of that feeling, that high. He wanted to live in the lie because it felt so good. He wanted to feel like the man he wasn't instead of truly earning the title by becoming the man that he should have been. Yes, I've got his number. How, pray tell?

And this is where I may lose some of you but I'm willing to put it out there and take the chance. Because as clear as their Facebook breadcrumbs were to me (now), it is precisely with that same clarity that my JC revealed all of these epiphanies after prayer. That's right people. My problem solver is on it people!

And that's how I feel like I know what's really good. Of course, knowing all of this does not make me believe that JC is some magic genie that will make my hubby come correct. Unfortunately not. I am only part of this puzzle. He's got a lot going on, and while he's doing what's right for me, he's also doing what's right for the heifer and my hubby. So what's a girl to do? Trust in Him. That's all I can do.
And when I feel the doubts threatening to overcome me, I get my pillow, toss it on the floor and bend my knees. I

don't know everything but I do know when this is all over, I'm going to be all right. And as my cousin Charmy says, well a dah! (All my GT posse say yeah). It's a Caribbean thang—you betta ask somebody!

Sense & Sensibility

It was Saturday. It had been a long week of ups and downs. I ran the gambit of emotions and still no word from C. No texts, no phone calls, no nothing. I can't lie. I was twisted up inside despite my Jesus's reassurances. My faith was at an all-time low.

Damn this human side of me, JC! On Tuesday, when I could no longer bear the doubting voices in my head, I gave in and texted him with a simple: "Are you all right?" He texted me back about an hour later with a succinct "yes." I thought the agony couldn't get any worse.

As C would say in his Trini accent, "you waste a thought," only it would sound like "ya wAse a taught." How could one generally positive word create so much negative emotion? My faithlessness was just rewarded, I suppose. I moved on and made it to Saturday without incident. Now that it had arrived, there was nothing but lonely, empty hours spread before me. My teacups knew something was wrong but would not press me. My sister was a little different. She called me last night and I found myself relaying the basics of what I had been going through sans emotion.

For the most part I really was fine. I felt fine. But there were moments when I felt acutely depressed and my outlook on my future seemed bleak. I did not need my man financially. I could make it on my own. That was somewhat of a relief. But no matter how logical or methodical I analyzed my situation, I couldn't always shake the weight of it.

I should have felt blessed that I was able to make decisions based solely on my wants rather than my needs. But I did want him. I wanted my husband of seven years beside me. I wanted him in my life. I wanted the we, not the me. After unburdening my heart a little to Nikki, she insisted on stopping in today to speak to me. She would have her boyfriend Drew in tow. It didn't bother me to speak my business in front of him. It is what it is. Gaia wasn't home yet. Friends were always in her midst and she was enjoying her life in a way that she had not in Jersey. Here were her own kind of people, and not just brown Caribbean people, Guyanese and Trinidadians but the whole mutt mix that NY is indeed famous for. She was much more accepted here, and her attitude reflected it.

I was grateful. The timing couldn't be better. Misery did not always love company. She didn't need to mope around here. I did that enough for the both of us and it was a relief to be able to break down sometimes without the fear of worrying her.

After Nikki and Drew were comfortably seated and nursing a steaming cup of tea and I a cup a joe, Nikki began.

"So what's your plan now?" She arched a freshly threaded brow, gazing at me intently.

I don't mind saying I was a little uncomfortable having this conversation. Nikki and I were like two peas in a pod in many aspects, but we were on opposite sides of the spectrum when it came to men and relationships. We picked up different tools that our parental counterparts put down. I had a softer side toward men.

Through my parents' relationship I learned a lot about men, how to be beside them, nudge them softly in directions they were resistant to exploring, encourage them when they needed it and dress them down when necessary.

Of course, these are very cut and dry ideals. Life is much messier, but those were my guidelines. Nikki was different. She had coldness toward men. She competed with them. She didn't trust them to lead, and so she was always the front runner, which might be well and good if you happen to be married to an Englishman, but on this side of the ocean men were a bit trickier. I knew what her position would be before we sat down.

I shifted in my seat uncomfortably. "I don't actually have one. I'm going to wait and see what enfolds before I make any moves."

My sister's facial features did nothing to hide her disappointment.

"Girl, if he's gone then you better see to yourself and Gaia."

"I hear what you're saying Nikki, and we're already seen too. There's nothing that I need to do in order to make us comfortable. We're good. Financially we're straight. I can handle all of my bills without him. I might have to give up the car at some future point, but that's no biggie. I'll do what I have to do when and if that time comes, but for right now, we're straight."

Drew picked up his teacup and took a long sip. He remained silent but graced me with a warm and sympathetic smile. He was a smart man and played his position well.

Nikki sighed loudly. "I really can't believe that he would do this to you girl. I just feel that you're in an extremely vulnerable place right now and he's in the driver's seat."

I reached across the table and held her hand. My sister's heart was in the right place but her head was calculating the best way to disentangle me from my marriage. She had the attitude that if something was broke, pick it up, throw it in the garbage and get a new one. I, on the other hand, reached for the crazy glue.

"Listen little sister. I hear you. I understand how you feel. But I am not ready to give up on the love of my life simply because he's in the middle of making one of the biggest mistakes of his life. He's not perfect. I'm not perfect. I can forgive him for this if and only if he comes correct. I am willing to let it all go if he's not. But I don't need to make that call right now. That would be rash and foolish.

Nothing's really happened yet except that he's gotten carried away with a feeling and that euphoria is causing him to engage in some foolish behavior. Hell, we've all been there. It's just that usually when we have we've been able to bear the cost and no one's the wiser. Let's not forget that he came clean after he got busted. That doesn't count for much, but it counts for something. One incident does not negate seven years of marriage Nikki."

She nodded her head, yet I knew she remained unconvinced. But she squeezed my hand in unity. She did not have to understand me in order to lend her support. I loved her more because of that.

"Okay, well, you know I'm available day or night if you should need me for any reason."

I smiled and pulled her hand close to my heart as we touched foreheads.

"That, little sister, I've always known."

The Queen Looks On at the King and His Pawn

Weeks passed in much the same way. I rarely heard from Christian. I assumed he was enjoying the freedom I afforded him and was dating the heifer. I was not so naive as to think the man was sitting in his brother's apartment making a list of pros and cons while watching Dr. Phil. I did, however, feel like Bobby Fisher in moments of empowerment, like we were all in the chess game and I was the only one who could see all of the angles and was certain of the outcome.

Yes, I know. Certain of the outcome? Oh contraire. But it's true. I knew that there was a possibility this could all go left and my man might leave me for some random, I really didn't believe that would be the case. Arrogance, you ask? No, not especially. Faith. I prepared for the worst but I genuinely expected the best. I can't explain it but I felt it was a matter of time before C came to his senses and returned home.

The tricky part was how long would that take? And if/when he wanted to come home would I have moved on in my heart, rendering his revelation useless? Who knew? I had to give it to God and try and move forward every day. And every day it was the same battle in my head and heart. They say when you give something to God, you have to remember to let go. It's not your problem to solve anymore. And I want to be able to say that I did. I want to.

A little after a month had gone by and one day UPS delivered two cabinets that I ordered from Overstock. Now Bob Villa I ain't. This was Christian's job always. He read instructions, looked over diagrams and then put shit together. I stayed throughout the process as a wingman lending moral support and handing him tools like a nurse to a doctor.

So when the cabinets arrived, I wasn't sure what the protocol was. Should I try and figure this shit out by myself? I barely cut through the tape without taking out an artery. Once I peeked inside and glanced at the boards and what appeared to be five million tiny nuts and bolts and screws, I instantly gave up. What the hell? I wasn't looking to build the atom bomb people. So I whipped out my phone and texted him all businesslike with a hint of managerial acid.

The cabinets I ordered for the kitchen came in. When will you be available to help me put them together?

After I hit send, I reproached myself just a tad. Was it really necessary to be so cold? Then I further insulted myself. Yeah bitch, that's your husband. Just because his ass decided to abandon his family doesn't mean you guys don't exist. You're still together whether he acknowledges it or not.

His return text startled me out of my own ass kicking.

I can come tomorrow around 2pm.

My eyes narrowed at his lack of warmth. Not even a shred of the man I knew. It kind of broke me at that moment. How is it that I can be so certain of the outcome most of the time but then something like this happens and I feel like there's no hope for reconciliation between us at all?

I took a deep breath and texted him back.

That's fine. I'll see you at 2pm. Please bring your house keys.

My sister had a point. I didn't have to head for the divorce lawyer's office just yet but I didn't have to play the sap either. It was time to take a few matters into my own hands. I snorted. I was getting angry. He wouldn't like me this way.

A Word to the Wise

I didn't see him yesterday (Sunday) as we planned via text. His brother lived in New Jersey and he was depending on him for a ride, which wasn't going to happen. So instead we amended the plan to meet at my job after work on Monday. This way we would both make our way home together in complete awkward fashion.

I was nervous, angry and curious. I took care in my appearance, which was nothing unusual but I wanted to make sure I did not look like I was the least bit frayed from his sudden departure. I hadn't. And when I went downstairs to meet him I was disappointed to realize neither had he. He looked absolutely wonderful, young and fresh. I recognized that look, that glow, and for the first time in seven years, it was not attributed to me. I felt like a jilted, wilted rose by his side. I hoped he wouldn't notice.

"Hi," I chirped a little too bubbly.

He smiled and said a quiet, "Hello," relief washing his face. I guess he hadn't known what to expect. I suppose now that he realized this wasn't going to turn into a Rihanna and Chris episode, he relaxed his pose.

I couldn't help it. I felt nothing but longing for him. I linked my arm in his as we strolled down Lexington together (if New Yorkers could do such a thing) as if nothing had changed. But I couldn't fool myself.

Everything felt different. His arm in mine felt stiff and cold. Our exchange of pleasantries was a load of bullshit. I didn't really want to ask how he was doing. I wanted to slap the shit out of him and ask how could he do this to me? And yet I remained rational.

It got worse when we were on the train. I can't remember a time when Christian and I were ever together that we weren't physically linked in some way. We were an affectionate couple, the absolute envy of everyone we knew. We were naturally inclined toward each other. Today it couldn't be further from the truth. We were both figuratively and literally distant.

I now knew what people meant when they said "it was as if there had been a wall between us." We both looked lost and awkward in the close proximity of the train. We barely looked at each other, communication had deserted us both.

I studied him for a few seconds when he wasn't watching. He appeared to be a beautiful stranger. And I couldn't help but note, he seemed happy. I could hardly bear it. I understood that I was an obligation now. He preferred to be elsewhere with someone else. I could feel my spirit dying inside. It surprised me that I was still standing, appearing so normal in the wake of these revelations.

We walked into the house and I immediately hit the kettle. I passed the bar and eyed the Patron for a second longer than usual. I never drank alone but frankly new traditions seem to happening all over the place without my say so. Why didn't seem as strange as why not these days. He took off his coat and hung it on the hook like a guest. The entire scene felt surreal.

"Would you like some tea?" I asked from the bedroom, hanging up my coat in our closet.

"No, I'm good."
His voice was distant. He'd already crossed into the living room. He wasted no time on me and was getting down to business in a hurry. He hadn't even said "no thank you."

He didn't seem like the man I married at all. He only looked like him. I took a moment to sit on the bed and gather my thoughts. Whatever I thought or was hoping to hear out of him clearly wasn't going to happen. What was happening was that he would do his duty for now and run out of here as fast as possible. I had to accept that. I had to consider what I wanted out of this meeting. I said a prayer and then joined him in the living room. I would forego the coffee myself. I would most likely be up all night without it.

He was ankle deep in boards and metal parts and diagrams. I took up a new position on the couch and made a study of him. If he noticed that I wasn't lifting a finger, he hadn't mentioned it. In fact, he hadn't mentioned anything.

"Christian?"

"Yeah?"

"It's been a month. What's really going on?"

"What do you mean?"

I gritted my teeth. If we were going to play this game, I would end up on the eleven o'clock news for murder.

"Please don't put me through any more bullshit. What's going on with you? What are your plans?"

"I'm not trying to do that to you babe." He sighed heavily, peering at the diagram. "I just don't know what I'm going to do yet."
"And what does that mean? You don't know if you're going to stay married to me?" Anger coated my words.

"I'm just not sure that I want to be married anymore," he stated matter-of-fact like, picking up another part from the pile.

I kid you not, I almost freakin' lost it at this point, and if there had been a weapon in the house, I might have punched his ticket. I was that pissed at his gall. But JC got a hold of me and would not let go. He soothed me and sense spewed forth from my mouth, surprising us both.

"Let me tell you something Christian, and I hope you're listening. I love you, even now with all of this bullshit that you are putting me through. And you know why? I'll tell you. Because I know you have no clue what you're doing.

You're letting a little ego stroking lead you down a path that will ruin your life. You can't see it, but I can. I wish I could give you a vision of your future without me. This sounds like arrogance but it's not. It's wisdom. We were made for each other and you're on the verge of fucking that all up because someone else made you feel good about yourself even though it's all based on a lie.

You want an escape from reality, and when the clouds clear you're going to realize what you've done and you're going to be miserable. I'm going to wait a little bit more for this foolishness to be over and for you to come correct."

He swallowed hard but remained silent.

"Don't get too comfortable. I said I'd wait a little while longer. But know this. Once I move on and I turn from you, it's permanent. There's nothing you can do to rectify the harm you've caused and get your family back. You better seriously consider that."

"I understand." He looked at me but I knew he still couldn't see.

I got off the couch and walked over to him, cupping his face, forcing him to meet my eyes.

"No you don't but you will," I said softly.

I kissed him tenderly on the cheek and walked to the bedroom.

"Holler if you need my help. I'm going in the room. And before you leave, please leave the house keys on the kitchen table."

If he was hurt, he kept it to himself. A few hours later I he poked his head into the room.

"It's all put together."

I pried my eyes from the television and focused on his face. I had no idea how long it would be before I saw him again. How strange that was.

"Okay. Thanks. I hope you take what I said seriously Christian."

"I will," he said before kissing me on the cheek hurriedly and quitting our apartment.

The tears came sliding down my face without my permission. I felt my heart breaking.

"JC, I hope you know what you're doing, because I do not. I do not." I should have gotten my pillow out from behind and dropped it to the floor. I should have gotten on my knees and prayed for strength, for clarity, for faith. But I was overcome with melancholy. I could do nothing but sit and let the tears wash my face.

From the Ashes

A chill swept through my body as I walked the city streets, my earbuds ensuring my fortress of solitude as I weaved through the crowd. I would take the long way to the train, walk to Thirty-Fourth Street and double back to Fifty-Seventh and Lex. It would give me time to think, formulate a strategy that would gain me some control. Weeks passed and I still heard nothing from my husband. He'd become entrenched in his new life no doubt and forgotten us completely.

It was an old, familiar feeling, only this time it descended upon me without the bitter aftertaste. My ex had flaunted his side pieces for far too long in my presence. Christian and I never reached that stage. Yes, even in the midst of this there are things for which I am grateful.

Speaking of, Thanksgiving was less than a week away. I always cooked up a storm and invited everyone over for food, wine and games. Afterward, on Sunday, we would have a relaxing day of leftovers and putting up the Christmas lights and tree. This was my favorite time of year. Aside from Nikki, I hadn't explained anything to anyone. I went into hibernation and left Nikki to brief the teacups.

All of my girls texted me with thoughts of encouragement and let me know they were there for me if I should need them. I was comforted though I did not reach out. JC and Nikki were holding me down. Gaia had her own thoughts I'm sure, but she was her mother's daughter. Odd how there was nothing unnatural about it just being the two of us again. She gave me frequent hugs, ran her elegant fingers through my hair in comfort and made me tea whenever she felt it was necessary. It was as if she was on a mission to keep the chill from penetrating my heart.

Truth be told, my unnaturally calm demeanor probably freaked her out. Her warm cups of tea always made me smile. It was such a kind and touching act from my little mama. And so she vowed to make me smile as often as she could, therefore making me tea every chance she got. If I didn't want to drown in Lipton, I simply had to find another reason to skin my teeth.

There were quite a few good-looking suits on foot, mostly of the Caucasian persuasion. I chuckled to myself. Don't get me wrong, I appreciated men of every color and creed but being comfortable enough to be intimate was a bit of a struggle. I just didn't think we had very much in common.

Whatever would we chat about? Politics and religion bored me. Nikki was more of the civic-minded and dutiful citizen. The only sports I was ever interested in were the ones my hubby watched, the X-Games. I didn't know a single adult who was down with that.

Was I going to have to pull out my cougar claws and date the teens? I rolled my eyes and shook my head. Laza Morgan's "One by One" filtered past my ears and straight down to my intimates. Dealing with myself was fast losing its appeal. This is precisely why my mind took a left from strategy and plummeted into the gutter. Yes, dammit, I needed some sex. But what were my options? A random stranger?

I simply could not see how I could pull that off. Of course, I was only contemplating a basic instinct, but for Pete's sake, who was I, Sharon Stone? I can't lie and say the theory itself didn't hold great appeal. To be able to hit it and quit it with someone I knew not and would probably never see again sounded like the perfect option to me. But the problem is that although I find just about everyone attractive, I don't personally find almost anyone sexually appealing.

And before you start shaking your head and giving me that "bitch please" stare, hear me out. When I dig a guy, which is not as often as one might think, I want to be around him. I want to get to know him a little. During this process, shit can go one of two ways. Either the initial appeal intensifies or they say or do something that flat lines. While I have the instant attraction, the panty dropper for me is a slow burn process. But once I'm there, oh baby, you better tighten up your sneakers and hang on!

Out of all the fellas I knew, there were only two guys that fit the bill, Marcas and Ray. Marcas was my boy though. One of my best friends, and I hadn't even texted him throughout this bullshit because I knew if I saw him, I'd be too vulnerable and we'd probably end up doing something that one or both of us would regret. I mean sure I'd probably end up getting it good, he looked like a man who knew how to work me over but in the process we'd probably screw up an awesome friendship. It wasn't worth the risk. I valued him too much. So I put him on ice.

Ray, Ray, Ray. He gave me the most delicious nasty thoughts from day one. But I never saw him but for random moments. How would I even approach that? Hey, your appeal to me is like one in a million, you think we could chill for a bit, and if we still feel each other can we hit it and quit it? I wouldn't want to quit it. If he was as good in the flesh as he was in my daydreams, that could be dangerous.

He was not a stranger. I would see him from time to time. And therein lay the catch-22! I would want to spend time and sleep with a dude that I really dig, and I can't really do any of that in my current situation. So guess I'm back to literally screwin' myself until I come up with another option! Awesome!

So back to, oh yeah, my life strategy in the midst of my tragic pre-divorce, hoping it will work out stage. I did actually have quite a bit to consider after my conversation with Nikki last night. She, of course, was more than ever of the mindset that C had completely gone off the reservation and that I needed to take action and disentangle myself from my husband of seven years, because as far as she was concerned, he'd already dropped me like a hot potato. I just hadn't read the memo.

Given the circumstances, I could hardly raise a rebuttal. So pray tell little sister, what would you suggest? I should have known she'd be prepared with the solution. It was ingrained in her genetic makeup. She would let me borrow $5000 to pay off all of our credit cards, both his and mine, and that way we would have no ties, at least of the financial nature.

He could not hinder me or screw me later with our joint accounts. After paying them all off, I could close them and we could move forward separately. She couldn't understand why I would pay his credit card that was in his name only but I insisted.

The man had no job. I was clearly financially better off at this point. I had no intention of giving him any money. That would be insane and, after all, he did have his unemployment. But I could give him a clean break. We would both have to cut our losses and move on. We did not have stocks and bonds or property. We be regular folk. She raised a brow instead of an argument and let it go at that.

I was grateful. I didn't have enough fight in me to take her on, especially in the face of her extreme generosity. I was not uncomfortable with borrowing the money. I had a good job and could manage my bills with a surplus. I was confident I could pay her back in no time. She was not eager for repayment. The plan was a win-win.

By the time I got to the train I felt lighter. I felt more in control. I felt stronger. I had made a decision and had taken a step to move ahead on my own. By no means had I given up hope that Christian would still come to his senses and we would find a way to work things out. But I had to respect myself. I had to show myself, Gaia and C that everything was not in his hands. There were moves I could make to secure Gaia and me. It wouldn't hurt that C would realize that I wanted him but didn't need him.

He was far too comfortable in the cryogenic stasis our marriage had become. I don't think he meant to be cruel, but he was just the same. My man that I loved had burned me. But little did he know, I was a Phoenix. He better ask somebody.

Eye of the Tiger

Facebook, the bane of my existence, was fast moving in the direction of becoming my salvation. Now that C found his muse on Facebook, it would seem that he was anywhere but.

He was far too busy living life than posting about it. I, on the other hand, had no life beyond work and home to speak of. Facebook became my window to the outside world of men. I was trying to get more comfortable in the virtual world. I was craving testosterone in an ungodly manner.

I found myself being way too flirtatious in every avenue of my life with the exception of my West Indian crew. I was avoiding them like the plague. Work got the brunt of my new attitude. Like I said, I was always flirtatious, it is my nature, but now I was just a tad extra, and it was obvious. The men loved it. The women in my work circle thought I was losing my marbles judging by the looks I was receiving.

Of course, what were they going to say? These were white women at work. We weren't chummy enough for them to question me.

Kris was different. I gave her the short version and she was as supportive as one could hope. I decided to take Kris up on her offer and accompany her to a bar called Bogart's on Park Avenue and Fortieth Street. It's been so long since I hung out at a bar with a coworker that I wasn't sure if I'd know what to do with myself but I desperately needed a break from the monotony. And I needed to hush the voices in my head that were spiraling out of control since Thanksgiving was two days away and Christian still hadn't called.

I already felt a kinship with the name of the joint. I mean, come on, Bogart's? Bogie is my favorite actor of all time. He's the perfect man. He's a good guy trapped in a bad man's body. What's not to like?

Kris looked smashing as ever. I adore my coworker but it's a good thing I'm a secure mama jamma 'cause this young thang is a size 2, with a lovely rack, long blonde hair and a dazzling smile. Kris is one of the smartest girls I've ever come across. She's the only person I've ever met who uses the appropriate word to describe anything. Her expansive vocabulary must be the envy of writers 'round the world.

The thing is, for Kris it's natural. I have to pull up a virtual thesaurus in my head and run a synonym search or I'll be using the word "nice" for every positive occasion. What could be duller? I digress.

Kris was wearing a red wrap dress that clung to her body like second skin. I was wearing leggings and a sweater dress that unfortunately clung to my body as well. I should clarify. I appreciate my thick and in my West Indian circle, my figure is celebrated. But when you run in the Manhattan scene, you can be painfully aware that thin is in and thick don't get you dick.

So Kris and I, not exactly the same picture mind you. In many ways we were quite the opposite if one were to compare. She was ten years my junior. She was blonde, I had jet black hair, she was thin, I was thick, she was proper, I was more of a down girl. She was more like "Catherine, come on," followed up by an effervescent laugh. I was more like "bitch please," followed by a burst of giggles. And despite all differences, we had genuine love for each other and got on swimmingly.

226

As Bogart's was coming into view, I spied a few smokers in front of the joint. They were of the thirty-something Mad Men suits type with two "Peggy's" in tow. One very nice- looking green-eyed fella did give me the eye as Kris and I passed. The gesture rather gave me some hope and put a pep in my step. Mayhaps things have changed and I've been out of the game too long to have noticed. We walked through the heavy glass double doors and were gladdened to find the joint was warm and filled with couples and singles throughout. Sean Paul's "Gimme the Light" was playing in the background and a DJ with some Dre Beats headphones was bumpin' while hanging in a cage from the back wall. I was pleasantly surprised.

Kris was a take charge gal, and I was only too happy to follow. The joint was set up with small tables and club chairs lining the outside square with the circular bar in the center. Kris picked an empty spot by the far back of the bar, right below the DJ. I dug it. We had the vantage point of everyone in the joint, plus we could see who was coming and going.

We shrugged out of our coats, placed them on the stool backs and made ourselves at home. There were two male and two female bartenders tending to guests. All of the male staff were dressed in black slacks, white shirts and black vests. The female staff, bartenders and servers were dressed in little black dresses. Everyone smiled, and I found it rather infectious. One of the female bartenders, a gorgeous redhead with a sexy Russian accent, asked us what was our pleasure.

I smiled wide, giggled and boldly declared, "Your number!"

She smiled wider and said "Aw, aren't you sweet?"

Kris threw me a shocked expression which only made me laugh more.

"I'm just kidding, but seriously honey, you are gorgeous!" I smiled back, reaching for my purse.

She smiled and winked. "I'm Katiana. Anything you need, call me. I'm all over the place, so wave and that will get my attention. What will you have dahrling?"

I passed her my I.D. and credit card.

"I'll start with a Malibu and grenadine. Kris, what's your poison girl?"

Katiana took my cards.

"You want to run a tab?"

"Yes please."

"Do you have any red wine?" Kris asked.

"Yes of course." Katiana gestured toward the top shelves behind her.

"Oh, I don't recognize any of them. What would you recommend?"

"Don't worry. I'll take care of you. If you don't like, it's not a problem. It will be on the house and you can choose another okay?"

"Sounds good." Kris nodded.

About two minutes later, Katiana brought us our drinks and waited for Kris to take her first sip.

"It's okay for you?" she asked.

Did this girl realize how sexy her accent was? I'm pretty sure I could listen to her all day. Hey, before you lose your mind, shut it down. I'm not a lesbo. I've got nothing against them, but I can't see the appeal. I want to be the only soft body in the equation, know what I'm sayin'?

Kris took a dainty sip and nodded her head. "Mmm. It's delicious. Thank you."

Katiana nodded, graced us with a smile that showed off her pearly whites and then was off like a shot to the other side of the bar.

Kris and I started to take in the sights. I gave the populace a once-over. There were a few eyes that attempted to hold mine. I wasn't interested, but I was happy that there were a few contenders who made me feel like I was at least in the race and not cheering from the sidelines. Finally my eyes settled on Kris, who started talking while just over her head I caught the eye of this fabulous Jake Gyllenhaal doppelganger. My mouth inadvertently watered. Damn. I was hungry. No, that's not what the kids say these days, they would say I was thirsty. Well, whatever the hell the kids would say these days, home-girl needed some man company big time. I took a sip of my drink and tried to refocus my energy on Kris.

"Did you hear what John was saying? I think he's pissed that we have four days off for Thanksgiving and then another four days off for Christmas."

"Really? What difference does that make? He won't be in the office the entire week, I'm sure."

While Kris prattled on, I snuck another peak in Jake's direction. Damn. He was checkin' me. There was no mistaking the fact that he was looking right at me. He did a small sideways grin and saluted me with his beer mug. I broke out into a ridiculous childlike smile which I hoped was as sexy as he made me feel.

Kris immediately stopped mid-sentence and turned around. There it was. The test. If he was only using me to get Kris's attention, it would become obvious now. What happened next only served to puzzle me. Once he got a look at Kris, he stopped smiling and returned his attention to his group of friends.

How should I interpret that? Did he wish to make it obvious he didn't give a hoot about Kris, or was he intimidated by Kris so he was too nervous to look at her? Oh for Pete's sake, was I really analyzing a nice gesture from a handsome man to this degree? I have been out of the game way too long. I sipped my drink and pretended I was above it all.

Kris returned her attention to me and smiled. "Well, well, he's very good looking."

I smirked. "Girl, that's an understatement."

I sipped my drink and made a quick inspection of him. He was dressed casually, blue jeans, white button down long-sleeve shirt with a sweater vest. He had an unpretentious air about him. He looked like a guy who rocked a cowboy hat and rode a horse on Sundays. Then again, maybe I've seen Brokeback Mountain way too much.

A handsome blonde was passing by and paused in between Kris and me.

"I don't mean to interrupt two beautiful ladies, and I realize this is going to sound like a corny line, but I think I know you." He smiled shyly, pointing to Kris.
I grabbed my phone and cigarettes out of my bag and hopped off the stool.

I tapped handsome on the shoulder and pointed to my empty stool. "Listen, why you don't have a seat ah—"

"Jason." My but he was quick on the take.

"Jason." I smiled. "Yeah, I need to make a phone call and have a cigarette. You guys have a mystery to solve in the meantime?"

"Are you sure you don't mind?" Jason asked politely.

I glanced in Kris's direction. We kind of left her out of the entire affair but she seemed intrigued.

"No." I shook my head. "Not in the least. I'll be back in a few minutes."

I headed out of the double doors, pulled my jacket on and lit up. I whipped out my phone and checked my Facebook and texts. There were a few new friend requests from guys I didn't know. Unfortunately none of them were my style. I texted Gaia that I would be home late. After my check-in, she texted me back that she was home, watching TV and yes, she ate yesterday's leftovers. Damn, I was already that predictable.

"Hey."

I looked to my left, and lo and behold Jake was beside me. Whoa! The closer he got, the cuter he appeared. How many drinks have I had? No, no this was accurate.

"Hey." I smiled back.
"I saluted you with my hearty ale earlier."

I smiled. "Yeah, I caught that. Very smooth." I smiled wider.

He laughed and shyly studied the ground for a second, tucking his hands in his jeans.

He seemed to have made up his mind about something and suddenly turned to me with his hand out.

"Sorry, my name is Eric. A-And you are?"

I dropped my cig into the ashtray outside and shook his hand. It was warm and firm.

"Catherine." My face was starting to hurt from smiling. It had been a while.

"You work around here?" He gestured into the air.

"Yeah. My coworker Kris and I just decided to give this joint a whirl on a whim."

"Lucky me." He smiled and his eyes found their way back to the ground and his hands back to his pockets.

Could this be construed as flirting, Jake, I mean Eric? Mmm, do tell. I probably should have said something encouraging at this point, but this moment of power over this handsome stranger was intoxicating. So I stayed silent and drunk him in with my eyes. And he continued. Can you imagine?

He rocked his heels casually. "I live just a few blocks from here but this is the first time I've ever been inside. It was one of those nights when you don't really feel like going out, but you know you don't want to stay in. I guess this was something of a compromise."

"It would seem it worked out for us both, Eric." I smiled while doing some Italian thing with my hands.

"Oh damn. I hadn't noticed that before." He pointed to my left hand.

I stared at my wedding ring and arched my brow, contemplating my situation.

"Well Eric, as strange as it would seem, I'm actually separated at present." I drew a deep breath.

"Would I sound like too much of an asshole if I said I wasn't disappointed?"

He smiled, and I couldn't help but smile back. He asked me for my phone and I found myself gladly handing it over. He punched in his name and number and handed it back to me.

"No pressure, but if it's all right with you I'd like to see you again. Call me up anytime."

His friends came out just then and handed him his jacket. You could tell they had a few in them. They were a bit too loud, pulling him good-naturedly down the street. He turned back to me and put his fingers to his ear mouthing the words "call me" before allowing them to shuffle him away.

I shook my head and smiled. As I made my way back to my seat, I found Kris alone. I heard a tune I recognized and glanced skyward toward the DJ cage. He winked and pointed as if to say, this one's for you. Kris started happily chatting with me about her mystery man, and my mind wandered to the song lyrics. I don't know if I had the eye of the tiger but I do know that I was a survivor. For the first time in weeks, the future didn't feel quite so daunting.

Mr. Telephone Man

Thanksgiving came and went without a word from my husband of seven years. I was astonished and expectant simultaneously. I sat at our dining room table hoping that he would call and at least say something kind, but he seemed done with me, done with us, Gaia and me, his family. The snake shed us like old skin! I was livid, and in that moment he was no longer the man I married. He was someone else, with someone else and I had to have my cry and let him go.

It had been two months. Things were not getting any better. I know God had a plan but I wasn't sure what it was anymore. I was gaining confidence in myself and losing it in our marriage. I wasn't ready to sign divorce papers just yet but I was no longer content with being stuck in limbo and waiting for him to make a move toward me when it seemed all but obvious he had already taken ten steps away from any hope of us.

I called him. I feel you judging me. Yeah, I called, but save it. The call went straight to voice mail. Good golly gee allow me to digest this for a moment if I may. My call on Thanksgiving to my own husband of seven years went to voice mail.

If my cuzzo Charmy was next to me, she would have let out a resounding Wooooooooooooooooooooooow. Scenes of him, this trick and her family sitting around a dinner table laden with turkey and shit filled my head and clawed at my heart. Could you really replace an entire family just like that? Did he prefer them to us? Shouldn't sitting down with another woman and her family feel downright alien to him?

I should wait until I collect myself and call him again tomorrow or even the day after. I should get this show on the road and lay out my brilliant extraction plan. Let him have it right between the eyes. That is what I was telling myself when I heard Gaia come out of her room. She plopped down into the adjacent chair and looked at me with more than a little pity.

"Mom, what's wrong?"

I wanted to be strong. I wanted to deny it all confidently and then busy myself with a task so she would let it go. But I wanted something else too. I wanted some small measure of my suffering to touch and infect him. I was tired and petulant and sad and angry. I didn't want to hide it.

"It's Thanksgiving and he didn't even call. I thought he'd at least call. I called him, but I got his voice mail." The tears slid down my face quite of their own accord, and I felt ashamed that I had allowed Gaia to witness my weakness. I was supposed to be stronger, keep control.

"I'm going to call him. I have a few things I want to say to him." She was a bit hesitant with her words. She looked to me for permission or censure. I considered this for a moment. Was it right for me to stop her?

Our family consisted of the three of us. He not only abandoned me, but her as well. Didn't she have a right to let him know how she felt? Yes, of course she did, but wasn't I absolutely horrid for hoping that her words ate away at him like the acid I withheld all of this time? Yes. But sometimes you do the right thing for the wrong reason don't you? And so I did.

"Gaia, if you want to speak to him you have every right to do so."

That daughter of mine didn't waste any time. She grabbed her phone, hit a few buttons and leaned back against the chair with her arms folded across her chest. She was in a "take no prisoners" kind of mood. Unlike my call, he did not ignore hers.

"Why didn't you call us? Where are you?"

I'm certain by now he wished he had. His response didn't thrill her.

"What does it matter? You didn't think to call us? Call Mom on Thanksgiving? Really Christian! Really!"

She listened intently and leaned forward using her free hand to point to the phone accusingly. I started to feel a little sorry for him.

"Yeah but it's like you forgot us. Like you even forgot you had a family. What are we supposed to do? How are we supposed to feel? Did you ever stop to think about that?"

I swallowed hard. I realized that this wasn't just my second time around, but Gaia's also. She hadn't said any of this to her father, but she was unleashing it all onto Christian. I wasn't sure if I was doing right by her anymore. My motives were not 100 percent pure, but now I think I might be causing Gaia pain. I couldn't have that. Maybe it was time to shut this down.

I motioned for her to give me the phone.

She put her hand up to stop me.

"No Mom. It's time he knew what was going on here while he's out there living his life as if we don't exist. I'm tired of this bullshit."

I blinked back the tears. Damn. She was my daughter, and she was angry, maybe even more so than me. She was on a roll and she was going to get her feelings across come hell or high water.

Christian wasn't saying much. He had a hard time expressing himself in a benign situation, this would keep him to a maximum three-word reply.

"Listen. I don't know what you're doing, trying to find yourself and whatnot. You ain't lost. You right there, just look in a mirror."

I damn near burst out laughing. Gaia had too much of Nikki's witticism about her.

"And Mom doesn't tell me much about what's going on with you two, and that's probably none of my business anyway but I do know that for you to just leave and never call, never talk to us, never even call me to find out what I'm doing is just bat-shit crazy. Don't you care what happens to us anymore?"

She stopped and listened to his answer. Her brows knitted together and then her entire hairline slid back. It was like watching her father in action. Weird.

"Does it matter? You should have at least called Mom for Thanksgiving. It's THANKSGIVING!"

She listened.

"Well you should be. I got to go. I just wanted to tell you that. Here, talk to Mom." She thrust the phone at me angrily. The moment I took it she stormed off into her room.

"Hey," I answered sourly.

"I'm sorry I didn't call. I didn't know what to say but she's right. I should have called anyway. Tell Gaia I'm really sorry."

My heart sunk.

"You're sorry. You want me to tell Gaia you're sorry. That's great. What should I tell myself?"

"What do you want me to say Catherine? I don't know what to say to you anymore, that's why I don't call. I thought it would make everything worse."

"I don't think it can get any worse Christian."

Silence.

"How could you forget about us so easily C? It took us seven years to build our life and you forgot us in two months? How is that possible?"

"I didn't forget about you or Gaia."

"You could at least call me and tell me what's going on with you? Have you made any decisions about you, this girl, us?"

"No. I'm still trying to figure this out." He sighed.

"Well I'm about at the end of my rope with this whole business Christian, and I've made a few decisions. When can you come over? I want to talk to you."

"Tomorrow. What time do you want to see me?"

"Two. Come at two."

"Okay."

"All right. Bye."

"Bye."

He was cold. He was heartless whether he meant to be or not. It was time I said no more. I made two cups of tea and headed to Gaia's room. It was also time to fill her in. He might have abandoned us, but I had only made it worse by keeping her in the dark. Illumination was at hand.

The Quick and the Dead

"Say what now? Who died?"

My cousin Charmy sighed loudly and reiterated, "My dad. I'll text you the wake info. It's tonight. You gonna' come right Cat?"

"Oh my gosh I'm so sorry girl. Of course I'm gonna' come. Text me the stuff, I'll send it to Nikki and the rest of the teacups. Who can come will come, but of course you know Nikki and I will see you there. You want me to tell my mom too?"

"Yeah Cat, that would be nice."

"All right, hang in there baba. I'll see you in a few. Text me if you need me to do anything or bring anything okay?"

"Okay, Cat, thanks."

"Don't mention it."

I hung up the phone and noted the time. It was almost 10:30 a.m. Wakes typically start around 7:00 p.m. I could see C at two and give him the dealEO before going to the wake. I mean, honestly, how long could it take? He wasn't one for standing around and making small talk. I'm sure after I give him the lowdown, neither one of us will have much if anything to say. Probably best to get it over with. I texted him a confirmation and then texted Nikki with the news and called my mom. While I was on the phone relaying the details, C reconfirmed our 2:00 p.m. meeting. Swell.

I thought about my cousin Charmy. I did not have the corner market on grief after all. You might be wondering why she was so calm in the face of her father's death. But hers is a strange tale of woe. Her father had been out of her life for decades. He walked out on Charmy and her mother and two sisters and four brothers many years ago. He left them for another woman with children of her own. It's strange how some men are perfectly apt at taking on the responsibility of other people's children while abandoning their own. About two years ago, he became ill and just showed up on Charmy's doorstep.

She took him in and cared for him. They had a strained relationship. He tried to make up for it a little by caring for Charmy's son Kris, his own grandson. But he was an irritable man, and frankly I thought he was more trouble than he was worth. But that's Charmy for you, a heart of gold. She couldn't say no to anyone who was down and out. I shook my head at the absurdity of us all and got to work.

I cleaned the house and cooked some chicken curry and rice. I hope his mouth watered up a storm when he walked in. By 1:00 p.m. I took a shower and tried to look fresh-faced and unaffected.

I was sitting on the dining room chair in the kitchen when I heard his keys in the door. I wondered if he would use them. Last time he was home I told him to leave the keys on the kitchen table. What he left instead were some leftover metal parts to the cabinet he put together. I was livid when I made the discovery. At this point, it mattered little because after today it would no longer be an issue.

"Hi." He half smiled and brushed my cheek with an awkward kiss before putting his jacket on the chair back and seating himself.

He was a degree or two warmer, but still all business. I decided to adopt a similar attitude.

"Would you like some food? I cooked some chicken curry." I intend to get down to it so keep your panties on, but I was still me, right. Wasn't I was hospitable to all who came through my door? It's what I told myself anyway. "No thanks. I just had lunch with my bro." He half smiled and fidgeted in his seat.

I nodded, folded my arms across my chest and pierced him with a frank eyeball.

"So since yesterday have you made any decisions about your life and where it's heading?"

"No, but I'm workin' on it."

Did I detect smugness to his voice?

I narrowed my eyes and continued. "Well I've been patiently waiting for you to tell me what exactly you're wrestling with? Are you in love with me, with her? Are you sleeping with her? Do you still want to be married?"

"I'm confused about everything right now Catherine. I don't know how I feel about her or you."

"Christian, honestly, do you know how stupid you sound?"

He didn't respond as I knew he wouldn't. I continued on. My hands took on a ghetto violent life of their own. I landed a great deal of backhands into the air behind me and conducted an entire symphony before me.

"Haven't you realized yet that you were in a slump and your lazy ass did nothing to get yourself out of it? None of this has anything to do with me, Gaia or our marriage. You started talking to some chick who knew you from way back when and knows nothing about the man that you are today. She can afford to make you feel good about yourself because she don't know shit about you. She ain't been through shit with you. You're essentially strangers to each other. You are simply infatuated with the newness of this thing, can't you see that? I really can't believe that someone this trivial could have you questioning your marriage. Dude, this is some real As the World Turns bullshit!"

I folded my arms across my chest. Both my hands and voice retreated, awaiting rebuttal.

He sighed and shifted some more but remained willfully silent like a child waiting for the lecture to be over.

"Seriously, a more mature man would have seen this for what it is and just banged this bitch and kept it moving!"

"That's what you want me to do?" he said angrily.

Well bless my soul, he can speak!

"No. Of course not. But honestly that might be easier to handle than this. I can forgive a mistake but by the time you figure out that you're making one, it might be too late for us. Did you sleep with her?"

He looked to the ground. "Yes."

I swallowed hard. "For how long?"

"We've only been together once and that was last week."

"You guys weren't together before that?"

"No. I told you, we were just friends, just talking to each other."

"So you slept with her after I told you to leave?"

"Yes." He hesitated and then continued. "It's difficult for me to be with her because I'm so use to being with you."

My man had no guile. A more experienced man wouldn't talk about such problems with candor, but he could precisely because he was so inexperienced. Christian was as simple and as painful as the truth. This both irked and gladdened me. I sat up straight and tried to remember what the purpose of this visit had been. I couldn't let this information sidetrack me because, although it gave me insight, it still hadn't made him come around. Chalk it up to useful yet pointless.

"Well I can't wait forever for you to figure things out. I made some decisions, and that's why I asked you to come."

"Okay," he said firmly.

"First of all, I'd like you to give me your house keys."

"Why?"

"Why? Did you really just ask me that?" I spat vehemently.

"Yes, why do you want my house keys?"

His calm nondescript John Malkovich monotone voice irked me to no avail.

"Because frankly there's no reason why you should have access to my apartment. You made a choice to leave."

"I didn't choose to leave. You asked me to."

Why this brazen little fuck. All sense of propriety has left the building.

"I demanded that you leave after you asserted that you weren't sure you still wanted to be married to me and had already started talking to some heifer you knew in high school, or have you forgotten?"

"We were only talking then Catherine."

"Who cares Christian? Did you forget that I caught you in a lie and that's how this whole thing started?"

He shrunk back down into his seat.

"You were already seeing her. It was only a matter of time before you two started sleeping together. Don't you know that? I told you from the start that I'd already been through this bullshit. I was not going to watch your romance unfold with the texts and the outings and the FB messaging right before my eyes. Are you retarded?"

"All right here are the keys. What else?" he said flatly, taking the keys from his pocket and tossing them onto the table.

I gave him a look of pure venom. "Was that freakin' necessary?"

"Sorry. What else did you decide?" He mumbled sullenly.

Wow, I guess now that everything's not in his hands and he's facing some consequences, it's making him a little uncomfortable. Oh well, tough shit. I felt, dare I say, good. It was nice to have some power over this situation at last. I ran with it.

"I'm going to pay all of the credit cards. I'm borrowing the money from Nikki, and I'm paying the two cards in your name as well as the ones in our names. The ones in our names I'm cancelling so don't use them anymore. The two that are in your name alone you can do what you want with those, but I won't be paying for them anymore. That will be your responsibility. So you better be careful because your unemployment only covers but so much." I managed the last line without too much vinegar.

"Okay, thanks."

At this point I wanted to say, forget it. Fuck you and struggle to pay for this shit yourself. But I couldn't. Although he was not bowled over by my generosity (and he damn sure should have been), it wasn't because of this particular situation. It was not in Christian's nature to be so. I had spoiled him during our entire marriage, let him get away with murder, and bought him everything like he was my kid and not my man. I had been ridiculous, and now there was a reckoning. I had to own my own bullshit.

"I'm doing this next week so don't spend one penny on the cards until then. I'm not going to be paying for your bullshit beyond today. Date the heifer on your own dime from here on out." My foolishness and mayhem could only go so far.

"All right."

I knew what he was probably thinking. He was probably thinking that he really was free of me. That I had cut every string between us and he could genuinely do as he pleased from here on out. I knew what he was thinking because only a foolish man would have such narrow vision, and currently he was the reigning champ.

"Well that's it. That's all I had to say. You have anything that you want to tell me?"

"Nope."

"Okay. Well, see ya."

He got up, put his jacket on, kissed my cheek and left as quickly as a jackrabbit.

I sighed, got up and hit the kettle. Fool. He hadn't seen that I had freed myself from him as well. Another hard-working, good-lookin', good cookin, West Indian sexy siren back on the market. Bloody fool. I could almost hear JC whisper in my ear, took you long enough.

It's Complicated

I "met" him on Facebook. I wanted to call that guy I met at Bogart's a million times but I wasn't entirely comfortable with that scenario just yet. Facebook seemed less risqué, anonymous. I just needed to get back that pep in my step. I wanted to feel wanted. I needed a guy to make me feel sexy and alive again.

It had been too long and I was starting to lose it. I smiled too hard at anyone with balls, stared two seconds too long, and worse was the air of desperation that surrounded me like stale cigarettes. I needed to get back my mojo. Where is Taye Diggs??? Stella needs to get her groove back!

Anyhoo, as per usual, I digress. So I met this dude on Facebook. He seemed harmless. He lived in Canada. I was in New York, safe distance away. He was attractive enough, but not my style. He didn't give me the shivers but he did have fingers and could type fast. My requirements were at an all-time low.

At first our chats were quite innocent. I had my Facebook up on my screen during work hours, and when we had downtime we were able to chat. Coincidentally, his name was Veran. Good grief! You'd have thought the name alone would convey some inkling of dissatisfaction. It had not. Not long into the game he started asking me questions of a more personal nature.

Normally I spurned such attentions. This time I welcomed them and found myself being quite candid about my situation. Who could have guessed that this would turn him on? His attention toward me intensified. We began texting each other consistently in the days ahead. After a while he asked if I would grant him permission to call me. I

249

hesitated before granting his request. I wasn't sure what I wanted, but I figured this must be the next logical step, right? Who wanted to text forever? I asked him to call me around ten when I had already closed the kitchen, kissed the kid good night and the rest of the evening belonged to me. He agreed.

I took a quick shower, got into my shorts and tank and hopped into bed with five minutes to spare. My phone buzzed at exactly 10:00 p.m.

I dropped my voice an octave in what I hoped sounded at least interesting, if not appealing.

"Hey Veran," I answered. He was prompt.

"Hi Catherine. It's nice to hear your voice after communicating with you for so long in text and chat."

My first impression of his voice was that it sounded a bit bland. I was neither impressed nor disappointed, which in and of itself was disappointing. I hadn't realized I was hoping it would have some appeal. I must dissect and analyze later.

Secondly, I thought to myself we've only been chatting for a week, what do you mean by so long? I silently chided myself. Really bitch? How many boxes have to be ticked in order to converse? I hushed my inner Sasha Fierce and played along.

"Nice to hear your voice too. So what are you up to tonight?"

"Catherine?"

"Yes."

"Where are your hands?"

"What? Why?" Okay, now this was getting weird. I started looking at my free hand like it was going to do something independent of my command.

"Pull down your panties and touch yourself for me? Don't you want me to make you feel good?"

What the fuck?

"Umm, what?"

His tone became even more assertive.

"Pull down your panties for me babe. Touch yourself. Are you wet? Did I make you wet?"

Was this fool for real? I couldn't contain my laughter any longer.

"What? You're not turned on?" He asked, adopting a more appropriate and humble tone.

"Dude, no. I just started talking to you and you're gonna' come at me like that?"

"I know, I know. But I figured you've been through a lot and by yourself for a while. I was hoping you would think it was fun."

"Well honestly, I've never really done the whole phone sex thing, but if I'm gonna' go that route with anyone, I'd definitely have to be comfortable with them. You can't just hit me with all of that during our first conversation."

"Yeah, I guess. Sorry."

I laughed. He wasn't a jerk, but I didn't quite know how to feel about what just transpired. What was clear is that I'd had enough for one evening. Justified was coming up, and this wasn't worth missing one second of Timothy Olyphant.

"It's all right, dude. No harm, no foul. I'm gonna' say good night now. We'll chat another time."

"Oh okay, hope so. Good night." he replied, disappointed.

"Good night," I said as kindly as I could before hanging up.

He wasn't important enough where his feelings would matter above my own, but I didn't want to be a dick about it.

I checked Christian's Facebook before shutting off my phone. My eyes widened. On his Timeline it didn't even have his status as a married man anymore. He hadn't changed it to Single or It's Complicated, he avoided the quandary by omitting it entirely.

Awesome sauce! NOT! I checked the time on my phone. Still had fifteen minutes before Justified. I flung the covers off, jumped out of bed and wiggled out of my poom-poom shorts. I rummaged through my bottom drawer before grabbing my prize and leaping back into bed. I took a second to engage the lock on my door and another minute to search for an appealing porn video. I was wound far too tight. I needed a release, and I sure as shit wasn't gonna'

252

get it from that lame ass conversation with Veran. Exit stage left. I've got business I must attend to. I'll be damned if this night was going to be a complete bust.

'Tis the Season

Why did it always seem like right after Thanksgiving, before you had a moment to collect yourself or your finances, Christmas was right up on you? I revel during this time of year. I have a routine and throw a soiree that generally keeps me jollier than old Kris Kringle himself! Christian and I host the only and most elaborate Christmas dinner party in town.

My Teacups (my girls), Teabags (the men), sometimes Teapots (my mama and aunties), and Crumpets (the kids) wait patiently all year round for the food, laughs, liquor and games. It's a big deal and I take my role as hostess incredibly serious, eh. Christian does his part by helping me decorate, shop and he's definitely our exclusive resident DJ. But one can hardly describe him as being as enthusiastic as myself.

We put up the tree right after Thanksgiving. I have a unique five-stone manger scene that ornaments our Z table in the living room. We prop the dining room table in the corner, cover it with a festive tablecloth and equally gorgeous runner and stagger the plastic champagne flutes I usually buy from Party City in a pyramid pattern.

After I've strewn the table with some plastic jewels and a Christmas potpourri of cones and twigs and all kinds of other goodies I get from Pier 1 Imports, the air is filled with cinnamon spice and everywhere you look is decorated with something nice. I don't mess around when it comes to my favorite time of year.

And let me tell you, not only can we eat, but we can drank people! The Patron, Kettle One, Grey Goose, Hennessey and Jack Daniel's liquor bottles are all placed just so on the

254

table with short stacks of the infamous red drink cups. Whenever anyone is ready to eat, all they have to do is pluck one of the plastic dinner plates, napkins and plastic forks, knives or spoons already laid neatly on the table. When our guests are ready for dessert, we hit the kettle and they can choose from any of the three cake plates laden with my baked goodies. Sometimes I bake a chocolate raspberry or better than sex or even a banana sour cream cake. I try to make two different varieties to tempt my guests. And if I've a mind, I might bake some sugar cookies and throw some vanilla and chocolate frosting with sprinkles for some color, get everybody in the festive spirit the moment they walk through the door.

One year I made sugar cookies, melted some Cadbury chocolate bars and dipped the cookies in them. Delish! Anyhow, you get the idea! We don't play!

We have a large kitchen and no dining room, which is why we chose to section off a corner of the kitchen and make it our dining area. We bought a beautiful round marble table with four tall pub chairs alongside a tall, white cabinet bar. It's such an elegant look and one of the first things you notice when you walk into my Jewel Box Joint.

Unfortunately, we don't have a whole lot of counter space, but I solved that problem by purchasing two very large cutting boards, one marble and one wood. I simply place them over the stove burners and then I can put my trays of food on the stove as if they were countertops! Can you tell that HGTV has been my favorite channel for like donkey years?

Bet you'd like to know what's on the menu? Succulent baked chicken, which I baste every few minutes so it's never dry, my famous corn cream casserole (and I do mean famous, my peeps talk about it year round), carrots and green beans baked in an apricot glaze, stovetop stuffing, and homemade mashed potatoes.

When everyone's done eating their fill, we have dessert which is already on the table aside from the liquor. Everything is decadent, everything is self-serve. No one is shy about getting seconds, thirds or whatever! By the by, all of my guests know, when you're at my joint, you eat hearty, you eat everything you want, because for Christmas we don't do doggy bags. Whatever is left over belongs to the house. Yeah, I said it. After spending five to six hours cooking, do you think I want to see the stove for at least the next two to three days? Ya mad or what!

Everyone's invited for 4:00 p.m., and the majority of my people show up around five or six. We sit around, watch the latest videos that my innovative hubby usually casts to the TV, have a drink to get started and wait for the rest to arrive, 'cause once they do, we eatin' like we never see food before. Come see never see for my West Indians out there—right? Right.

Once we're talked out and had dessert, Christian casts more interesting videos on our big TV, and when we can move again we play Charades and other games that require you to act out a word or scene. We're loud, we're loose, we're brass and we're hysterical. The entire evening is filled with nothing but laughter, food and love.

You can imagine my depression this year. My man is gone, and it would seem he took my Christmas spirit with him. It's so weird to be high and thankful and confident, really feeling that you're doing what you're supposed to do, having confidence that you're on HIS path, and the very next day feeling absolutely the opposite. You feel lost, afraid of the future, depressed, questioning yourself, are you on HIS path or your own? It's exasperating. Being bloody human sucks some royal arse!

I considered all of this as I sat down to write out my checks to my yearly charities. The more I continued to write my checks, the more thankful I became despite my circumstances. I thought about the United Veterans, the Coalition for the Homeless, the Food for the Poor, the Cancer Research, Diabetes Foundation and even the little "manimals" as I wrote out my last check for the ASPCA. Yes, my situation was sad. I was losing my husband of seven years, and I didn't know if my marriage was over or if this was simply a trial. The not knowing kept me in limbo. I could not move forward, yet I was not secure in my stasis. I was waiting to hear from him, even though I had made some moves to protect myself from a complete turn of events, and it was all but killing me.

I sighed deeply and decided Christmas was going to go on with or without my man. I shot a text to my teacups confirming our usual date for my Christmas Dinner Party and set to planning my grocery list.

I had to remember what Christmas was about. It wasn't about celebrating myself. It was about celebrating the birth of my savior, and no matter what was going on in my life, I was sincerely thankful for that! I opened my Bible App and read my favorite Psalm, Psalm 23. Afterward a peace came over me that made me surprised at myself, and I heard these words in my heart, this too shall pass.

Don't Tell Your Father

I took a deep breath, turned down the volume and shut off the car.

"Jesus, please help me get through this. I don't know what I'm going to say, but if you guide me I know everything's gonna' be all right, but if you leave me to my own devices—well, it's gonna' be a hot mess. Amen. Here we go."

I shuddered and turned my collar up against the wind. It snowed the night before, and even though it hadn't stuck, there were pockets of fragile thin ice sheets over water puddles. I navigated the treacherous path safely and rang the side doorbell. By now they had surely sealed the back sliding doors as if they were under quarantine so it didn't make any sense to go around. A few seconds later I could hear my mother making her way toward the door.

"Catherine?"

She always called out to me before opening. It was a good safety habit. I watched too much ID Channel to snicker.

"Yeah Mom, it's me." My voice revealed a hint of impatience. Involuntarily, of course. Damn. I might have swayed her entire mood.

"You there?" she asked.

"Yes, Mom, it's me." I sighed, relieved that she hadn't heard me the first time. "Thank you Jesus," I whispered before ducking through the doorway.

"Watch yourself! Don't fall into the basement!"

Even after all of the years that my sister, my daughter or I have been visiting my parents, my mom never missed the opportunity to warn us of the impending doom of falling into the basement. Unfortunately, one could easily misstep and in fact capitulate down the brick stairs onto the basement floor, but she warned us so much that even if she suddenly ceased, you'd still hear it.

"Hi madre," I sang cheerfully.

"Hi padre," Mom threw back at me before covering her mouth while she laughed as if she'd said something forbidden. She had her shy old school habits that I found both endearing and sometimes annoying. Geez, I needed a flogging. She was being so sweet, and my mood couldn't be more foul. One day my daughter might feel the same about me. I had to get over myself! I chuckled. JC was working on me. This would not be my last revelation of the evening, to be sure.

"Put your coat there." Mom pointed to kitchen banquette and then spread her arms wide, waiting to enfold me. "Come let me see you my child."

I sat down on the green bench and pulled my boots off first. Once I took my coat off, I wanted to be standing so she could see me at my thinnest. I had every intention of faking it until I made it!

"Come here, let me kiss you."

I was a little more than a foot taller than Mom. I had to bow from the waist. She took my face in her hands and kissed both of my cheeks and then my forehead. She performed this ritual with the reverence of a beloved pope, all warmth and love. Then she touched my shoulders and gently set me back a pace so she could get a good once-over.

"You look good." She nodded approvingly.

"Thanks Mom." I smiled in relief.

"We all have to watch what we eat. And it's not because of looks. Weight is not healthy. Everybody these days is watching their figure. I hear it every day on the news. Weight cause over mark problem." If JC hadn't kept my eyes pinned to my mom's cherub face, they would have been rolling.

"Yes I know, Mom. Anyway, how are you? You look very nice."

Weight was never something I cared to discuss. I had deep seated issues about the subject. When I was married to my ex, and we began to have issues, I ate, he drank, I got bigger, he came home later and later, and you can guess the rest. It's not an especially original story.

As time went on, I became more and more depressed and eating became my solace. I gained some weight. I went from a size eight to a size twelve. My mother, being an old school West Indian woman, felt that my weight gain to some degree had prompted my husband to step outside of our marriage.

Even after all was said and done and it became obvious that my ex was simply a man who could not be satisfied with one woman, my mother still held on to her ideas about my weight. For the better part of my life since that point she's given herself permission to vocalize her opinion. I was angry and hurt for many years over this, but nothing prepared me for the day my father jumped on the bandwagon, in front of mixed company no less.

It was at that point that one day during dinner after my mom brought up weight, that I shut them down with no mercy. Now my father is all crickets and my mother includes a sentence or two like "everyone watches what they eat" kind of thing, and so I wage no further war.

I think having my own child sit around a dinner table while my parents were discussing me as if I were a child just hit me one day as grotesquely wrong. I realized they were completely crossing serious boundaries and I had to beat 'em back with a bit of force since they were enjoying free rein at my expense for far too long.

"Me? Really? You think so? I lost a couple of pounds, but not as much as I wanted to."

"Mom, there's nothing wrong with your weight. You look great. But if it would make you feel better to lose some weight than by all means go ahead. But you look great. Your face looks bright and young. What have you been using?"

I'm not using misdirection, hush up. My mom actually does look great. She doesn't have but maybe one wrinkle and she's in her sixties. And I find she's quite proportionate. So put that in your pipe and smoke it.

"You hungry? I cooked some nice chicken curry and spinach and dahl and roti."

My mouth watered. "I'm starving. I only had breakfast today, I was so busy."

"Good. I glad. You wash your hands and sit down. I'll dish out now. You want a hot cup of tea now or later?"

"No thanks Mom. I'll drink water while I eat and have tea with some dessert later."

"Okay, good. I'll dish now."

Later that evening, after dinner and before my father arrived, my mom popped the question.

"So where's Christian?"

I must have hesitated a little too long. Truthfully, I hadn't prepared an answer. I thought everything would have blown over by now.

"He couldn't make it, Mom."

She leaned forward on her elbows and tucked her hands under her armpits, a habit I mimicked and hadn't realized until just then.

I folded my arms across my chest and leaned back into the chair for support.

"Look, Mom, I guess I should tell you what's going on."

"Quick before your father comes. I could see that something was bothering you all night but I wanted to see that you eat first."

The air went out of me. She was sooo my madre, making sure I ate first before asking me about my troubles. Whatever our differences, she was first and foremost my mama, and she was worried about me in that way that only moms can be.

"He reconnected with someone he used to go to high school with. When I found out he was seeing her, I asked him what was going on and he couldn't answer me. Long story short, I saw where this was going. He was infatuated with this girl and I couldn't stand there and watch it happen right in front of my face any longer, so I asked him to leave. I gave him some time to figure out what he wants and he's been staying with his brother ever since."

My mom took her hand and covered her mouth.

"I would never have believed this of Chrish-tan."

Now when my mama enunciates and breaks your name down into syllables, you know you're in trouble.

"Well that makes two of us," I joked without much humor.

"Is he sleeping with this woman?"

"Not when he was with me but since I asked him to leave he continued to see her and he said he slept with her twice."

"So if he wasn't sleeping with her then why did he leave you?" Confusion etched my madre's usually unwrinkled forehead.

"He left because I asked him to mom. He was running around dating this girl while I was at work. It was only a matter of time before the two of them ended up sleeping together. I couldn't watch it happen under the same roof all over again," I explained defensively.

Oh Lord, please don't let this be one those things I have to defend. Please don't let her adopt the, if he ain't beating you, sleeping with your sister, an alcoholic or a drug user, you shouldn't leave him defense.

Instead mi madre sat back and seemed to consider all that I revealed.

"So what you doing about all of this?" she asked, pitching forward and rocking back.

I leaned forward. "I guess I'm waiting for him to figure out that he's being a jackass and come back home." The truth was simple. The truth was painful. My shoulders slumped after the confession.

She pushed her chair back and came to me. She hugged me hard, a real face to bosom hug. She cradled my face with her hands and kind of rocked me side to side.

"You're doing the right thing. Pray for him and pray for you and Gaia. I will say a prayer too. Don't do anything rash. Don't make any decisions and don't tell anybody what's going on. Some people will give you wrong advice."

"I haven't," I whispered into her ample bosoms. The scene filled me with warmth and not a little humor.

"You're right. He's a damn fool but he'll ketch he-self. And Catherine?"

"Yes mom?"

"Don't tell your fada a word." Mom dropped her British proper and easily backslid into her creole.

"I won't."

"Because I tink Christian will come to his senses but your fada mightn't find it easy to forgive him."

Go dad. I felt a sense of childish pride. My daddy loves me. He won't tolerate no bullshit!

A minute later we heard the side door and my father call out.

"Hello there."

"We're here dear." And she slid back to British proper without missing a beat.

Mom started to move toward the kitchen, but not before she turned around, gave me an encouraging smile and put her finger to her lips.

Guess Who's Coming to Dinner?

I put a few drops of olive oil and swirled it around to coat the carahe before chipping an onion and throwing in some ready minced garlic and turning on the stove. The shrimps were soaking in lime juice and the rice was in the cooker. Dinner would be served in T minus thirty-five minutes. I turned the hood fan on low, but the sautéed garlic and onion fragrance was heavenly. I heard my phone ping as I set to washing the shrimps.

A few minutes later after I turned the shrimps, set the heat on low to simmer the stew and covered the pot, I dried my hands and picked up my phone.

My eyebrow shot up. A text from Christian. Will wonders never cease?

He wanted to talk. I suspected the veil was no longer obscuring his vision and reality was fast setting in but who knows? Maybe he wanted to tell me he was filing for divorce. No way to tell but I highly suspected he wanted to come back home. Maybe it was my wishful thinking, I can't say.

I sat at my table studying my French mural trying to decipher how I felt.

I hadn't changed my mind. I still wanted my husband back. But I had conditions. I didn't want the life I had with him. I wanted a new one.

I wanted him to be the man I imagined he should be, not the man I accepted, not the man I settled for and celebrated even when he did stupid, unworthy shit. Throughout this entire experience and my daily if not hourly conversations with JC, I had come to realize a great many things. I had a part to play in creating the husband that I had. Some of the distractions in my life might have led my husband to believe he had latitude in the same arena. So what's good for the goose! I also accepted so many things in our marriage that were wrong. When my husband spent more money than we had, when his tastes exceeded our budget, when I asked him to do something and he never got around to it and the list went on and on.

I realized this man hadn't been present in our life for a good, long time. He'd been allowing me to carry us both in more ways than one for much longer than I imagined. I had been so swept up in the routine, in trying to keep the machine running, that I hadn't stopped to think just because I can doesn't mean I should. I've been in this by myself and using distractions to get me through instead of forcing him to work on us with me. It's so strange that the physical nature of him sleeping with this chick seemed the least important to me, but there it is. Surprisingly it was hardly a blip on my radar.

I sat down to make my list of demands and then texted him back.

Tomorrow at 6pm works for me.

He confirmed with the last ping.

I sent my boss an e-mail that I had to leave early tomorrow. This time when I saw C, I planned to be prepared.

Apparition

"Bye Chris!" I waved cheerfully to our day shift guard as I made my way through our lobby. It had been under construction for months, and when they finally finished no one could tell there had been much of a difference or improvement.

I think the idea behind it was to modernize the look in the cheapest possible way. The end result looked like an incomplete art nouveau light installation from the 90s. It hardly mattered. A good day for this building was all three elevators working. Half the time I travelled in freight with a ladder threatening to clobber me if the painter moved a fraction of an inch to his left

I had a million things on my mind as I made my way across the street. There had been a light dusting of snow during lunch and just as I made my way to the curb I slipped. A hand shot out of nowhere to steady me.

"Eh girl, you payin' attention to where you going or what?"

I whirled around and couldn't believe my eyes.

"What the hell?" I barely contained.

He laughed but still hadn't let go of my arm.

"That's no way to thank me. I just saved your life. You all right?" he asked, gently leading me back from the curb.

I swallowed hard. I still couldn't believe what I was seeing. Could the timing have been any worse? Why couldn't I have seen him a week ago?

I shook my head in disbelief. "Yeah, sorry. Thanks Ray."

"You surprised to see me here right?" He laughed easily.

Damn, I could smell his cologne from here. The GT lilt in his voice was hypnotizing. He wore a hat, but his collar wasn't all the way up, exposing just a sliver of neck. Like a vampire I was drawn to it. What would he do if I just leaned forward and bit him?

"I'm surprised to see you anywhere," I said stupidly.

He pointed to his work van across the street. "That's my van over there." He pronounced there like dare, and I found it sexy as hell.

"I'm workin' in that building. We're putting in the ducts. You work around here?"

I shivered, but not from the cold. Seriously, are you shitting me? I've been in a drought for months and now, now the one man I've been feigning for is actually working across the street? This has got to be some candid camera moment!

"Yeah I, ah, work right over here." I vaguely pointed behind me.

"Which building, the one by the deli?"

My eyebrow did its high lift thing. He wanted to know precisely which building I worked in? Hold up now, say what?

I cleared my throat and became as precise as one could be.

"Yeah, 369 Lex. We're right there on the seventeenth floor."

He smiled as if he caught my play then checked his watch. "Girl, you only work half day? What kind of job do you have?"

I laughed. "No, no. I have some things I gotta do so I had to leave early. Usually I'm here 'til six."

He nodded and looked toward his van.

"All right. Well I don't want to hold you up. Tek care, walk good. Don't fall you know." He hit me with all the Guyanese fit to print and left. I barely had time to nod.

I crossed the street, and when I was far past I looked up. "I am not able. If this is a test JC, I'm already on the wrong side of it." I shook my head but thoughts of Ray kept knocking about.

The Mirror Has Two Faces

"Well of course I don't trust you, so I need you to call this girl right now in front of me and break it off."

"But I did that already." He shuffled in his seat.

"I don't give a shit. You want to come home, you're gonna' have to do it again. Either we're gonna' start from ground zero or not at all. What's it gonna' be Christian?"

"Yes. I'll call her. What else?" he asked, softening his tone.

"I will not allow you back into this house without a job. You need to get a job if you want to come home."

"Okay."

He didn't sound enthusiastic but did I expect him to be someone else entirely? Sure, would have been nice. But I created this monster and this is who he was. It was time to help destroy him and create something else.

"I want you to change your phone number and make your e-mails and FB accessible to me. If there isn't total transparency between us until I feel like I can trust you again then we can just drop this right here and now. Don't ask me how long it's gonna' take because I have no idea."

"Okay. What else?"

"That guy that you used to be, the one who whenever I needed something done and you would delay and act the fool and never get around to it until it suited you, that's not gonna' work for me any longer. If you intend to be who you were, forget it. This is not going to work. I've learned a few things in your absence Christian. One of them is that the way you were, that guy, isn't good enough for me. I accepted him for some reason unknown to even myself. I let you get away with things as if you were my kid and not my husband. I settled for what you chose to do instead of what you should have been doing, and I made it seem like I was grateful to have that guy in my life and as my man. I was absolutely ridiculous and I will never repeat that bullshit ever again. So either you're going to be the man I want or you're going to be someone else's man."

"Catherine, I'm sorry that I was so far from the man I myself wanted to be. I don't know how it happened. But it's not who I want to be. I want to be your man. I want to be the man you deserve, and if you give me a chance, I know I can show you that I can be."

Yes, it was words, but they held meaning and they moved me. I had prayed a long time for this moment and it came. Now that it was here I had to be careful. I had to lean on my JC's guidance and not my own understanding of things.

If Christian was willing to change then I had to give him that chance without using the past against him. If I was going to forgive him and make a new start, then I would have to do just that. I couldn't pretend to forgive him and then punish him later. If that was my intention, I would create a bigger mess than we had now, and I would be victimizing him.

I couldn't have it both ways. I understood all of this in an instant as if it were written on the wall. In my mind I told JC that he was wizening me beyond comprehension. I knew myself, and it was clear that these revelations were NOT coming from me.

I would get in my own way of what I wanted if left to my own devices. Anger would control me and my words would end up pushing me further and further from the very things I wanted. Once I understood this, once JC showed me the light, nothing else mattered. The choices I had to make were clearly mapped out. I simply had to walk the path.

I took a deep breath and made ready.

"Okay. I'm going to give you that chance. You can start by calling her."

Sucker Punch

"Hello?"

I tried to read into her voice, to add or subtract from my previously formulated opinion, but I already knew. I viewed her Facebook page and summed up that she, in and of herself, was nothing special. She hadn't displayed any extraordinary charm or wit, or even tits for that matter. Oh, trust me, I scoured her FB pictures and posts with all the subtlety of a 1980s' stalker. Epic

Don't act like you're above performing such tasks. This is my husband, not some sidepiece. All's fair in love and war. Her state of dress regularly consisted of T-shirt and jeans. Her body didn't hold any secrets that would compel a man to unveil.

Quite frankly, she was boxy, and I knew my man liked to ride curves. There was one unique attribute to her physicality that I could remark upon with all sincerity; that of her startlingly clear blue-green eyes. It was easy to imagine a man loosing himself in them. But the sum total of her appearance and her words, seductress she was not.

I presumed she showered him with attention, made him feel special, wanted. Yes, I was pretty confident that I had the 411 on that score. Of course, we all know that bullshit is all an illusion. Once it fades, one is forced to confront the stark reality of the situation.

He must have started to question why he thought leaving me for this girl was beneficial. I suppose the feelings were fading and he was starting to catch on to the real deal and that things weren't comin' up roses no mo', ya feel me?

Truth is, she could have been a fine gal. Who knows really? I just knew she wasn't for him. I was made for him. It's just that simple, even if the fool didn't know it.

"Hi, it's me," C answered, nervously rubbing his forefinger with his thumb and staring at the motion, mesmerized. He exhibited anxiety like a Scarlett letter.

"Yeah, I know. What's up?" She sounded nervous, like she knew the hammer was about to drop.

"I'm sorry Lisa, but I'm going back to my wife."

I was kind of shocked that he put it to the girl like that, and for a moment I felt a twinge of sadness for her. But then I remembered this trick was grown and starting some shit with a married man was a fuckin' stupid bitch ass move to begin with. I stiffened my spine. She better put her big girl panties on and drink her medicine. I was under JC's counsel for sure, but I wasn't JC.

"What you mean? Why didn't you figure this out before you messed with me? Before we did anything I told you that if you wanted to be with your family you should leave me alone."

"I know, and I'm sorry. I don't know what to say. But I'm going back to my family."

"I can't believe this shit. I—"

"Listen, this isn't gonna' be one of those long drawn-out discussions. You should have known better than to deal with a married man in the first place. What did you expect?" I interjected. I was tired of this shit, and I wasn't gonna' stand for some back and forth drama. Bitch, I have a list to go through. You're only the first thing on the damn paper.

"Who the hell is that? You have me on speaker Christian?"

"Listen, Lisa, is it? I'm Catherine, his wife. We 'met' on FB already, remember? Remember that message I sent you about the fact that you were texting and messaging my husband to the point where I said you could have his ass and made him leave my house? Remember your reply was that you two were 'just friends'? Well I suppose that wasn't entirely accurate, now, was it?"

"Yeah, but when I sent you that message we weren't doing anything but talking."

Christian sat back in the chair with a look that translated he'd rather be anywhere but in the middle of this. But my look was even more priceless and could have frozen water, such was the ice in my veins. So he took a deep breath, sat back and strapped in for the ride. He was also smart enough to speak only when spoken to.

"I realize that Lisa; however, where did you think dealing with a married man would lead? What did you expect would happen eventually? You were having problems with your own baby's father, weren't you? Didn't you have enough experience to recognize when a man is just using you to make himself feel better? You really expected a married man to be honest with you when he was dealing dirty with his own wife? Seriously?"

"Listen, I don't know what was going on between you two, but he said that you guys were through and over with. Only after he told me that did we become intimate. I've known him for a long time, much longer than you, since high school."

"You know Lisa; it really pisses me off when people say they've known someone since high school. That's some real dumb shit. You've known him from high school. But it's been twelve years since then, twelve years that he's been growing and changing, and for seven of them he's been married to me. So allow me to correct you. You did know him. You actually don't know shit about him now."

"Whatever. I just want to talk to Christian for a minute." She sounded frustrated and beaten. What more could I want?

I almost laughed.

"Yeah, you do that. You go ahead and talk to Christian. Get it all in girl because this will be the last time you ever talk to him, okay?"

"Sure. Whatever. Christian, why didn't you tell me you were gonna' go back to your wife when we were together the other night? Didn't I ask you if there was something wrong? Did you really have to call me up in front of her and tell me this bullshit?"

"I talked to you about this before. I told you that I wasn't sure what I was doing."

"Yeah but you didn't say all this."

"I'm sorry to have to tell you like this but I'm going back to my family. I made a mistake. I'm sorry."

"Well, I should let you know that I'm late."

I felt dizzy. Was I hearing this bitch correctly? Bitch what you talkin' bout,' late for church? Let the church say Amen. I snapped my head to the right and glowered at C. He beat me to the punch. The blood drained from his face and a tear escaped from his eye.

"How many times were you together?" I barely could formulate the question. I was trying hard to maintain my composure.

"Twice or three times. I can't remember," She replied dismissively.

"And you slept with a married man without protection?" I accused. I was pissed beyond all reason, but I treaded lightly. I needed answers more than I need to expel my anger.

"Yeah, well, he didn't think it was necessary. Anyway, it happened. I should have gotten my period two days ago, and it's late, so I thought he should know. If I don't get it by tomorrow, I'm gonna' take a test."

I gritted my teeth and tried to steady my thoughts. I banished JC from my mind. I could only see red. Christian hung his head low as the tears continued to flow from his eyes.

"Will you call us with the results of the test once you know?" I maintained control. I needed her to continue to be reasonable until we knew for sure one way or the other.

"Yeah. But I don't want to hear from either one of you ever again. I'll call you."

She disconnected the call. He hadn't bothered to answer. I turned to him, far too angry to shed tears. They would undoubtedly visit later.

"Christian, you slept with this bitch, and you didn't even use a condom?"

He kept his silence, still facing the floor.

I was enraged.

"You, who don't even want or like kids, slept with this Spanish bitch and didn't even fucking use a condom? And you know this beatch has a freakin' four-year-old son already from some freakin' baby daddy and you know how some of these bitches be droppin' children like fucking stray cats all over the fucking place, and you didn't think to use a condom? Are you this fuckin' stupid?"

He looked up at me then, his eyes red, his face tear stained, his lips trembling. I knew he was sorry. I knew he was sorrier than he'd ever been in his whole life. And I spoke to HIM- then, in my mind. JC, I did not sign on for this. You didn't tell me about this monkey wrench. I am not able to take this on. And then I found my voice and I spoke to him.

"Christian, this negates everything."

"I know," he whispered miserably.

"If this bitch is pregnant, I can't take you back. I cannot deal with you having a baby by some trifling dumb bitch you had an affair with."

"I know."

"If she's pregnant, you're fucked. She has you by the balls. And this will not be my problem. I will divorce you."

"I know," he repeated like a zombie.

I almost felt sorry for him. His entire life would change in the blink of an eye. He never wanted kids. He didn't much like them. I could see him becoming a statistic; yoked to a woman he barely knew and no longer wanted because they now shared a child. I could see him dying before my very eyes.

"I'm sorry that I put you through this," he said sincerely.

"Yeah, me too. I think you should go now. Come back in two days and we'll call her together. Don't call her before then. Don't contact her. I don't want to have to investigate and search and dig. Trust me, it's in your best interest to do what I'm telling you to do. If she even thinks that this might be a way to keep you, she might do something drastic or devious. Stay away from her. If she calls, you don't answer the call. In two days time, come back here. We'll call her together and find out what's the story. Once we know, we'll go from there."

He nodded, got up and put his coat on. He came back and kissed me on the cheek.

"Christian?"

"Yeah?"

"All this time, going through all this crazy shit that YOU put me through, I've been praying. Praying every day."

He nodded. "Yeah."

"It's your turn. You better pray that that bitch isn't pregnant." I said coldly.

"Yeah. I will be." He swallowed hard and left our home.

Divergence

The sky was dark. It was cold. It was raining, and I had no clue in what direction I should head. I didn't feel like going home. And yet it was too cold and miserable to be wandering aimlessly in the city. Her words kept replaying in my head. I might be pregnant. I might be pregnant. I stood in front of my building, threw up my hoodie and lit a cigarette. I watched the smoke stream reach out into the night and disappear, fascinated by it's movement.

"I never seen a girl love smokin' so much."

"Wha." I turned toward the voice in my dreams and shook my head.

"You stalkin' me, boy?" I laughed. He grinned.

"No." he said simply, reaching into his pocket and digging out his own pack.

"I see you have your own stash now. Ain't depending on me for your nicotine fix anymore huh?" I grinned, pointing to his half-empty pack of Newports.

"I don't like to depend on nobody yo." he stated seriously.

I rolled my eyes skyward and took in a long drag. My situation at home had me twisted enough that as much as I longed to catch a glimpse of Ray, he still managed to annoy me with his GT bravado. Homie don't play that.

"You finish work? You goin' home now?" He puffed.

"Yeah, I guess." I gave a noncommittal response. "You?"

"Yeah, I done for the night. Let's go take a drink man." he said casually.

"With you?" I sputtered, losing all my cool points.

"Who else? Yeah me." He laughed.

 He was easy. Easygoing, easy to look at, easy to be next to. And he was confident while I was anything but. I was pretty sure he could read me like a book, so why shouldn't he be? Every time he was near my eyes widened like a doe in headlights, and if you held up a mirror I'm sure my tongue would be hangin' out. I didn't take but a second to weigh my options.

"Sure. Lemme just text my daughter and let her know I'll be a little late."

"You got a daughter?" he asked, clearly surprised.

"Yeah. Gaia."

"That's a boy's name yo."

My eyebrow went up and my eyes narrowed. This boy was far from my style. He was a straight-up coolie. I might have been attracted to his look but his attitude was probably going to be a whole different story.

"Actually, that's a name that could belong to either a boy or girl. It's unique and the only name her father and I could agree on." I proudly enlightened. You're welcome grasshopper.

"Did I ask you all that?" he stated, not the least bit impressed.

Right about now I was quite certain he was regretting asking me out for a drink, and I was damn sure regretting taking him up on the offer. I was about to give him a tongue lashing when I noticed he was grinning from ear to ear.

"Yo relax kid. I'm just playin'. You finish your smoke? Let's go. My van's right across the street."

In spite of myself, I smiled back. I couldn't explain this coolie appeal. Normally if someone came at me like that I would run in the opposite direction. But on this particular man, I found the same type of behavior I generally found appalling, appealing. Good grief, how fucked up was I?

"Where we going?"

"Relax" he stated, holding up his talk to the hand.

I sighed loudly. This was going to be a lesson. In what, I couldn't quite gather, but I knew he would test my patience in every way possible. He hung beside me, almost touching my sleeve. I was surprised. I thought he'd be ten paces ahead of me like most of these coolie dudes be doing to their girls.

That was Ray for you. Just when you thought you had him figured. He stopped just short of the passenger door, fished out his remote and held the door open for me. He held my elbow to prop me up on the high seat. I could smell his cologne. It was heavenly. And for a second I closed my eyes and let it take me.

"Thank you." I recovered.

He nodded, closed my door and went around to the driver's side. I reached across and opened the door. It was raining and I was sure his hat was soaked through.

He gave me a strange look before coming in and sitting down.

"Thanks." He dropped the keys in the ignition and started the car.

"Sure." I was back to one word answers from here on out. I looked around his white van which he kept meticulously clean. I laughed. The man had a clean, white van, like most serial killers. I have been watching the I.D. Channel way too much.

"Why you laughin'?" he asked seriously.

"Nothing, nothing." I said and cleared my throat. I made another assumption that either he wouldn't understand what the hell I was talking about or I would botch the explanation and it wouldn't sound so funny after I said it. I chose to shut it. I hoped he didn't take it personally.

"So where's your daughter now?"

"She's at home."

"By herself?"

"Yeah." He was beginning to sound like my mother. This was going to be a tennis match between elation and irritation.

"How old is she?"

"She's fifteen." Now here's the part where people usually say, what? You have a fifteen-year-old? Wow, you don't look a day over twenty yourself. How is that possible? But not this cat. To impress him, I'd have to clap ten roti.

"Okay. What's she gonna' eat?"

I must have stared at his profile for a few seconds before answering.

"I have leftovers." I was on the verge of asking him if he worked for my mother.

"Okay." He seemed satisfied with my answers and kept driving. We both kept a tight lip for the next ten minutes. Finally he pulled into a parking spot. I could see we were in the Village somewhere. I didn't frequent this part of town so I was more than clueless.

"We're here?" I asked skeptically.

"Yeah. Pull up your hood, it's still raining." He threw back over his shoulder as he opened the door and hopped out.

Man, I sure wasn't used to this type of conversation. C never really talked to me like he was my dad. What surprised me was how much it grated my nerve, and yet awakened some part of me that I had no idea existed. Some part of me that, dare I say, liked to be told, not asked. What the hell was happening up in here? He opened my door and helped me out.

"We goin' across the street. Follow me."

"Okay." I managed, while holding up my hoodie and hurrying alongside him.

I hadn't managed to look up and catch the name of the pub we tumbled into, but once inside it had the warm feel of an old speakeasy. The place was dimly lit and smelled of wood polish and whiskey. The rectangular bar catered to a handful of customers, and the tall pub tables and chairs throughout the establishment contained specks of the after-work crowd enjoying a Willie Nelson doppelganger on the piano spotlighted in the corner.

He steered us to the end of the bar and held out the stool for me. I climbed into it and barely put my bag down on the ledge below when a bartender in casual slacks and a button-down shirt with the over the shoulder suspenders moseyed over. He looked like an old-fashioned Chicago gangster. He put down his cigar and gave Ray and me the once-over.

"What can I get you folks?" he asked smiling.

I dug that he hadn't introduced himself or had a nametag.

"I'll have a Johnny Walker Black no ice. Catherine, what do you want?"

"I'll start with a Malibu and grenadine, please." I smiled politely.

"Comin' right up." Our mystery bartender smiled and disappeared to the other side of the bar.

I was impressed. He might have been the only bartender who hadn't questioned my drink. Most of them ask me if I really want grenadine. Did I realize how sweet the drink would be? He had a slight twang to his voice, reminded me of Sam Elliot, except he was about twenty years younger.

I turned to Ray. "How do you know about this joint? You come here often?"

He smiled. "I know this city like the back of my hand." He was bragging. I dug it. I wanted to slap myself.

Every quality that annoyed me thus far in other men he openly portrayed: arrogance, a controlling quality, that old-school coolie judgment thang that they hand down like the word of God. Yet I either overlooked or dismissed the traits entirely, and in some cases responded to them like a plant to sunlight.

You ever watch the Discovery channel? The scene where the lion gets in back of the lioness ready to mate but she snaps her head back, bites him and moves on as if to say "child please!" That's my usual response to guys like Ray. But this cat bit the nape of my neck just right, invoking a submissive nature completely foreign to me.

Where does one go with an answer like that? Luckily our drinks came and I sipped instead of speaking.

I sat back and spun a little to the right to enjoy the piano player while coolly sipping my drink. The bartender, whom I secretly dubbed Sam, was magical. He made my drink to my exact preference, more grenadine, less rum. Out of the corner of my eye I could see that Ray was making a study of me. My neck felt hot. He made me nervous.

When I turned back around there were two shots of something before me. I screwed my eyebrows together in puzzlement.

Ray laughed. "It's Patron. You look like you got a lot on your mind. You need to get loose. Let's have a shot."

I wondered if I was incredibly transparent, or he was unusually perceptive.

I slapped both hands on the bar and nodded my head.

"Okay, let's do it." I picked up my shot. He picked up his shot. I clinked his glass. He looked confused. Guess his peeps don't do that. I smiled, wide, all teeth.

"Bottom's up." I saluted and downed it like a pro. He hesitated, polished his off and ordered round two.

"Dude, you tryin' to get me twisted?" I asked, half serious.

"Relax." He put his hand up and grinned.

The shots came and we repeated the process. This time he clinked my glass. Quick study. The conundrum that is Ray, indeed.

After an hour and a few more drinks, I hardly knew what we were discussing, but I felt weightless and giddy and we were laughing. Several times I placed my hand on his shoulder to emphasize a few points during the course of the evening. He, however, made no such moves, no hand on my thigh, no hand on my hand. Nada. Zip. Zilch. ZerO. I was disappointed.

It was after nine when he mentioned that it was getting late, and he would take me home.

Oh geez, he's going back to being my daddy again. I wanted to stay longer, but he was right. I did tell Gaia I was going to be late, not stay out all night.

It was harder to climb back into the van. I felt Ray's hands circle my waist as he redoubled his effort to help me. I was not twisted, but definitely had a nice buzz going. He looked straighter than Thor at a gay convention. Considering he was the gent behind the wheel, this was welcomed news. I hadn't tried to reach over and get the door, but I was staring at it like I had telekinesis. He sat down and gave me an amused look which inexplicably annoyed the shit out of me. I sensed judgment.

"Catherine?"

"Yeah?" I said, my eyes Bambi wide, my mouth watering.

"What's your address?"

I sobered immediately. I rattled it off and lurched unattractively when he put the van in gear and pulled off. Oh just shoot me.

We drove in relative silence. I was trying to remember to take an Advil the moment I got home or I would wake up with a hangover from all of the rum.

It seemed like he pulled up in front of my house in minutes. Clearly not sufficient time to admire him from a distance.

He hopped out and around to help me out gracefully. I didn't make it easy. I was having a hard time keeping my eyes open at this point.

We walked up to the front steps and he held the door open for me. I fished around the bottom of my purse for my keys. When I had them in hand, he gently took them from me and opened my door before returning them to my palm. I smiled and rolled my eyes. I'm quite certain after six or seven tries I would have managed.

"Thank you," I said condescendingly, marveled by the pattern on the floor.

He placed his index finger under my chin and pushed my face up. I blinked twice before catching the intensity in his eyes. He leaned forward as I leaned back and caught my lips in a quiet softness. His lips and his finger were the only parts of his body touching mine. He did not lean into me. The kiss was almost chaste, and yet I could feel him slightly tremble, a betrayal of his surety. I wanted to open myself to him, open my mouth, feel his tongue rake against mine, but I remembered myself. To do so would be the beginning of something. This kiss felt more like an ending.

He withdrew gently, and I stared at him in shocked silence. He smiled and said not a word but turned and, with an easy gait, walked back to his van. I was glad I drank so much rum. It would be the only way I'd get any sleep tonight.

Change Is In the Air

While I was waiting for my life to begin or end, work was
slowing down. I was told this is how it went in the
financial field. The summer, things were running at two
hundred miles per hour, and during the winter, things
grinded down to a mere fifty. It made me nervous. I didn't
want to lose my job when I had just begun.

I loved being at the office, and frankly I needed the
distraction from what was going on at home. If I was
sitting at home contemplating this mess 24/7, I would lose
my mind. Kris reassured me, explaining that during her six
years of working at NGN, this schedule was par for the
course and that I shouldn't worry. I was glad; it was one
less thing off my plate. By 4:00 p.m., the office was empty
but for Kris, Len and I. By 5:30 Kris insisted I hit the road.
I immediately complied.

After work I stopped in front of the building to light up. I
was almost hoping to run into Ray, but of course I didn't.
Beside the fact that I was early, he never did show up when
I wanted him to. I hadn't noticed his van when I got to the
curb either. Probably better this way, I reasoned inwardly.
After all, who needed the complication? Hadn't I had
enough going on? I needed a pep me up.

I decided the window mannequins looked dandy when I
passed K&G and pushed past the revolving doors. A cute
salesman greeted me with a smile and asked if I needed any
help. I returned the smile and shook my head. This store
was rather a home away from home. I knew every nook
and cranny! I skipped downstairs to check out the latest
dresses, shoes and bags.

After scouring through the countless racks, I found one dress that I liked, two blouses that I absolutely had to have, work appropriate, and a nice pair of black pumps, also suitable for work. I tallied it all up and it was just under $100—gotta love this store! I tended to shop on a whim. Sometimes I needed a pick me up and buying something that I could use would make me feel better, sue me. I could do it without the guilt as long as it was under my "mad money" budget.

Thoroughly pleased with my purchase, I placed my shopping bag on the floor in front of the revolving door so that I could fetch my gloves from my bag. As I was putting them on, my eyes automatically lingered at the front of my building. My jaw nearly hit the floor. Ray was having a smoke, peeking inside, clearly waiting for me to come through the lobby. I felt both giddy and uncertain. I wanted to run out and flag him down but something stopped me.

Instead, I crossed to the front of the store and exited. He wouldn't be able to see me from this angle. Suddenly my purchases weren't the reason for my high. I shook my head and blasted Daft Punk on my headphones. I had to shelve this bullshit. Tomorrow C would come by after work, and we would finally know if this bitch was pregnant or not, if we had a future or not. I didn't need to have anything else on my mind. Once I got inside the train, I took my usual position, back against the door, pocketed my headphones and pulled out my nook. It was time to get lost in Winterfell. Who needed Ray when I had Robb Stark?

Checkmate

He arrived without ceremony. I beat him to the apartment only twenty minutes prior. I barely had time to hang up my coat and hit the kettle. However nervous I might have been to hear the truth paled in comparison to him. His face was ashen, looked like he'd dropped a few pounds from only two days ago, and his eyes were puffy and red.

I'm not going to lie, I felt sorry for him more than I felt sorry for myself or the potential loss of us. If things went south, I would eventually move on but his life would be irrevocably damaged by one foolish mistake. Yes, I was angry, but I was not without pity. I softened my demeanor and made him tea without asking. I set our cups on the coasters before us and sat down heavily. I said a little prayer in my mind, please God, don't let her be pregnant.

I held my cup in my hands, enjoying the warmth. "Have you spoken to her?"

He looked up surprised. "No. You told me not to call her."

"Yes, I know, but that doesn't mean you listened." I stated simply.

"I did. I didn't call her." he replied just as simply, without attitude or malice.

"Did she call you?"

"She called once yesterday but I didn't pick up and she didn't leave a voice mail."

"Okay, that's good. Well, I guess we'd better call her and find out what's going on."

He hesitated, fumbled in his pocket for his phone and pressed some buttons.

The phone rang five times before she answered.

"Hello?"

I said nothing but looked toward Christian. We hadn't rehearsed this part.

"Hey."

"Hi. Are you alone?"

"No. I'm here with my wife."

"So why are you calling me?"

My eyes went wide and C put his head down. This was not a good sign.

"You know why we're calling." I said, holding back my fear and anger.

"Yeah. Well I took the test and I'm not pregnant."

Christian's body literally sunk into itself with relief. All the weight he had been carrying was suddenly lifted off of his shoulders. His tears came in quiet streams. I closed my eyes and thanked my Jesus.

"That makes things a lot less complicated. Do you have anything you'd like to say to Christian? Do you need to resolve anything else between you two?" I looked at C as I asked the question. I was asking him too.

"Christian, you have anything you want to say to me?" she asked cynically.

C dried his eyes and addressed his phone on the table. "I'm sorry." he said heavily.

She would have to assess a great deal from those two words. She wouldn't get any more. I didn't feel bad for her. This was an old game that all women were hip to. She chose this path. She chose to deal with someone who was married. She had a man, she knew how they worked. She was not a newborn kitten.

"Yeah, you're sorry all right" she said bitterly.

Clearly she still carried feelings for him. Oh well!

"Yeah, okay, so this is a wrap. I don't expect you two to be communicating anymore. This is finished. My husband and I have some work to do before we figure out if there's something salvageable between us. If you two do communicate, see each other, text, talk, whatever, I'm done with it all and will file for divorce the same day any bullshit comes to light."

"Why are you telling me this? I don't care." She threw the only lame jab she could.

"I'm telling you both because I don't want to be a part of any bullshit in the future. All of our cards are on the table. Now we can proceed accordingly. I hope to never hear from you again." I finished the last words with a sharp edge. It wasn't necessary, but I was feelin' myself now that we were out of the danger zone.

"Yeah whatever," she said before hanging up.

I looked over at C. "The very essence of maturity, that one. You sure can pick 'em."

It didn't come out angry as much as matter-of-fact like. He looked at me, eyes shining with more unshed tears.

"From this day I'm going to show you how much I love you and how I will never let anything or anyone get in between us ever again."

I shrugged. That was more than two words, anyway.

"Not so fast C, there's the matter of my list. I'm not even going to consider allowing you back through those doors unless my list has been met." I had to be all business. It wouldn't do to crumble now. One hurdle had been crossed but there were many other obstacles between us, and as my papa always says, words are wind.

He got up, dried his eyes, held my face in his hands and planted a tender kiss on my forehead. He opened the door and looked back.

"I'm on it." He smiled and closed the door softly behind him.

I closed my eyes and thanked my Jesus. I had no more moves left to make. The rest was in God's hands.

That Which Does Not Kill

I saw him many times after, and we fell into an easy friendship in betwixt after-work smoke breaks. He never mentioned the kiss, and with my life in transition, I was content to let sleeping dogs lie. Christian kept close to home. Odd that whenever he came to walk me home from work Ray was nowhere to be found. A lucky coincidence, no doubt. I didn't give it too much thought.

Meanwhile, C showed up at least twice a week, after work, with flowers or a card or chocolate. The man mercilessly exploited my weaknesses, but I was as cool as a cucumber even though the light in my eyes was dancing. He called and texted me several times a day and explained his whereabouts without prompting.

I didn't want to play detective, so his transparency and willingness to relinquish the information was important and silently appreciated. It helped to reassure me that he was serious about wanting to come back home. He earnestly looked for a job and went on quite a few interviews. A few times when he came to pick me up, he was dressed in his suit. I couldn't help but notice how handsome he appeared, how well he filled it out. I could feel things were slowly coming together.

In the meantime, at home, JC was working on me. I could feel it every day, and I was surprised by my own attitude, which hardly seemed like my own at all. I was not bitter. I did not harbor anger toward C or the girl. In fact, aside from my initial involvement with her, I felt that she was a non-factor in our situation. I viewed her as a symptom not the problem. At first I thought I might have been fooling myself, that perhaps I was only covering my anger with a speedy need to move forward. But as time went on, I realized that wasn't the case. I wasn't angry with them, and I couldn't pretend to be. I wasn't angry with myself either. In fact, the more C and I talked and texted and walked together, the more I realized that my life with him prior was not the way I wanted it to be.

I had accepted too much and now, in the strangest turn of events, here was a chance to obtain what I'd always wanted, what I had been afraid to ask for. Here was a chance for Christian to be the man I wanted him to be, and because he seemed to want that too, we had a good chance of turning a tragedy into a miracle.

Christian was demonstrating a willing spirit to do the things I asked for, things I needed, except now he had a sense of immediacy. Usually when I asked him to do something, he did eventually, when he got around to it, and not without kicking up a bratty fuss. But these days he prioritized my wants and needs at the top of his list. It was a novel experience for us both.

We began sharing our hopes and dreams in a more realistic way than ever before. I was able to be truthful this time around. I expressed that I wanted a home. I wanted money in the bank. I wanted to be able to break away from the "check to check" living. And instead of blindly agreeing like he always did and then spending money and giving in to his whims, he came up with a plan where I would take care of the finances and we would both have one credit card with a reasonable $300 to spend and payoff as we saw fit.

It would be our personal "mad money" that would never get out of hand. I could see that he'd given our situation a lot of thought and even came up with a plausible solution.

This was definitely a contemporary C that I had not known before.

Two months passed in this manner, and though C met everything on my list, he still had not yet found a job. But something lit a fire under that boy, because in the interim he started taking online courses at DeVry. I couldn't help but be impressed. I was a bit apprehensive that this new C might not last, but there was no way to guarantee that one way or the other.

I could tell by now he was hoping he'd be back in the fold. He hadn't come out and asked, but he was hinting around the idea. I still wasn't sure. I needed more time to sort things out in my mind and pray about it. I didn't want to give in too fast and send a message that what transpired between us didn't have serious repercussions.

It wouldn't do for the man to think he could get away with something this serious too easily. By the same token, I wanted him home. I wanted him near. I wanted my cold feet tucked under his warm, solid calves at night. I wanted … So I stalled. So I prayed.

As the World Turns

Call me when you can. I want to discuss Gaia's Sweet Sixteen.

"Next on line. NEXT ON LINE PLEASE."

I returned to the present, shoving my phone in my coat pocket and reaching for my debit card. On second thought, I was going to need more than this cheese Danish to get me through my morning.

"Sorry," I mouthed to the cashier before turning to the suit behind me. "You go ahead. I changed my mind."

He nodded curtly and charged past me with his apple and yogurt in hand.

Never fails. I always seem to be the only one on line who screams "healthy don't live here no mo." Frankly, some of these damn fools need to have a cookie and move the frig on. Would it really kill your ninety-pound frame to have some gluten every now and again?

I put the Danish back and headed out of the deli and crossed the street to my other favorite joint.

"And what did you get, miss?" the cashier asked.

"A banana chocolate chip muffin," I answered with much joy.

"A dollar ninety, please."

I happily forked over my $2.00, savoring the thought of devouring this delectable goodness with my cup of coffee.

The owner was in the front holding the door for his customers on their way out and bidding us a good day. What a nice guy. He's not bad looking either, but a bit older for my taste. I'd put him in his early fifties, but he rocked a svelte, solid physique and was always dressed impeccably. He had style and manners that made him noticeable in a crowd.

"Have a great day Catherine."

Did I mention the memory of a salesman?

"Thanks Steven, and you as well." I flashed my pearly whites as I glided past him.

I saw Spartan having a ciggie at the usual spot in front of our building. His actual name was Alex, and he was like the little brother than I never wanted. However, he was a doll in his own annoying way, which is to say I loved him completely.

"Hey Spartan." I smiled in greeting.

"Hey Cat. We're getting ready to do the capital calls for this quarter," he whined. "Oh joy!" He took a serious drag.

"Awesome," I returned in heavy sarcasm.

It was about that time for us to hound our investors for their quarterly commitment. Not a fun time. We had to get all of the investment company stats in order as well as a number of other documents. The process was wearisome and far from logical—something Kris developed eons ago. It worked for her, and as long as she was content to give me instructions, I was content to follow. I wasn't interested in tearing down the system.

I was contemplating whether I should begin my day with fresh nicotine when I caught Ray crossing the street toward me. He looked delish. End of debate. I lit two cigarettes simultaneously, a little trick I picked up a few years ago from my sister.

He didn't wait for me to fork it over but pinched it straight from my lips.

Alex cleared his throat, stubbed out his cig and declared he'd see me inside. I nodded. I'd forgotten he was there.

"So where you been hiding? I didn't see you last week," he asked, suddenly serious.

"Oh, I've been here. My husband picked me up a couple of times after work, but I should be asking you that. I haven't seen you around lately."

Was it my imagination, or did his eyes squint at the mention of my hubby?

"We've been working overtime now for a while. This whole week too, it's gonna' be like that. I figure I'd ketch you before you go inside."

Oh, you can catch it, all right.

I smiled, trying to keep my cool. If I don't start nothin', it won't be nothin' right? Right.

"So whatcha gonna' do this weekend?" I asked noncommittally, taking a drag.

"Girl, it's Monday and you already askin' about the weekend?" He raised his eyebrows in irritation.

I laughed. It took me a while, but by now I'd gotten to know Ray a little. He generally bounced between two expressions, happiness and irritation. He had no grasp on middle ground.

"Yeah, you're right. Way too soon for all a' that." I smiled and took my last drag. He, on the other hand, was only down to three-quarters on the cig.

"Well, I better get inside and start my day. We've got a lot to do."

"Did I ask you all of that?"

"Oh, hush and just give me a kiss and let me go."

"Never," he softly murmured, unsmiling.

I cocked my head to the side like a confused puppy but said nothing. Instead I continued with our usual routine. Of course, with Ray nothing routine was ever routine. Instead of exchanging a kiss on the cheek like I do with practically everyone else, he never kissed me. What he did instead was present his cheek to be kissed. He always found a way to stand apart from everyone else without trying to. I found it adorable.

And so he did. And so I did. And like two schoolkids on the corner, we parted. As I was waiting for the elevator, I turned back. He was still there, unsmiling but for his eyes. And as I turned around I couldn't help but smile and wonder about the tingles in my tummy.

Respect, Reflect, Reject, Regret

"What's this?" I smiled up at C, unfolding the paper he handed me.

"It's the last thing on my to-do list, my love." He caressed my cheek, smiling with pride.

I read the paper excitedly and glanced back up at him. With the sun behind him, silhouetting his frame and beaming off of the top of his beautiful bald head, he could have been an angel. I could almost hear Halo playing in the background, and with that last move of his my walls came tumbling down. I hugged him fiercely, tears flowing freely from my eyes.

"I love you," he whispered with abandon, cupping my face with a gentle firmness.

When I opened my eyes I could see that he had been crying also. I looked around at the strangers walking to and from my building, passing us without so much as a glance, a few even annoyed that we'd dare to take up space so close to the entrance.

Christian must have realized the obstacle we created and maneuvered me gently to the spot closer to where Ray and I had our routine fag. I thought about how far C had come within the last three months. He had done everything I asked for and more. He gave me space while being completely transparent about his moves. I never asked, though I was comforted by the voluntary information. He spent most of his days on the computer at his brother's house taking online classes and most of his nights he managed to procure a dinner date or walk me home from the train even though it meant that he had to turn right back around and go all the way back to the Bronx. He never asked to come in, and he never gave me the puppy eyes routine about it either. Now that he had done this last thing, there was no valid reason for us to be apart.

I fished out his keys to the apartment from my pocket and dangled then in front of him enticingly.

"I believe these are yours, Christian." I smiled, pressing them into his palm.

He grabbed me with such ferocity I thought my neck would snap.

When he released me he said nothing, but I could tell it was because he couldn't. After a minute or so he managed to find his tongue.

"Let's get a salad from Pax and head home. Game of Thrones rerun is on tonight and I missed that episode."

It dawned on me that I wouldn't be calling my own shots anymore. I actually might mourn the fact that for the past few months I had no one to answer to but myself. I won't lie. I'd been lonely, especially at night when C and I would usually talk about our day, have dinner together, shower together, cuddle and sleep together.

On the other hand, I'd discovered a certain independence in the absence of a partner. I could laugh as loud as I wanted during a show, guffaw even, yell at the characters, eat without having to consider ladylike decorum, pass gas without embarrassment like a man, wear my grandma duster on the weekend if I so chose. Of course I would miss these things. Damn right I would. But when weighed against having my man at home with me, there wasn't much of a competition. I wanted him. And I wanted him with me in our home sharing our life together.

I linked my arm in his as he started leading us toward Pax. I smiled halfheartedly at something he said. He was laughing and joking and going a hundred miles per hour. I tossed him all of the right gestures but was lost in my own mind, a million thoughts circling my brain.

I wondered if there was any room for Ray in this new turn of events. Would we share a laugh over a cloud of smoke ever again? Could I keep those tingles that he inspired at bay? Could I forget the erotic daydreams that his crooked smile designed and put him in the friend zone for my own safety's sake?

Would he even want to continue a friendship now that I was no longer in limbo and had made my definitive choice? What the hell was my problem? Now that I had obtained everything I wanted, why should I care what happens between Ray and me? Nothing really happened thus far, and now that I was here, I should make damn sure nothing ever happens from here on out, right? Right. Right. Right.

"Hey?"

C stopped short, snapping me out of my thoughts.

"Huh? What'd you say?"

"I was just asking if you were sure about this? About me?"

I shook my head to clear the cobwebs.

"What? Of course I am. Why would you ask that?" I said squeezing his arm reassuringly.

"You just seem to be in another world, and I wondered if maybe you were having second thoughts." He smiled nervously.

I smiled reassuringly.

"You know me. I've got a hundred things I'm contemplating in my head right now, moving myself back to the other side of the bed, putting out a towel for you, moving my charger to the other outlet. You know how I do. But none of the things I'm thinking are about regretting my decision. It's time for us to move forward together and leave the past behind us, all right?" I nodded.

"Okay." He smiled.

And just before we resumed our walk, a black and white jacket from across the street caught my eye. He'd planted himself in front of K&G, a long white harpoon of smoke preceded him. I tried not to stare as Christian resumed his chatter but it was next to impossible. The intensity of his eyes nearly blinded me. I glanced back only once, casually when we hit the corner and were waiting for the light but by then, like the smoke, he was gone.

I ran through all of the scenarios in my mind. Except for that one kiss that seemed like a hundred years ago, all we had shared was conversation and nicotine. He asked about my status, and I was truthful. I told him I was separated but we were working it out, so why then did I feel so strange, as if I owed him some explanation, as if I'd somehow led him on? It wasn't illegal to enjoy the company of men now suddenly, was it? I have a ton of male friends, do I not? But none who made me feel like he did. But he didn't know that. Right? Right. Right. Right.

Things That Make You Go Hmm

I reached across the table and took the Bed Bath & Beyond sales flyer beckoning me from atop the Sunday newspaper pile while munching on my cinnamon raison bagel.

"Babe?" I managed, in between munches.

"Yeah honey?" C answered, lowering the Best Buy flyer, dazzling me with a secret smile, gracing me with his full attention.

Nothing like a little lovemaking first thing in the morning to set a man in the right frame of mind.

"I was looking up umbrella stands for a while now, and they're so expensive for no logical reason."

"Umhm." He furrowed his eyebrows, cocking his head to the side expectantly.

"Well, I was thinking that we take a walk later today to Bed Bath & Beyond and check out their small bathroom garbage cans."

"Why?" He snapped his head back, screwed up his confused face and reached for his green tea.

I took a sip of my coffee, savoring the oncoming explanation I would give. Sometimes I really think I have my own HGTV show.

"Because it's practically the same look, form and function at a fraction of the price, don't you think?" I said, fingering the picture illustrating my point. I'm so gifted I can even incorporate props.

The corners of his mouth turned south, eyebrows turned north and he tipped his head back then pitched it slightly forward. His nonverbal thumbs-up response.

I smiled, backed out of my chair, placed his empty plate on top of mine and kissed his bald head. I would have to imagine the applause.

"You know I love my repurposing, Schmoops!" I declared, depositing the dishes into the sink.

"Babe, you got a text."

"Yup, I heard, thanks." I shut the water off and wiped my hands on the hanging kitchen towel.

I pressed the home button and raised my brow before coding in.

You gonna' be at work tomorrow?

I hadn't heard from Ray in weeks. This was a surprise, and yet it wasn't.

Yeah.

I kept my response brief.

He answered right away as if he had been waiting.

I want to see you.

I glanced over at C. He was still reading the Best Buy flyer. I had not attracted his attention.

When?

I mean, what was I supposed to say? I didn't want to have a full conversation via text now. I was in the middle of family time. What was the big deal? I texted my friends all of the time. And yet the nature of these few words felt so covert.

Tomorrow, before work.

I wasted no time. I was way too happy to hear from him, and even more excited that I would get to see him tomorrow. This was wrong on every level, or was it? I mean, what were we going to do but share a forbidden cig and chat a bit. No harm, no foul, right?

Ok. Now let me go, I'm in the middle of something.

I figured with his personality, once he saw that he wouldn't answer back, and just as I was pressing the home button to quickly check my calendar before getting off of the phone entirely, I heard a ping.

Without looking at C. who was sure to be a little curious by now, I feigned exasperation and sighed loudly while checking the text.

Never.

That one word stopped me in my tracks and made my heart sing. The tingles that I hadn't felt in weeks were suddenly out in full force. I distanced myself from the phone and went back to the dishes.

"So babe?"

"Hmm?" C said, turning the page and sipping on his tea.

"You think in an hour we could head out?"

"Well, I could be ready in five minutes. It's you who usually has the fifty million things to do."

I chuckled. Couldn't deny that.

"True that, but after these dishes I'm just going to get ready. I did everything yesterday. There's nothing left to do today." I smiled, studying him for a moment.

He was a good man. He was a handsome man. He was my man, and Ray was a passing fancy, and if I wasn't careful here I could end up making the same mistake that Christian made almost a year ago. Why would I want to put C or myself through that bullshit again, right? Right. Right. Right.

Epilogue

Two a.m. and I was still awake. Wide awake. My mind was busy revisiting every scene of my life that Ray had been a part of, every conversation, every twinkle in his eye, every subtle innuendo between us. And at the very end, I would replay the kiss that we never spoke of, the single kiss that we never repeated.

I slipped out of bed as quietly as I could. I watched C's sleeping face intently, looking for any sign that he might awaken. When I was certain he was out like a light, I softly closed the door. I padded into the living room, scrounging around the bottom of a large decorative vase for my secret stash.

When I was finally out on the front stoop, I lit up and took a long drag.

I had a sense of urgency to talk to him. I could feel my willpower slipping, and I knew that if I relied on him he would keep me steady. This, of course, is precisely why I hadn't sought his counsel at all. I knew he would tell me all of the things that I didn't want to hear. He would bid me to walk in the light when my heart of hearts sought anything but.

Even now I had the audacity to try and reason with him, when we both knew I was as wrong as wrong could be. And yet I prayed to him and thanked him for his mercy and forbearance. I wouldn't think beyond that. I was afraid he might smite me where I stood, contemplating my wicked thoughts, inhaling death and reveling in it all. Foolish, weak human that I am.

I washed away all traces of the cig and slipped back into bed. It's a good thing we have a king-size bed and my movements couldn't be felt. I turned away from C, half in shame, half in excitement. The early light already started to penetrate the room.

I could not deny that C's infidelity left me with a dark sense of freedom. And as I closed my eyes, I thought to myself, could I not continue to do a bit more of the wrong thing before deciding to do the right? Right? Right. Right.

About The Author

Amanda Sohan was born in the heart of New York City to a set of parents from British Guyana. While growing up with one foot steeped in the strict cultural boundaries her parents held dear and the other rooted in modern teenage American angst, reading and writing became the main medium for her journey toward freedom.

In her dark poetry she grew to love the meaningful depths hidden in a collaboration of words. There was nothing odder than the music she and her only sister Rowena grew up with; two American, West Indian girls bumping to the sound of Eazy E as Video Music Box flashing across the tube. Her teenage years were a graphic rebellion of words that could sneak under the radar of her parent's watchful eye. How ironic that her first work would be a gentle, humorous children's book. But stay turned as she intends to showcase her more adult side in her fourth book entitled HER.

All of Amanda's work is currently self-published under her own label: At Home With A Teacup.

www.ingramcontent.com/pod-product-compliance
Lightning Source LLC
Chambersburg PA
CBHW062116170626
46813CB00002B/467